"It would help considerably if you'd just be in a few exterior shots. We'll shoot in shadow and substitute another actress later."

Jerry was delighted. "Go for it, Mac."

Gaskins called for quiet. "All right, let's get started. Davis, you and Madeline come around the side of the house."

Davis grabbed my arm and pulled me with him. We ran around the side of the house about thirty times before Gaskins was satisfied.

"All right, I want one more here in front of the house. Stephanie, where's my drink?"

Stephanie handed him his cup. He took a noisy slurp and said, "Lance, come out the front door, look around, and go back in."

Henderson did this until Gaskin had the shot he wanted.

"Now I want everyone out here around the tree looking back at the house." Gaskins took another annoying slurp of soda. "Just stare at it like it's the worst thing you've ever—"

I'm sure he meant to say, "seen," but he never finished his sentence. He shook his head as if to clear it and fell over.

Davis said, "What the hell?"

Stephanie screamed, "Josh!" and knelt down. She looked up, her face ghastly white in the moonlight. "Get a doctor!"

Previously published Worldwide Mystery title by
JANE TESH

A CASE OF IMAGINATION

A HARD BARGAIN

JANE TESH

W⦾RLDWIDE®

TORONTO • NEW YORK • LONDON
AMSTERDAM • PARIS • SYDNEY • HAMBURG
STOCKHOLM • ATHENS • TOKYO • MILAN
MADRID • WARSAW • BUDAPEST • AUCKLAND

Recycling programs
for this product may
not exist in your area.

A HARD BARGAIN

A Worldwide Mystery/December 2011

First published by Poisoned Pen Press

ISBN-13: 978-0-373-26779-8

Printed in U.S.A.

But heaven knows,
I had no thought of evil;
My only wish, my only longing
Was love, tender love,
Good and true.

—From *Faust* by Charles Gounod

ONE

THIS CASE STARTED WITH a hamburger, specifically a double deluxe three-cheese hamburger with tomato and pickle at Deely's Burger World. Jerry and I were having a late breakfast in town while Nell finished painting the upstairs bedrooms at the Eberlin house. Nell's smoldering gaze had warned me I'd better get Jerry out of the way before she stapled him to the wall. Since he'd already knocked over one paint can and torn the drop cloth, I understood her concern.

Jerry hit the bottom of the ketchup bottle with unnecessary force. "I don't know why she doesn't want me to help. It's my house."

"Because you create more mess than you're worth," I said just as a huge glop of ketchup fell on his plate, splattering his dragon-patterned tie. "Get over it. Besides, I want you to see my new office."

The letters "Madeline Maclin, Private Investigations" weren't quite dry on the door of my new office in the Arrow Insurance Building on Main Street. I had a desk, though, and a filing cabinet. All I needed now were cases to solve.

Jerry tried to wipe the ketchup off his tie and succeeded in adding new shades of red to the already garish dragons. Since it was a sultry Monday morning in July, he'd left his jacket at home and rolled up the sleeves of his light green shirt. I'd opted for khaki shorts and a pink tank top.

"Any jobs yet?" he asked.

"No, but lots of interested phone calls."

"You should have tons of cases. Everybody knows you caught Juliet Lovelace's killer."

Two weeks ago, ex-beauty queen Kimberly Dawn Williams had been convicted of the murder of aspiring beauty queen Juliet Lovelace. Juliet's death had been only the second murder in ten years in Celosia.

"That doesn't translate into more work for me," I said. "Although, I'd be happy with missing objects and philandering spouses."

Most of the phone calls to my new detective agency were offers to judge local beauty pageants or coach contestants. My fame as a past Miss Parkland had caught up with me. People take one look and assume I'm only useful strutting down a runway. It doesn't matter that I've cut my hair shorter than Jerry's and just wear sunscreen on my face. Something about me screams "Beauty Queen." I have my mother to thank for that.

I must have let my glum thoughts show on my sun-screened face, because Jerry looked sympathetic.

"It'll work out, Mac. Just give it a little more time."

Jerry is rarely serious, and even when he is, he still looks so damn cute I could glob ketchup all over him and eat him up. He's the main reason I can't go back to Parkland. Our friendship is teetering on the brink of full-fledged romance, but we can't seem to get in sync. When we met ten years ago in college, Jerry was ready for a relationship, but I was involved with an art career that never got past one disastrous exhibit. Then, a few weeks ago, I was just about to declare myself when Jerry told me something that made me back off. He believes he's responsible for the fire that killed his parents. Until I solve this mystery, I'm going to have to keep my feelings inside.

It'll work out. Just give it a little more time.

I hope those are prophetic words, Jerry Fairweather.

Burger World filled up. People waved and smiled and

said hello. Gwen Macmillan, a tiny little woman with her hair cut in an unflattering bowl style, stopped by our table and spoke to Jerry.

"Don't forget to look up that incantation for me, Jerry. I want really big tomatoes this year."

"I'll have it for you by the end of the week, I promise."

She patted his hand. "Good, good. I've got a cousin who beats me every year at the county fair, and this time, I'm going to be ready for her. How are you today, Madeline?"

"Fine, thanks."

"You keep this young man on task. Make sure he finds the right spell for me. I intend to win as many blue ribbons as I can."

She went to the counter to pick up her order. I swung a skeptical gaze to Jerry. "You're using spells to grow vegetables now?"

He grinned. "It's just some advice out of an old almanac. Gwen likes to think there's magic involved."

"You're not getting involved in witchcraft, are you?" Jerry has a distressing habit of running scams, the more paranormal, the better. "That's all you need."

Before he could answer, Delores Epstein, who goes by the nickname Twenty, came bustling up. As usual, Twenty was dressed like a runway model in some alien fashion show. Her skirt had zigzag stripes of lime-green and pink, and her off-the-shoulder blouse was lined with tiny red beads that jingled and clacked together like the rows of bracelets on her arms. Today, her hair was the sort of orange you see on traffic cones.

"Hello, Madeline. Hello, Jerry. Have you two heard the latest news? We're all going to be in the movies!"

"We are?" I said.

She slid into the booth next to Jerry. "I heard it from Lois at the beauty parlor. A film company is coming to Celosia to do a movie, and they're going to need tons of extras. And guess who's starring in the movie? Lance Henderson! Isn't this exciting?"

I'd heard that name before. "Lance Henderson. Wasn't he on *Sheriff of the Plains* back in the fifties?"

"And *Destinies,* and *From These Hills,* and *Jupiter's Moons.* I absolutely love him. Do you suppose Laura Costos will be with him? Oh, I'd die to see those two in person."

I wouldn't exactly die, but it would be interesting to see how old Lance and Laura were holding out these days. For a while, they starred in every big-budget TV movie and mini-series. Lance was a solid, square-jawed man with minimal acting skills. Laura got by on the strength of her wild green eyes and a couple of other outstanding features.

Jerry offered Twenty a french fry. "I remember *Jupiter's Moons.* Didn't he play the captain?"

"Oh, yes. He's so dashing."

"Why would he be coming here?"

"I'm not certain of all the details, but I think the director is looking for an unspoiled small town. This will put Celosia on the map."

Jerry brightened. "It could really help the Eberlin house."

I tried not to sigh out loud. Jerry's uncle Val left him the Eberlin house, eyesore of Celosia, and to my amazement, he's decided to fix it up and live in it. So far, Jerry has decided the house would be a perfect New Age retreat, a haunted bed and breakfast, and a murder mystery tour. Movie stars in the neighborhood would not help my cause.

And what is my cause? To convince Jerry to find a real job and leave all the psychic nonsense alone. This is not just an uphill battle. This is a climb-several-hills-and-cross-many-valleys-during-a-hurricane battle. I watched as he chatted animatedly with Twenty. Now his gray eyes gleamed with a light I knew and feared. Jerry was about to have an idea.

"Wait a minute! I just thought of something terrific. What

if the director needs a big old house for his movie? The Eberlin house would make a great set."

Twenty, curse her, said, "Oh, you're right! It would be perfect."

"There's plenty of room if the actors want to stay there. Then we could bill the house as 'Seen in so and so's production of *Small Town*,' or whatever he's going to call it. That would be excellent." He wiped his hands on his napkin and dug in his pocket for his wallet. "When is the film company coming to Celosia?"

"I don't know," Twenty said. "You could check with the Chamber of Commerce."

Jerry tossed some bills on the table. "Come on, Mac."

"Whoa, hold on," I said. "Let me finish my cheeseburger. It might be the last calm meal I have for a while."

"If this works out, we could advertise the house to other film companies. We might even get an entire film industry going, just like Wilmington's."

Twenty said, "Wouldn't that be exciting? I'll see you later. Must dash."

Twenty hurried off to spread the news. I couldn't see sleepy little Celosia as the next Hollywood East, but then, I hadn't expected to find murder here, either.

Jerry gulped down the remains of his soda. "Let's go."

"Think about this," I said, which is useless to say once Jerry's got a plan.

"But this is great publicity. Once word gets around that the Eberlin house was seen in a movie, people will want to come tour it. We can use the haunted house angle, or the attempted murder angle. Either one is golden."

I was still trying to head Jerry off. "The director might not need a big old country house in his movie."

"That's what we need to find out."

I was about to say something else, but reconsidered. Jerry looked at me impatiently. Even then, I had to admire his

youthful face and wide gray eyes and the mouth I longed
to kiss.

"Are you ready?" he asked.

Better believe it, buster. "Okay, let's go."

WE WALKED THE SHORT distance up to Main Street. Thanks
to a great bookstore, a drug store that recreates the soda
fountains of the fifties, and several other clever and creative
artsy shops, Celosia's Main Street is alive and well, despite
the Walmart hovering at the edge of the city limits and the
close proximity of Parkland, one of North Carolina's largest cities. The Chamber of Commerce has its offices in a
neat little building across the street beside the First Savings
Bank and Trust. Although there's not a lot of traffic, Jerry
and I were waiting at the corner for the light to change when
I heard a glad cry from down the street.

"Madeline!"

I looked and wished I hadn't.

"Oh, wow," Jerry said. "It's the Pageantoids."

"What the hell are they doing here?" I said.

"Ten bucks says they'll mention 'visiting queen.'"

The two people who charged down the sidewalk looked
average and sane, but I knew from long experience they are
two of the craziest people in North Carolina—possibly in
the world. Jerry nicknamed them the "Pageantoids" because,
although they never compete, they live and breathe beauty
pageants and all the attendant fuss. I'd met them years ago
when I was serving time as a Junior Miss. I'd made the mistake of being polite to these groupies. Now they feel they
know me well enough to shriek and gush whenever they see
me.

Cathy Sloop, a plump, bug-eyed woman, got to me first.
"Madeline, you look fabulous! We just knew that was you.
I told Mitch that was you."

Mitch Hutton, bone-thin and balding, shook my hand.

"We heard you were in Celosia, and we thought we'd come see for ourselves. We heard you'd given up pageants and left Parkland to run a detective agency here. Is this true?"

"Yes, it is," I said. "Do you know my friend, Jerry Fairweather? We were on our way to a meeting, weren't we, Jerry? It's very nice to see you."

It was a good try, but not good enough. The Pageantoids stood in disbelief, blocking our way.

Cathy Sloop's eyes bugged out even further. "A detective agency? But why? You had a shot at Miss North Carolina, even Miss America!"

"Anyone can be a detective," Mitch Hutton said, "but very few people have the looks and the talent to win a major beauty contest."

"We thought you were here for the Miss Celosia Pageant," Cathy said. "Wasn't that a few Saturdays ago?"

Before I could explain that the pageant had been cancelled, Mitch said, "I can't imagine you being a detective. It's so dirty and low-class. Don't you have to sit in your car for hours outside crummy hotels?"

Jerry came to my defense. "Mac just solved a murder here in town."

The Pageantoids looked at me with horror.

"A murder?" Cathy said. "Wasn't that dangerous?"

"Not really." No need to go into detail about gunshots and deadly hairspray. "But the Miss Celosia Pageant was cancelled."

This horrified them even more than the idea of murder.

Mitch stared at me. "Cancelled? But Celosia's had one of the longest-running pageants in the state! Since 1983, right, Cathy?"

Cathy shook her head. "1984. Did they reschedule, Madeline?"

"No."

"Now, that's a crime! What about the other girls?"

I truly resent the way pageant contestants are referred to as "girls." You might as well go all the way and call them "bitches," as announcers call female dogs in dog shows.

"They'll get over it. It was good seeing you again, but I really need to go."

Cathy Sloop clutched my arm. "You can't possibly consider detecting as a career. The pageant world needs you, Madeline. I wish you could see the pitiful group of girls we have this year for Miss Parkland. We're on a mission to recruit someone who can win it all, and that someone is you."

I pried her off. "That's very flattering, but I've aged out of the Miss Parkland category."

This stopped them only a few minutes.

"But you could be a consultant," Mitch said. "Or a judge. Or at least a visiting queen."

I ignored Jerry's snicker and said, "No, thanks. Excuse me, please. I really have to go."

Jerry and I left them on the sidewalk, still talking about their next plan of action.

"Don't look back," I said.

When we were a safe distance away, Jerry held out his hand.

"Pay up."

I ignored this. "I can't believe those two are in town. Don't they have lives?"

"Everybody has a hobby," he said. "Their hobby just happens to be you."

A blast of cool air greeted us as Jerry opened the Chamber of Commerce office door. "Forget the Pageantoids. We're on a mission here, remember?"

Patricia Hargrave, the Chamber's secretary, confirmed the rumor. Yes, a film crew was sending a scout this weekend, and yes, Lance Henderson was scheduled to star in the movie. She wasn't quite sure when he would arrive.

"But we are very pleased Voltage Films has chosen

Celosia," she said. She patted her hair and adjusted her collar as if preening for a screen test.

"Do you know what kind of movie they're planning?" Jerry asked.

"No, but the director promised to meet with the city council as soon as he got here. His name is Josh Gaskins. He sounded very nice on the phone. I wonder if he's related to the Gaskins up at Middleton? Oh, by the way, Madeline," she said. "I may have a job for you. You find lost objects, don't you?"

"I try," I said. "What have you lost?"

"My very best umbrella. I know I had it last week when I went to church, and I know I had it when I went to the monthly sing along at the theater, but I can't find it anywhere."

It was a struggle, but I remained professional. "What color is it?"

"It's red and has a duck head handle. It's really the best umbrella I've ever had. It opens so smoothly, and it dries off in minutes. I bought it out of Riverside Rural catalog. I suppose I could order another, but they're all out of red."

"I'll see what I can do, Patricia."

She looked worried. "Do you charge a lot for something like this?"

"Consider it a favor."

"Thank you, Madeline. That's very generous. I know you want to get established here in town."

And if it takes finding red umbrellas with duck head handles, then I'll do it. "I'll look around and get back to you."

Jerry had managed to keep a straight face during all this. He waited until we were back on the street before laughing.

"Could you call this an open and shut case?"

"Only if I find the damn thing."

"Sorry, Mac. Life can't be all thefts and murder."

"If finding her umbrella brings me some good PR and

more business, I can't complain." It wasn't the kind of business I'd hoped for, but I had to remind myself this was Celosia, not Parkland, and I'd made the choice to move here. Still, I didn't want all my cases to be so dinky.

Jerry and I walked back down Main Street toward my office.

"Voltage Films," he said. "I've never heard of them."

"I'll bet Georgia would know."

We stopped in Georgia's Books, the large, exceptionally well-stocked bookstore on Main Street, and asked the owner, Georgia Taylor, if she'd ever heard of Voltage Films. Georgia is a slim, efficient woman of about sixty with auburn tinted hair and half-glasses she wears on a pearl necklace. She peered over her glasses.

"They're probably listed in one of the film guides." She pointed. "Right down there next to the movie magazines."

We looked in several guides before finding a listing for Voltage Films.

"'A small, independent company specializing in thought-provoking and experimental films,'" Jerry read aloud. "'Recent films include *Heart Songs, Cabbages on the Windowsill* and *The Ever-Prevailing Theory of Invisibility.*'" He grimaced. "Doesn't sound like they make the kind of movies that go well with popcorn."

"If they pay well for the use of the house, that won't matter."

"That's true, but I was kind of hoping for something more exciting than cabbages on the windowsill."

"I'm sure that's a metaphor for blood, guts and fast cars."

Georgia had followed us down the aisle. "Did you find what you were looking for?"

"Yes, thanks," I said.

"Has it anything to do with the movie company that's coming here? I haven't seen the town in such an uproar."

"Yes, Voltage Films is the name of the company."

"Well, they haven't even gotten here yet, and they're already causing a wealth of confusion." She readjusted her half-glasses. "Madeline, I may have a case for you."

Great, I thought. She probably needs a subscription renewed.

"Hayden and I have noticed some things out of place. I'm afraid we have a shoplifter. I was wondering if you could come in and walk around the store and keep an eye out for our culprit."

"Of course."

"We think it's one of the Yates boys, but we're not sure. They're usually in here in the late afternoon. I hate to accuse anyone, but I know my store and what's in it, and things are not where they're supposed to be."

"When would you like me to start?"

"Whenever you could drop by. Hayden is coming in after lunch. He can tell you more about it."

Jerry and I thanked her for the use of the video guide and left the store.

"Shoplifting. Now that's more like it," Jerry said.

"Yep. A regular crime wave."

We walked on to the Arrow Insurance building near the end of Main Street.

"Okay," I said, "don't expect much, but it's a start."

Once inside the building, we took a short walk down the hall to my office. Jerry admired the sign on the door.

"Wish I had my camera," he said.

I unlocked the door and pushed it open for him to enter. I had a small but serviceable desk, a new beige filing cabinet and two chairs, a swivel chair for me and a beige-and-green armchair for my clients.

Jerry plopped into the armchair. "This is nice. It'll make people feel comfortable when discussing those embarrassing secrets."

"I hope so." I sat down in the swivel chair. "The computer

and printer will be delivered next Monday. The phone lines are already in."

The window offered a view of the side yard, grass and trees and the swing set in the backyard of the neighboring house, a far cry from my hot little cubicle in Parkland. There, I had a splendid view of bricks.

Jerry looked around at the bare walls. "Any plans for decoration?"

"How about a big picture of me as Miss Parkland? That would inspire confidence."

He grinned. "I was thinking a couple of original landscapes would brighten up the place."

My glare warned him to drop the subject. At one time, I'd dreamed of a career as an artist. Lately, the urge had surfaced, but I kept pushing it down. The memory of my one disastrous show was still too painful.

"Maybe I'll just get a big fish, like Ted," I said.

As if invoking his name called him to my door, Ted Stacy looked in and said, "I thought I heard you in here. Good morning. Hi, Jerry. What do you think?"

"This is really nice," Jerry said. "We were just saying all it needs is a big fish on the wall."

"Oh, I've got a new one. Come have a look."

We walked next door to Ted's office. An impressive sailfish was mounted above the bookcase.

"Wow, that is neat," Jerry said.

"Took me five hours to land."

As the guys talked about fishing, I indulged in one of my ongoing comparisons, in a desperate attempt to talk myself out of wanting Jerry. Here's Ted Stacy, tall, dark, handsome and successful, a real Southern gentleman, who arranged for me to rent the empty office in his building, who took me to dinner, complimented me and made me feel welcome in Celosia without feeling I owed him anything in return.

And here's Jerry. He's not as tall as Ted, which means

he's not as tall as I am. His light brown hair has a tendency to stray. He could easily be the poster child for attention deficit disorder. He enjoys making people think he has connections with the spirit world and will relieve them of their money if they let him.

But that smile. Damn.

Ted finished his fish tale. "So I guess you've heard about the movie."

"Yeah," Jerry said. "I'm hoping they'll use the Eberlin house for a set."

"Depends on what kind of movie they're making. I thought it was going to be one of those slice of life pictures where nothing happens but a lot of talking."

"There has to be at least one car chase, or I'm not interested."

"Excuse me?"

A timid voice made us turn. A dark-haired woman stood in the doorway clutching a large pocketbook. "I'd like to speak to Madeline Maclin," she said.

"I'm Madeline Maclin," I said. "What can I do for you?"

She looked anxiously at Jerry and Ted.

"Please come to my office," I said.

The woman came into my office and sat down where Jerry had been sitting. "I've never hired a detective before. I'm not sure if I need one."

"What's the problem?" I asked.

She kept the pocketbook in her lap as if using it for a shield. "Well, it's not exactly a problem now, but it's going to be. My name is Frannie Thomas, and about six months ago, I let a man named Kirby Willet store some things in my downstairs guest room. I wasn't using it, and he needed a place to keep some things. I thought I was doing him a favor."

"But he hasn't come back for his stuff."

Her eyes went wide. "Yes. How did you know?"

"I had a roommate like that once."

"See, I didn't really mind at first, but now my mother's coming to live with me, and I need that room for her and her things."

I had this solved already. Frannie Thomas was too shy to confront this freeloader. "You'd like someone to contact Mister Willet and tell him to come get his property."

"That would be great, except I don't know where he is."

"He didn't leave an address or phone number?"

"Oh, yes, but the phone's been disconnected, and there's no one living at that address anymore."

"What kind of stuff are we talking about? Clothes? Books? Anything of value?"

She clutched her pocketbook tighter. "I don't know. It's all in boxes. I haven't looked in them. I don't want to go snooping through his things. I just want him to come get all that out of my room."

"Okay. Why did you agree to store his things in the first place?"

"My friend Bernice Coleman told Kirby I had extra space in my house. He seemed like a nice man, just a little down on his luck. I wanted to help him out."

"Your friend Bernice doesn't know where he is?"

"No one knows where he is, and I haven't the slightest idea of how to look for him. That's when I thought of you. I figured if you found Juliet Lovelace's murderer, you could find Kirby Willet."

I was glad I already had a good reputation in town, but Juliet's case had been overloaded with suspects. This case had the slimmest of clues. Still, it was a case. "I'll need to have a look at the boxes. There might be something in one that can help me locate Mister Willet."

"Can you come tomorrow afternoon around four? I'll be over at Mother's till then helping her pack."

We agreed on a time and my fee. Frannie Thomas took

her pocketbook and left. I went back to Ted's office. Ted and Jerry were still talking about fish.

"If you want to go fishing, the best place around here is Carson's Lake. I've pulled bass out of there by the bucket loads." Ted spread his hands apart. "One this big, I swear."

"I have another case," I said.

"Great," Jerry said. "Murder? Kidnapping? Drug busting?"

"Leftover boxes."

"Boxes full of money?"

"That would be nice. Are you guys setting up a fishing trip?"

"Next week, Carson's Lake. Want to go?"

I tried to remember if I'd ever been fishing. "Sure." And then I said something that always gets me into trouble. "I don't think this case is going to take me very long."

JERRY'S NEGOTIATING WITH his pal Buddy to buy Buddy's Volkswagen Bug, so my blue Mazda's been our only form of transportation lately. As we got in the car, I gave him a sideways look. "Speaking of money, how's your cash flow these days?"

"Except for the ten bucks you owe me, no problem."

I thought there was a big problem. Jerry has declined his share of the Fairweather fortune, but somehow always has plenty of money. I know whatever he charges for his séances and Ouija board readings couldn't be enough to live on.

"When are you going to tell me about this mysterious bankroll of yours?"

"No mystery. I'm doing just fine, thanks."

He wasn't going to tell me, and I knew from past experience that nagging wouldn't help. I changed the subject. "Did you look at the college catalogue?"

"Still thinking about that."

In an attempt to steer Jerry in some direction, I'd suggested he take some classes at Parkland Community College. He's never done anything with his history degree. I thought he'd make a good teacher. He's smart and entertaining and likes kids. He's even mentioned he might like teaching. That was several wild schemes ago, back before he inherited the Eberlin house. I refuse to give up. The fact that he's kept the house and decided to live in it is a huge step toward settling down.

Celosia's such a small town it doesn't take long before you're out in the country. A couple of turns and we were on the road to the Eberlin house. Even though the July morning was hot, I left the windows down so I could smell the fresh air and honeysuckle. A few cows looked up as we passed the fields. Jerry, as was his custom, mooed at them. Kudzu vines twisted around the abandoned tobacco sheds and rail fences. We passed more fields until we came to our own, an expanse of long grass and clover that leads up to a large house surrounded by oak trees.

"Jerry, you're right. The house would be perfect for a horror movie."

He pretended to be insulted. "You have to admit it looks a lot better than the first time we saw it."

"It still has a long way to go." I saw a flash of gray-and-white as a mockingbird sailed over the daylilies to perch on the battered mailbox at the end of the driveway. "Too early for the mail?"

"I'll check."

I stopped, and he got out to see if the mail had come. I gave the house another look. I'm still staying in one of the upstairs bedrooms. At first, living in the same house as Jerry was a throwback to our co-ed college dorm. We ate junk food, we talked about our day, watched TV on his new giant-screen television. We still do those things, but now that there's a chance for a permanent relationship, I find myself thinking of the Eberlin house as home.

Jerry got back in the car. "Nope, not yet."

Not yet.

I drove up and parked beside the white van under the large trees in the front yard. We got out and walked up the porch steps.

"Let's see what Nell's done so far." He pushed open the screen door and called up the stairs. "Nell, are you through yet?"

"Hold on," came her voice. "I'm coming down."

Nell had on her work clothes, grubby white paint-splattered overalls and sneakers. Her dirty-blond hair was stuck in a ponytail and covered with a white baseball cap. She gave Jerry a look from her small blue eyes. "Don't touch anything till I say so."

"Yes, ma'am."

"And get me a beer."

Jerry keeps a supply for her in the fridge. Nell followed us into the kitchen. Jerry got her a beer and one for himself. I chose a Diet Coke.

Nell popped her beer can open and took a swig. "So when's this movie crew going to arrive in town?"

I haven't been in Celosia a month, but already I've found out that Nell hears and knows everything. "Patricia's going to let us know."

Nell nodded. "Wouldn't mind having a look at Lance Henderson. Been watching him for years."

Jerry offered her a doughnut. "You might get the chance to work with him."

She gave him another look and then glanced at me. "What's shorty been up to now?"

"He thinks the house would make a good movie set."

To my surprise, Nell agreed. She took a doughnut from

the box. "Hadn't thought of that, but it sure would. What kind of movie they making?"

"We don't know, but it could be the start of something good."

"Hmm." Nell took another drink. "Oh, you had a call from your brother, junior. Wants you to call back. Something about a wedding."

Jerry set his beer can on the table, his face suddenly serious. "Okay. Thanks." He got up and left the kitchen.

Nell's eyebrows lifted. "It's a long story," I said.

"Not your wedding, is it?"

"No."

"So tell all."

"Tucker's getting married in a few weeks, and he wants Jerry to come."

"What's the problem?"

"The wedding is going to be at the Fairweather mansion. Jerry hasn't been back home in over twelve years."

"Family troubles?"

"Not exactly." I wondered how much of Jerry's strange history I needed to share with Nell and decided the answer was none.

She reached for a second doughnut. "So why doesn't Tucker get married in a church?"

"I don't know."

"Seems like a fine detective such as yourself would find out."

"It's really none of my business."

She chuckled. "Everything about that man is your business, and you know it." From the first day, Nell had seen right through me. She finished her doughnut and her beer and tossed the can into the recycle bin by the back door. "I've got floors to sand."

I thought of something I needed to ask her. "Nell, has Jerry paid you for all this work?"

"Yep. All caught up."

"I'm a little concerned where he's getting his money."

"Ask him."

"I have."

She shrugged. "As long as I get paid, I don't really care." She cut her little eyes at me. "You think it's dirty money?"

"I don't know. I keep hoping he'll tell me."

"Probably shaking down Bigfoot for some cash."

"That's what I'm afraid of."

Jerry was still on the phone, so I followed Nell upstairs. I admired the paint job she'd done in one of the guest rooms, a very nice light blue. Then I went to my room. The room's very plain. I have a large bed, a dresser and an old-fashioned chair. The walls are still their original beige. I don't spend a lot of time in it. I'm hoping to move across the hall into Jerry's room.

Outside, a car horn honked. Movie people already? I went to the window to see who had come to visit. A tall, rangy man with a hawklike nose climbed out of a Buick sedan.

"Damn!" Rick Rialto, one of Jerry's former partners in psychic schemes. Of all the people in the world, this was the last person I needed right now. The only word to describe Rick is "shifty." He is shifty from his wiry black hair to his fake alligator shoes.

He came up the front porch steps and knocked on the door.

"Mac, can you get that?" Jerry called.

Oh, I'll get that, all right. I came down the stairs and opened the door. Rick grinned that grin that never reaches his shrewd dark eyes.

"Hello, Mac, old pal."

Jerry's the only one who can call me Mac. I gave Rick my frostiest stare. "Rick. What are you now?"

"Rick Rialto, Animal Psychic. Where's J?"

I continued to block the door. "He's on the phone."

"They told me in town this is his place now." He looked over my shoulder at the living room, which had been gray and Victorian and now, thanks to Nell, gleamed a modern blue and white. "Nice, very nice."

"Thanks."

"And you two are what? Married? Living together?"

"Friends."

He smirked. "Still friends after all these years. That's so sweet."

"What do you want?" I asked.

"Nothing. I was in the neighborhood and just stopped by to see my old pal."

I didn't believe him for a minute. "Celosia's a little off the beaten track for you."

"I'll say. What a hick town. But that's to my advantage."

Jerry came up behind me and I had to stand aside. "Yo, Rick! What brings you to the country?"

"I kinda wore out my welcome in Charlotte." The two men shook hands and smacked each other on the back. "You've got a great setup here, J. Nifty old house. Must be perfect for séances."

"Thanks," Jerry said. "We're working on it. Come on in. You want a drink?"

Rick interpreted my stare and grinned again. "Nah, just stopping by to see what's up. Anybody around Celosia got a troubled pet? Goldfish a bit peaked? Cat coughing up too many hairballs?"

"Not that I know of."

"This animal psychic deal is the best. People will believe anything you tell them about their pets. You've got tons of room out here. We could do cows and sheep and everything."

"We're kind of hoping the movie folks will want to use the house."

"Oh, yeah, I heard about that. More gold, pal. Those actor types are way into astrology. Some of them have their own personal psychics." He snapped his fingers. "Hey! We could get on board with this crew, whadda ya say?"

"Sure."

I'd forgotten how easily Rick could sway Jerry. Most of the time Jerry comes up with his own wacky ideas. He doesn't need Rick's dubious input.

"Can you stay for supper?" Jerry asked. "I've got a grill out back. We can do hot dogs, steaks, whatever you like."

"Can't stay tonight. Got a few things cooking of my own. Just touching base with you. I'll stop by tomorrow."

"Okay, great."

I walked Rick out to his car to make sure he got in and drove away. He paused, one hand on the door. He grinned.

"You don't like me, do you, Mac?"

"Not especially," I said. "And it's Madeline."

He put on a little boy voice. "Gee, Miz Maclin, I didn't mean to keep Jerry out so late. We were just riding our bikes backward down Dead Man's Hill."

"Very funny."

"It was Jerry's idea to put that bag of flaming shit on Old Man Robbins' doorstep, but I totally claim letting the air out of Coach Bob's tires."

"I don't doubt it."

He switched back to his own voice. "This is harmless, Madeline. All we have to do is tell people how wonderful they are. Actors are paranoid with low self-esteem. They love compliments."

"But you take their money under false pretenses."

"Always have, always will."

"I don't think Jerry should get mixed up in this."

He shrugged. "I can do it with or without him. Just thought he might like a piece of the action."

"He doesn't need your kind of action."

His grin turned into a smirk. "You've convinced him to go straight, have you?"

"Well, let me put it this way, Rick. I've convinced him to take up the piano again."

The smirk disappeared. "No way. He was through with music."

At that moment, the sweeping melody of "Till There Was You" came from the parlor. Jerry couldn't have timed it better. Rick's mouth dropped open.

"He's playing for *The Music Man* in town," I said. "He gets in about two or three hours of practice every day. Sometimes he just plays for the hell of it."

Rick looked at me with a new respect. "Well, I'll be damned. Maybe you and I should team up. If you can do this, you can do anything."

"I believe you were leaving."

He gave me another grin and a salute and left. I went into the house, planning to sit in the parlor and listen to the music, but the phone rang.

"I'll get it," I said. I picked up the phone on the coffee table. "Hello. Eberlin house, Madeline Maclin speaking."

"Oh, good," a woman's voice said. "You're the very one I need to speak to. You're the detective, right?"

"Yes. What can I do for you?"

"My name is Joan Ribileau. I'm head librarian at the Celosia Public Library, and I could certainly use your help. Do you suppose you could stop by sometime today?"

Another case! Things were picking up. "Certainly," I said. "I can come right now, if that's convenient."

"Wonderful. I'll be at the front desk."

I hung up and went to the parlor. Jerry brought "Till There Was You" to a close. "I've got another case," I told him.

He took his pencil and made a mark in the music. "Told you things would get better."

"The music sounds really good."

"Thanks." He turned the pages until he found "Lida Rose." "I think this one's my favorite."

I wondered if he and Rick had something going he wasn't telling me about. "Kind of odd for Rick to show up here, isn't it?"

"Yeah, I haven't seen him since we had the Take Your Picture With a Live Unicorn business."

"This pet-psychic thing sounds pretty lame."

"Worth a try. I'd rather see what I can drum up with the film crew, though."

"Everything okay with Tucker?"

He kept his expression neutral. "Oh, yeah. Everything's fine."

He started playing "Lida Rose," but I know "Don't Talk to Me About This" when I hear it. However, if he thought this was the end of our discussion, he was mistaken.

I waited a few minutes and then reached over and closed the book. "Jerry, if you want me to find out what happened to your parents, you're going to have to be a little more helpful."

He stopped playing. "I don't know what to tell you."

"Well, for starters, you could come back to the house with me and look around. You might remember something."

"That's the trouble," he said. "I don't remember anything about it except what Harriet told me."

"Did she tell you you were responsible for the fire?"

He paused as if thinking back over the years. "I knew I'd done something very wrong, but she told me everything was okay. She would take care of things. She would take care of us."

"But I don't understand. Did you have your own flame-thrower? Were you building fires in the living room?"

"I liked playing with matches."

I took a deep breath. "Whew. Well, that's not good."

"I'd already been spanked for it twice."

"So you think maybe you were playing with them again and started the fire?"

"I don't know what else to think. There was a fire, my parents were killed, Harriet took what was left of our family and did the best she could."

I sat down beside him on the piano bench. "Isn't it possible something else caused the fire, and Harriet either didn't know what it was, or knew and decided to cover up the truth?"

"But why would she do that?"

"That's what I'm trying to find out, but you have to cooperate. You're going to have to talk to Harriet."

"Oh, man."

"Unless there's someone else who knows what happened."

He finally managed a smile. "That's why I hired you."

"I'm not sure you can afford me."

"Oh, yes, I can."

"Which brings us back to your mystery bank."

"It's the Harriet Fairweather Savings and Loan."

I was so surprised I almost fell off the piano bench. "What? Harriet sends you money?"

"She said she'd always take care of us, and she has."

I couldn't believe he told me. "But you swore up and down you didn't want any of the family money."

"And she made me swear up and down I'd never tell. So you'd better not let on." I was gaping at him, so he said, "I'm cooperating here."

"And I appreciate it. Does she bankroll Des and Tucker, too?"

"No, they have their own money."

I was still trying to process this information. "She just sends you money."

"Yes, every month. Fire insurance."

"Jerry." The fact he could make a joke, even a black one, was encouraging.

"Well, obviously, I need help."

I thought there could be another reason Harriet felt the

need to be generous. "You do need help, and I'm going to help you. Call Harriet and tell her to expect us very soon." I opened the music book and smoothed the pages. "Then you can get back to 'Lida Rose.'"

TWO

THE CELOSIA PUBLIC LIBRARY was a plain beige building right across from the Post Office, and Joan Ribileau was a plain beige woman, her glasses pushed back on top of her dark hair. She smiled and got up from her seat behind the checkout desk.

"I'm so glad you could come. Let's go back into my office. Bernice, will you watch the front for me?"

A thin woman with gray hair like a pad of steel wool looked up from a computer and nodded.

Joan Ribileau's office was as neat and organized as the rest of the library. She sat down behind her desk and opened a folder. "I have all the information right here."

I sat down in the chair across from the desk, wondering what sort of crime I needed to investigate for the library. Ms. Ribileau slid the folder across to me.

"These are the main offenders. I don't know what else to do. Maybe you can reason with them."

I looked at the list of names and titles of books. Beside each name was a date written in red. I felt a sudden sinking feeling. "Are these overdue books?"

She pursed her mouth. "Way overdue. I've tried calling, writing letters, email, everything."

"And you want me to see if I can collect fines?"

"I really don't expect any of these people to pay, but I do want to get the books back. If you could manage to get what they owe, that would be extra. It's a nickel a day, except holidays."

I almost got up and tossed the list back. Almost. Hang on here, I told myself. It's a case. You need the money and the good public relations. Even if you got one or two of these books back, that would be something.

When I told Joan Ribileau my fee, she didn't even blink. "I say it's worth it."

"I'll get started on this right away," I said. "The woman named Bernice who works here, is she Bernice Coleman?"

"Yes, she is."

"May I speak to her for a minute?"

"Of course."

Bernice Coleman was gluing the torn edges of a paperback book. She frowned as if resenting the interruption. "It's about Kirby Willet," I said. "I understand you told him Frannie Thomas had a spare room where he could store some of his things. She's a little concerned he hasn't returned for them."

Her expression didn't change. "I have no idea where he is."

"When did you last see him?"

She set the repaired book aside. "Months ago."

"Is he the kind of person who would just dump his stuff and go?"

She picked up a stack of index cards and began to look through them. "He's not very dependable, if that's what you're asking, but I don't think he'd leave his personal items behind."

"What does he do? Does he have a job?"

"He flits from one thing to another. Last time I saw him, he was working for the paper."

"As a reporter?"

She made two stacks of cards, doing her best to ignore me. "Nothing that grand. More like a paperboy. Or maybe he was going around getting all the quarters out of the newspaper stands. Something like that."

"Is there anything else you can tell me about him?"

She kept her eyes on her cards and spoke curtly. "No."

I hadn't encountered this level of rudeness in Celosia, which made me more determined to continue. "Does he have a home here? Any kind of address?"

"Try the Wayfarer Motel. He stayed there sometimes."

"Where did he usually keep his stuff?"

"I don't know. He just said he had some boxes of things but couldn't afford to store them. Frannie had this big empty room. I was just trying to do him a favor."

"Why?"

I'd asked the question innocently enough, but Bernice Coleman finally looked up from her cards and bristled to the top of her wooly head.

"Because, unlike people in the big city, we try to help each other around here."

By being snippy and prickly? "Seems to me that's quite a favor. How long was he supposed to leave the boxes at Frannie's?"

"There wasn't a time limit."

"He didn't say, 'Oh, I'll be back for these in a couple of weeks,' something like that?"

"No, he did not. As I said, he flits. He's probably flitting around somewhere and just forgot."

Something about this woman made me want to get a rise out of her. "How about if Frannie and I put the boxes out on the curb?"

"She'd never do a thing like that."

"I would."

She glared at me. "That wouldn't be very good publicity for your detective agency, would it?"

Round one to Bernice.

I WENT DOWN MAIN STREET to the offices of the *Celosia News* and inquired about Kirby Willet. Brandon Bergman, the editor, was in his office sorting through photographs of Celosia's Clean Up Day. He had pictures of teens wading in the creek to fish out old tires and rusty cans, children gathering paper cups and cola bottles, and older citizens hauling away bigger piles of trash.

"Oh, yeah, Kirby. Worked for us a short while, mainly collecting subscription money. Haven't seen him in a while."

"Any idea where he might have gone?"

"Nope."

"Did he ever mention any relatives? Friends?"

Bergman held up a picture of two teenage boys grinning from their pickup truck. "What do you think about this one? These guys carried off six loads of garbage from the high school."

"I like this one," I said, pointing to a photo of a toddler trying to use a broom.

"Yeah, there're a lot of great shots."

Now, why would I find that particular picture appealing? I wondered. The toddler reminded me of the children in Bill's photos, and I certainly didn't want to think about children or Bill.

Bergman put the picture of the teenagers in the pile. "Getting back to your question, Madeline. Did Willet have any friends? Not that I know of. He wasn't very friendly, to tell the truth. He did his job okay, but he spent a lot of time tinkering with things. He called them his inventions, but they usually screwed things up or made ungodly noises. I told him he needed to invent someplace else. Guess he took me up on that."

"What kind of inventions?"

"Useless stuff. Something that would reshape paper clips that had been straightened. Who needs that? And one time he took the copier apart to see if he could improve it. We're still getting toner out of the carpet."

My gaze strayed back to the child in the photo. Maybe I'd

been drawn to the way the light picked up the gold in the little boy's hair. Yes, that's it, I decided. I'm admiring it from an artistic standpoint and not from any latent maternal stirrings. "Bernice Coleman said he lived at the Wayfarer Motel."

"That's where we sent his last check. So, you like the shot of little Bucky and the broom? I've already got a whole page of kid pictures planned for Farm Festivities. I'll have to use my dad's favorite trick." Bergman closed his eyes, let his hand wave over the desk, pointed a finger and brought it down on the photos. He opened his eyes. His finger had landed on a picture of a group of young people tidying up around the "Welcome to Celosia" sign at the city limits. "Perfect," he said. "Works every time."

Bergman's method would save a lot of time and effort, I thought as I drove out to the Wayfarer Motel. The next time I have a complicated case, I'll spread out pictures of all my suspects, close my eyes, and let my finger "finger" the culprit. A technique as reliable as Jerry's Ouija board.

The Wayfarer Motel is a long cream-colored building with green doors, a plain building the owner has tried to spruce up with buckets of geraniums and hanging baskets of petunias and ferns. A picnic table and a swing set fill one corner of the front lawn. The other corner has an array of plastic chairs arranged around a small swimming pool. Two small children splashed in the pool while an elderly man in faded jeans and a baseball cap sat watching them and smoking a pipe. The man was Elijah Grimes, a retired fireman. I'd met him at Deely's.

He tipped his cap. "Morning, Madeline."

"Have you graduated to lifeguard?" I asked.

He took his pipe and pointed it toward the children. "Got my grandkids visiting from Pennsylvania. The pool at the park's too crowded, so I brought them here. Tilda don't mind."

"That's very nice."

"Yeah, I can keep an eye on them better. Jennifer's five, and her little brother, Toby, is almost four." He raised his voice. "Jenny! Toby! Come here a minute."

The children climbed out, shook themselves like puppies and trotted over. The little girl's bathing suit was pink with purple flowers. The little boy had on neon-green swim trunks almost too big for him. With their dark curly hair and dark eyes, they looked like twins.

"Want to meet somebody," Grimes said. "Jenny, you know how you like to watch *Miss America* on TV? This is Miss Madeline Maclin, and she's a real live beauty queen."

For a brief shining moment, I thought he was going to say "real live detective." I should've known better.

Jennifer stuck her finger in her mouth and looked me up and down. "Where's your crown?"

"It's at the cleaners."

Grimes laughed. "She don't wear it all the time."

The little girl frowned as if this didn't make sense. "I would, if I had a crown."

"She loves beauty pageants," Grimes said. "I've told her mother to enter her in one of them Little Miss contests. I think she could win." He gave his granddaughter a hug. "What do you think, princess? Win some money and a big gold crown?"

She clapped her hands. "A lot of money!"

Her little brother wasn't impressed by the conversation. He looked longingly at the swimming pool. "Can I go back in the water now?"

Grimes tousled the boy's wet curls. "Sure can, sport. Say good-by and nice to meet you to Miss Madeline."

"Bye, nice to meet you," Jennifer said and ran back to the pool.

Toby looked up at me. "Well, you are pretty," he said as if doing me a favor, "but I want to swim."

Grimes gave a hoot of laughter. "Go on, then, you rascal."

He grinned as the two children hopped into the water. "They're a sight, aren't they? Never know what that Toby will say."

Like Toby, I was ready to escape. I knew what Grimes was going to ask me. Sure enough, he asked it. "You think Jenny could do well in one of them contests?"

How to discourage this without hurting his feelings? "She might be a little young."

He looked surprised. "I see babies winning on TV."

"And it can get very expensive. Registration fees, pageant clothes, travel to different cities. Some people even hire coaches. The expenses can really add up."

Now he looked doubtful. "Guess we'd have to work on that."

If I didn't change the subject, I was going to start having flashbacks to the horror that was Backstage At Little Miss. "Mister Grimes, do you know anything about Kirby Willet?"

"Kirby Willet. That's a name I haven't heard in a while." He took a few puffs on his pipe. "He tried to fix the hose on Number Seven once. Thought we'd never find all the pieces. Tall fella, skinny, kind of absentminded. Used to work here, I think."

"Can you recall where you last saw him?"

Grimes shook his head. He called to the children. "Toby! What'd I tell you about no spitting? Don't spit water at your sister. Sorry, Madeline. Maybe Tilda can help you."

"All right," I said. "I enjoyed meeting your grandchildren. I hope you have a nice visit."

"I might be calling on you later if we decide to enter Jenny in a pageant."

And I might be way out of town if you do.

The owner of the Wayfarer Motel, Tilda Sorenson, a large untidy woman with unnaturally red hair, was more excited about the possibility of Lance Henderson staying at her motel. She didn't have a lot to say about Kirby Willet. She leaned her meaty arms on the front desk.

"He just worked here a few months, cleaning up, mostly. Took out trash, vacuumed. Didn't cause any trouble."

A younger woman in a maid's uniform was cleaning out the ashtrays in the lobby. Her long brown ponytail was tied with a rubber band. I could see a large wad of pink gum as she chewed. "Well, he worried me," she said. "Always taking things apart."

"Yeah, well, he did that." Tilda chuckled. "Got the drink machine all screwed up. Wouldn't give out nothing but diet sodas and the occasional bag of chips."

The young woman came up to the desk, popping her gum. "And he'd get me all upset about room sixteen. Said it was haunted."

"He just didn't want you going in there." Tilda Sorenson turned to me. "See, I let him stay in sixteen 'cause it wasn't one of my best rooms. Needed a lot of things done to it. He said he'd fix it up."

The young woman wasn't going to let go of her story. "He said somebody died in there. Killed themselves, he said."

Tilda gave a snort. "Well, now, that's a bunch of bull. Nobody's died in my motel. Don't you think I'd know it? Just some of Willet's stories."

"Could I see room sixteen?" I asked.

"Nothing to see. It's just like the other rooms."

"There might be something that could help me find him."

"Go show her, Sue Ann."

Popping and smacking, Sue Ann led me outside to room sixteen and unlocked the door. The room was a typical motel room, two beds, a long dresser, curtains in an ungodly shade of plaid.

"Watch this," she said. She flipped the light switch and water ran in the sink. "You have to flush the toilet to get the light to come on, and the TV won't play unless the air conditioner's running, too. He's got this room completely messed up, and I haven't even started on the peanuts."

"The peanuts?"

"Dry-roasted peanuts. He ate them all the time, so I found them everywhere, on the floor, behind the cushions, even in the shower. I told Tilda it would attract mice, but she never did anything about it. He'd only eat Blue Ribbon brand. It was really stupid."

"Why do you say that?"

She pulled out a long strand of gum and tucked it back in her mouth. "Because one time I was trying to be nice and bought a big old jar of Planters for him for Christmas, and he wouldn't even open them. He was weird."

"Or just extremely loyal to Blue Ribbon peanuts."

She looked skeptical. "Maybe. Anyway, we got to hire someone to fix this room, and I still say it's haunted."

"When was the last time you saw him?"

She tugged on the curtain cord and made a surprised noise when the ugly plaid draperies opened. "Well, at least one thing works in here. Last time I saw Willet was about a month ago. Tilda fired him because he never got around to doing what he was supposed to do. He came by to pick up his clothes and his peanuts. He didn't have much."

That's because everything else was stored at Frannie's. "Any idea where he was going?"

She shook her head. "We didn't talk a lot. I got the impression he didn't like girls. He wasn't no catch, neither, let me tell you. Tall and skinny with these wild eyes. Seems like he was staying with someone in town, but he could've just been saying that."

I borrowed a piece of paper from the pad by the phone and wrote my number. "If he should happen to stop by, give me a call."

She took the paper. "What do you want him for?"

"He needs to claim some property."

"Probably just junk," she said and blew a large pink bubble. The bubble popped, and she wadded the remains into her mouth. "That's all he ever had. Junk."

I THANKED SUE ANN AND went back to Georgia's Books to scout for shoplifters. One of the nicest things about Georgia's Books is the man behind the counter. His name is Hayden Amry, and he's worth looking at, if only for the startling color of his eyes, a sort of blue-green color that makes me think of Caribbean seas. The rest of Hayden is perfectly fine, as well, but he's spoken for.

"So what's missing?" I asked.

"Not so much missing as rearranged," he said. "Sometimes it's a pack of baseball cards in the children's section. Sometimes it's a best seller over in the magazines. Our thief hasn't established a pattern."

"When did all this start?"

"Not long after the last full moon." His worried voice made me suspect this conversation was heading into supernatural territory. "I think it might be something more serious than Georgia will admit."

"Gremlins?"

He looked startled. I should have known better than to tease him. Hayden believes in everything.

"I hadn't thought of that," he said.

"I'm just kidding."

"I was afraid it might be some sort of poltergeist activity, but there hasn't been any damage. Gremlins steal things, though, don't they, and move things around."

"Hayden, I was being facetious."

"Then I remembered the store had been built over another building that had burned. If anyone died in that fire, they may be trying to tell us something."

Now I was really sorry I'd said anything. Hayden fixed his marvelous eyes on mine, his expression concerned.

"Do you think Jerry could come and hold a séance here? If we get in touch with the spirit, he or she might tell us what they want."

"I don't think the store is haunted," I said. "Georgia suspects it's one of the Yates boys. How about if you fill me in on them? They're alive, right?"

"Yes, Clarence and Terrance Yates. Clarence is fifteen, and Terrance is thirteen. They're always in trouble."

"Well, point them out the next time they're in the store. They sound like more reasonable criminals."

Hayden wasn't convinced. "They're the kind of boys who'd steal comics or candy, not hardback books or gift items."

"If they're on drugs, they'll steal anything." I glanced up. "You have a closed-circuit video surveillance system, don't you? Have you got these guys on tape?"

"The tapes have all been snowy," he said. "Georgia says something's wrong with the cameras, but I think it's interference from the spirit realm. How much does Jerry charge for a séance?"

"I'll let you two work that out."

I wandered around Georgia's for about an hour, but neither the Yates boys nor gremlins put in an appearance. Promising to ask Jerry about a séance, I left Hayden still eyeing the books as if they were going to hurl themselves off the shelves and went by the Goodwill store in search of duck-head umbrellas. There weren't any duck-head umbrellas, but I did see a very nice easel for only fifteen dollars.

"That's a good deal," the woman at the register said. "Just brought in. It's practically new."

And tempting. I'd had one just like this.

"I'm looking for a certain type of umbrella," I said. "Red with a duck's head handle."

She shook her head. "Got plenty of regular ones."

"Does Celosia have a pawn shop?" I asked.

"Jim's Park 'n' Pawn on Highway Three. Doubt he'd have umbrellas, though. He deals mainly in electronics and furniture."

"Thanks."

I started out and she called, "Sure you don't want the easel?"

No, I wasn't sure. "I'll think about it," I said.

I leaned on my car and called Jim of Jim's Park 'n' Pawn. He didn't have any umbrellas. He had plenty of VCRs, camcorders, digital cameras and sleeper sofas. I had just turned off my cell phone when the Pageantoids rounded the corner.

"Madeline!"

Celosia is just too damn small. I sighed and tried to smile. "Hello."

They rushed up to me. I don't know if they plan this, but they always dress alike. Mitch had on khaki slacks and a pink golf shirt. Cathy was wadded into a khaki and pink jogging suit.

"Madeline, we had no idea!" she said. "When you said you were a detective, we didn't dream for a minute you solved actual crimes!"

Mitch grabbed my hand and shook it. "The people in town said you fought off a real murderer!"

Hadn't these two been listening when Jerry told them I'd caught a killer? I pulled my hand free. "Yes, that's true."

Cathy could hardly speak. "Mitch and I have just had the most fabulous idea. You have to go on tour. A crime-fighting beauty queen would inspire millions of little girls."

I laughed. "No, thanks."

"But it's perfect! You can be beautiful *and* tough. That's the message girls need to hear."

Just when I thought these two couldn't get any nuttier. "Cathy," I said. "Mitch. Calm down. I'm not going to tour around selling any sort of message. I'm going to stay here and do my job."

Cathy wouldn't give up. "But this is so amazing. It's like something out of a movie!"

This gave Mitch another idea. "Cathy, we need to talk to the director of Voltage Films. I'll bet he'll say it's a story that must be told."

Anything to get them away from me. "That's a great idea."

"What crime are you investigating now?" Mitch asked.

Let's see. Should I tell them about the umbrella or the library books? "It's confidential."

"A murder?"

"No. Some missing items."

"Some sort of treasure? A lost will?"

"Some valuable items that mean a lot to the owners." That much was true.

He looked at me as if I had answered the Final Pageant Question to thunderous applause. "How do you go about looking for things like that?"

"You ask questions, follow leads."

"Is it dangerous?"

"No, but it takes a lot of time, so if you'll excuse me." I opened my car door.

Cathy beamed at me. "This adds another dimension to our relationship, Madeline."

"It certainly made my day, Cathy," I said and drove away.

WHEN I GOT BACK TO THE Eberlin house, I found Denisha Simpson and Austin Terrell sitting with Jerry on the front porch. Denisha's a self-assured little black girl. Austin's a rugged little white boy. They're best friends and Jerry's biggest fans. They met Jerry while sneaking into the house via a secret passageway. Apparently, they've never met an adult willing to burp, climb trees, throw rocks and roll down hills with them. They come over almost every day, in awe of Jerry's giant-screen TV, his diet, which consists mainly of pizza, cookies and soda, and his enthusiasm for their most outlandish schemes.

Denisha jumped down the steps. "Madeline, did you hear about the movie? It's going to be here, and Austin and I are going to be in it!"

As usual, Denisha's sweeping statements caused a violent reaction from Austin. "We're not going to be in the movie, Denisha! It's a horror movie for grown-ups. There aren't any kids in it. You always get everything wrong."

She rounded on him. "I do not! I heard Mrs. Danbury tell Mrs. Forsythe they're looking for kids to be in the movie."

"Those two old women don't know beans."

Denisha flipped her hand up as if to say, I'm not listening to you any more. "Jerry, isn't there going to be a movie at this house?"

He nodded. "I'm hoping they'll film some of it here."

Austin still wasn't convinced. "When will they be here?"

"Patricia's going to call me when they get to town. You want a Coke, Mac? The kids and I are having a snack."

The kids could count on a snack every time they dropped by the house, as if Jerry needed an excuse.

"That would be nice, thanks. Did you make your phone call?"

"She wasn't home."

I wasn't sure I believed that, but I let it go for now. Jerry went inside. Denisha checked out my dark jeans and red tee shirt. "You're looking very nice today, Madeline. Do you have another murder to solve?"

"No, but I have some very exciting cases."

"Tell us!"

I sat down in one of the rocking chairs. "Well, there's the Case of the Leftover Boxes, the Case of the Missing Umbrella, and now, the Case of the Overdue Library Books. I really don't know which one to solve first."

She gave me a look. "You're not being serious, are you?"

"No. That's called irony. You run into it a lot when you're an adult."

Austin caught on, too. "So there's nothing really exciting, huh?"

"No, but these jobs will pay the bills."

"What bills?" Denisha asked. "You're living here free, aren't you?"

"Yes, but I want to get my own place."

"How come? Ain't you and Jerry a couple?"

"Not yet."

"Oh," she said. She thought it over and nodded wisely. "Kinda like me and Austin."

Austin was scandalized. "Denisha! I told you not to say things like that!"

He bolted into the house. Denisha just sighed and flipped her hand up again, this time as if waving Austin away. "Men," she said.

"How true, Denisha, how true."

Jerry came back with my Coke in time to hear this. "What's true?"

"Denisha and I were just having a girl talk."

"Well, what do you girls think of this?" He took a piece of paper out of his pocket. "Des's latest CD is coming out this fall."

"That's great." I took the Coke and the paper. It was an article from a magazine with a review of the CD. "'Masterful control of the keyboard, sensitive rendition, amazing technique.' Nice, very nice."

"This your brother that plays the piano like you?" Denisha asked.

"Way better than me." Jerry sat down. "He's on tour right now. Japan, Italy, Australia. All the big concert halls."

The phone rang. From somewhere in the house, Austin called, "I'll get it!"

In a few minutes, he came out, scowling. He still hadn't

forgiven Denisha for her remark. "That was your aunt, Denisha. We've gotta go."

"Okay. See you later, Madeline. Bye, Jerry."

Denisha and Austin picked up their bikes from under the trees and rode off down the driveway. I handed the review back to Jerry.

"Will Des be back in time for Tucker's wedding?"

"I don't know." He immediately changed the subject. "This is such a great review. I knew he could do it."

"I think all you Fairweather boys are very talented."

"Well, you have Des the Musician, Tucker the Gardener and me the Screw-Up. One in every family."

"You aren't a screw-up."

"Not much of anything else."

"Have you tried being anything else?"

"Aimless. Carefree."

"Besides that. What do you want, Jerry?"

He started to say something. Then he shook his head, took a drink of Coke and said, "I don't know."

"What about the history course at PCC? Are you interested in that?"

"I don't really want to go back to school. My studying days are over. Not that I ever did that much studying."

"Something in the theater, maybe?"

"It's fun, but I don't think it's something I'd want to do all the time."

I didn't want to suggest anything remotely paranormal, but I'd promised Hayden I'd ask about a séance at the store.

"Hayden's worried the bookstore may be haunted. Could you say a few magic words and make the boogeymen go away?"

"Sure. That's my idea of fun, too."

"But it's not a real job, Jerry."

"I wouldn't charge Hayden, anyway. He and I oughta

work together. I've never met anyone so sensitive to the spirit world."

I was going to continue my argument with the fact that Hayden was prone to mental breakdowns, when a small red Ford Escort drove up the drive. Twenty hopped out, her hair in wild curls.

"Jerry! Have you rented your house to the movie company?"

"Not yet," he said. "What's the matter?"

"I just cannot believe this! The movie is going to be about Mantis Man!"

Jerry and I exchanged a puzzled glance. "Mantis Man?" I said.

Twenty flopped into a rocking chair. "We'll be the laughingstock of the entire country. Poor dumb rural hicks seeing giant insects. It's awful!"

Jerry leaned forward. "Giant insects?"

She sighed. "Here I was, hoping for a sensitive portrayal of our wonderful little town, and all we get is a second-rate horror film."

Jerry said, "But it could be a really good second-rate horror film."

She glared at him. "Jerry, just because you like all that supernatural stuff."

"Well, I don't know anything about Mantis Man," he said. "Fill me in."

"It's ridiculous. It's like that stupid story about the Hook. Teenagers out on a lonely road, their car won't start, they see glowing red eyes and some ghastly creature tries to eat them up."

"So people have seen this thing?"

"Drunk teenagers and old coots who have nothing better to do than run around in the woods all night."

"What's Mantis Man supposed to be? A mutated insect? An alien?"

"Oh, there are all kinds of stories. He's a hobo who fell into some radioactive swamp gas. He's a pet let loose from a UFO. He's an escaped experiment from Peterson Air Force Base."

"And he looks like a praying mantis?"

"Yes, a great big, stupid, bug-eyed praying mantis."

Jerry looked at me in mock anger. "Mac, why have you kept this from me?"

"I knew it would stand in the way of you getting your doctorate in history."

Twenty blinked, trying to follow our exchange, and gave it up. "Well, I had to come out here and tell you the bad news in person." She pointed a shiny orange fingernail at Jerry. "And Jerry Fairweather, if you let those movie people use the Eberlin house to make a gory movie about Mantis Man, I'm not sure I'll ever speak to you again."

"Take it easy," he said. "They may not want to use the house."

"I'm going to start a campaign against this, see if I don't."

"Are there that many people in town who'd object to a movie about the Mantis?" I asked.

"Everyone in my gardening club, for starters."

"Guess they wouldn't like any kind of insect," Jerry said with a grin.

"That's not funny."

"Twenty, all you need is a really big fly swatter."

"If you're not going to take this seriously!"

"I never take anything seriously."

Twenty turned to me. "You know what I'm talking about, don't you, Madeline? You see how the town could be overrun with awful Mantis Man stuff? Cheap tee shirts that say 'I Saw the Mantis Man,' or 'Celosia, Home of the Mantis Man.' We'd never live it down."

"It could be a lot of fun," Jerry said.

Twenty was almost in tears. "You're not from here. You don't know how people feel."

"Just wait before you get too upset," I said. "The movie might not even happen. Voltage Films is a small company. They could run out of money. They could decide to go somewhere else."

She set her mouth in a grim line. "I'm going to see to that."

Twenty left, still grumbling. Jerry did a little grumbling, too.

"There's a giant praying mantis in the neighborhood and you didn't tell me?"

"I've never heard of Mantis Man. Didn't the Fairweather boys try to find him?"

"The Fairweather boys were dealing with other issues. But I want to find him now. Where does he hang out?"

"Why don't you ask Austin and Denisha? They've probably seen him."

"I think it's terrific. Our very own monster. Twenty's just overreacting. Do you suppose we could catch it?"

"And have you tramping through the woods all night with a net and a can of Raid? We had enough trouble with the disappearing cows."

"I don't care what that farmer said, those cows were taken by aliens."

"No, those cows were taken by college students who had a very warped sense of humor." During our college years, some kids had spray-painted cows in Day-Glo patterns. Jerry had gone on and on about aliens. "This Mantis Man is just some kid dressed up."

Jerry wouldn't give up. "Or it could be a real scientific find."

My cell phone beeped. "There he is now, calling to tell you he doesn't exist."

My caller wasn't Mantis Man. It was Ted Stacy. "Hello, Madeline. Just calling to see if you're free for dinner."

Despite all his good qualities, Ted is just, well, not Jerry. Like me, he's divorced, but unlike me, he often expresses his desire to have children. I keep hoping this is enough of a wedge between us, but Ted doesn't seem to mind.

Still, dinner wasn't a bad idea. Ted might know something about Kirby Willet. "That sounds very nice, thanks."

"Pick you up, or meet here?"

"I can be there in about twenty minutes."

"Okay. I'm looking forward to seeing you."

I closed my phone. "Dinner with Ted. I'll ask about the Mantis for you."

I was a little surprised by Jerry's frown. Usually, my going out with Ted doesn't even register with him. "That's the second time this week, isn't it?"

So he had noticed, after all. This was new. "I'm hoping Ted can tell me more about Kirby Willet."

He looked as if he wasn't sure what to say. Then he said, "Oh. Okay. I'm going to see if Nell needs any help."

As I put on one of my sleeveless sundresses and matching sandals and tugged my comb through my short dark curls, an odd thought occurred to me. Was it possible Jerry was jealous of Ted? This was so unlike Jerry, I had to dismiss the thought—still, the way he'd frowned, as if he didn't like the idea of me having dinner with Ted, even though I'd been out with Ted several times. Jerry knew it wasn't serious. Didn't he?

TED AND I DECIDED TO eat at Celosia Square, a new little complex of shops and restaurants. We like the Peach Garden best, a Chinese restaurant featuring shrimp and rice. I wondered briefly what Jerry was doing at the house, if Nell had stuffed him up the chimney or hung him out on the clothesline.

Stop it, I told myself. You're with Ted. You're working.

Ted held my chair for me and then sat down. We ordered the special and hot tea. Ted still had on his crisp pinstriped shirt and gray slacks. His tie, I noticed, was plain gray. Dull plain gray.

Get a grip.

The waitress brought the tea in a fat blue-and-white pot and two matching cups. Ted thanked her and poured the tea. "I see you've been busy, Madeline. I was afraid there might not be enough work for you in town."

"More than enough," I said. "Missing umbrellas, missing library books and a missing Kirby Willet. Do you know him?"

Ted passed one cup to me. "Quite a character. Always trying to invent something new. Invented a self-propelling lawn mower a few years back, but it never did work the way he wanted it to. Made some interesting patterns on the Methodist churchyard, though. Need sugar?"

"One pack, please. He worked at the Wayfarer Motel and at the newspaper. Anywhere else?"

"He did a lot of odd jobs to support himself while he invented things. I think he worked for a while at the paint store, and I know he bagged groceries at the Super Food for a while."

I tore open the sugar pack and dumped it into the tea. The tea was way too hot to drink. I blew on the cup and managed a cautious sip. "Any idea where he might have gone?"

Ted shook his head. "Sometimes he'd leave town for months. I think he went to Washington on occasion, to the patent office."

"But none of his inventions ever worked?"

"No. Poor guy. He kept trying, though."

Our food arrived. We ate for a while, and then I asked Ted about Mantis Man.

"Just a rumor," he said. "Somebody had a few too many

and started seeing things. When we were kids, my brothers and I used to dare each other to go into the woods by the covered bridge. If you spent the night there, old Mantis Man was supposed to suck out your brain—not that my brothers had that much brain to begin with."

I scooped up a plump shrimp with my chopsticks. "What do you think of Voltage Films making a movie about Mantis Man?"

Ted passed the little square dish of ginger sauce. "Well, I understand some people are upset about it, but I can't see that it will do any harm. Probably bring in some tourists, and that's a good thing. We could have our own Mantis Man Days."

"Twenty's very unhappy. She says this kind of thing will hurt Celosia's reputation."

"The movie might be a flop. No sense getting upset over something that might not even happen."

I liked Ted's straightforward approach to everything, but I couldn't help thinking how differently Jerry reacted to the idea of a Mantis Man. Ted has a good sense of humor, but I couldn't see him running through the woods at night chasing spectral insects.

He did, however, insist on paying for dinner.

"No, now, we haven't had a chance to go out for a while," he said, as I reached for my billfold. "It's my treat."

"Thanks."

"Madeline, may I mention again how glad I am you decided to stay in Celosia?"

"Thanks, Ted. That's really nice of you."

"I know it was rough for a while."

"It's tough being the new kid in town."

He smiled. "I know you want people to take you seriously. I think most of them do now."

"I can't really do anything about it if they don't," I said. "There'll always be some people who can't see past the tiara."

WHEN I GOT BACK to the house, Jerry, Austin and Denisha were running in the meadow, chasing fireflies. I sat down on the porch to watch. There was a great deal of yelling, whooping and triumphant cries of "Got one!" After a while, Austin came running to the porch steps, his jar full.

"Seventeen! I win!"

Denisha came panting up. "I have eighteen."

"You do not!"

Jerry came next. All three sat on the steps and counted their fireflies. Fortunately for peace and sanity, Austin and Denisha each had seventeen, and Jerry had fifteen.

"And to our lucky winners goes the grand prize of brownies and ice cream," he announced.

The kids dashed into the house for their snack. Jerry held up his jar and watched the yellow-green glow of the fireflies.

"How was dinner?"

"Fine."

"Learn anything useful?"

"Pretty much the same information. Willet's a hopeless inventor. Mantis Man will suck out your brains."

His gaze was still on the jar. "I want to talk to you about something."

"Sure."

"I don't exactly know how to say it."

I was suddenly aware of how loud my heart was beating. "Sounds serious."

I don't know what he planned to say. I never got the chance to hear it. Austin and Denisha charged out of the house, arguing fiercely.

"Jerry, Denisha took all of the corners when she knows I like them best!"

"Well, you poked your finger in the ice cream, your dirty bug finger!"

"Okay, okay," Jerry said. "Settle down."

He took them back into the house, and he must have settled their quarrel because I didn't hear any more fuss. Of course, by the time he got back to the porch, his serious moment had passed.

"What did you want to say, Jerry?"

He shrugged. "That's okay. Maybe later."

He tipped the jars on their sides and set the fireflies free. As the little sparks of light danced back across the meadow, I thought, When I find Kirby Willet, I'll ask him to invent something that will stop any and all interruptions!

THE NEXT MORNING, I came downstairs, expecting to have breakfast with Jerry and hoping he might feel like talking. Instead, I found Rick Rialto sitting in my chair. Jerry and I get up around eight. He likes to cook, so I look forward to pancakes, french toast, or whatever he decides to make. Now here was Rick in my chair, eating my pancakes and drinking juice out of my favorite glass. He even had his shoes off.

I sat down at the opposite end of the table. "Make yourself at home, Rick."

He saluted me with his glass. "Thanks. Already did."

Jerry turned from the stove. He'd flipped his pink flamingo patterned tie over his shoulder to keep it out of the batter. "How many pancakes do you want, Mac?"

"Two."

"Coming up."

Rick shoveled another mouthful in. "Great pancakes, J. I forgot what a good cook you are."

"Is there some reason you're here this morning?" I asked.

"Just stopped by for breakfast."

I knew this wasn't all. "And?"

"And to let J know the pet-psychic thing is going well."

"I'm so happy for you."

He chuckled and reached for the syrup. "Mrs. Klumpforth was delighted to find out little Perkie, her parakeet, enjoyed the special seed mix she bought for him."

"How delighted?"

"Fifty dollars delighted."

Jerry flipped two pancakes on my plate. "Mrs. Klumpforth can afford it, Mac."

I wasn't going to ruin my breakfast explaining to these two that wasn't the point.

I could tell Rick enjoyed my discomfort. "And Mister Blakely was happy to know his dog Roger liked his new doghouse, although Roger mentioned he'd like to sleep inside when it got colder."

I didn't answer. Jerry brought his plate to the table and sat down. He and Rick shared a glance I couldn't interpret. I wondered how long Rick had been here and what they had discussed before I came downstairs.

Rick took another drink of juice. "So, J, when are the movie people supposed to get here?"

"Sometime today, I think."

"Well, I can't believe no one here has taken advantage of this Mantis Man thing."

"I think most people are embarrassed by it."

"But think of the possibilities! Mantis Man Mania! They could have a street festival, a Mantis Man fair, Mantis Man tee shirts, key rings, mugs—it'd be bigger than Christmas."

Twenty's nightmare coming true. "Maybe somebody tried that already."

"It sounds like gold to me. Then Mac can quit worrying about old people and their pets."

I still didn't believe his being here was a coincidence. "How did you hear about the movie company coming to Celosia?"

He shrugged. "It's all over Parkland."

A minor-league company like Voltage Films? Rick's story was getting shadier by the minute.

"Plus I have connections with people in the business." He shot me a glance before saying to Jerry, "So how are things with Olivia?"

Leave it to Rick to remember Jerry's old girlfriend. "That's over."

"Really? My, my." Rick grinned. "What's this world coming to, eh, Mac?"

Before I could answer, Rick looked at his watch and said, "Oh, hell, I gotta run. Some cat's peeing all over this lady's sofa, and she wants me to delve deep into pussy's soul and plug the leak." He got up and shoved his feet into his shoes. "Gotta push off. Thanks for the snack, J. I'll get back to you on Mantis Man. Mac, you look radiant, as always."

Glowing with anger, I thought, glad to see him leave.

Jerry looked at my plate. "Aren't you hungry?"

"Sorry," I said. "Being around Rick makes it hard to swallow."

"Those pancakes are cold by now. Let me fix you some more." He went to the stove and poured batter on the grill. "Rick won't be around for long. He never stays in one town more than a week."

"Just enough time for the citizens to get wise."

He nodded. "I used to do the same thing."

"'Used to.' That sounds promising."

He flipped the pancakes. "How long have we been living here, Mac?"

"Almost a month. That's some kind of record, isn't it?"

"I like it here."

"I do, too," I said. "You still going through with the B&B idea?"

"Maybe." He put the fresh pancakes on a clean plate and brought them to the table. "Here you go, madam. Deux flapjacks à la Fairweather."

"Merci, Gaston."

He sat down and passed the syrup. "What's up with you today?"

I got the Celosia Public Library overdue list out of my pocket. There were four major offenders. James World owed *101 Ways to Cook Spaghetti.* Mazie Hurwitz had yet to return *Tatting For Beginners.* Bruce Selden was hanging on to *The Complete Works of Emily Dickinson,* and Pat Fenner had decided to keep *Stories From Great Operas* for her own personal library.

I handed the list to Jerry. "Want to ride with me, partner? I'm headed out after some mean desperados."

"The Library's Most Wanted? Sure." He set the list by his plate and read the first name. "*101 Ways to Cook Spaghetti?* He should've worked his way through all one hundred and one by now. And Mazie Hurwitz must be a champion tatter." He poured more syrup on his pancakes. "What is tatting, anyway?"

"Some kind of lace-making technique."

"Oh, here's a good book, *Stories From Great Operas.* I have a copy of that."

"Don't start singing."

"You're just jealous because you don't know any Italian."

"Or French or German. No opera. It's too early in the day."

He finished his pancakes. "Okay."

"And no Mantis Man scheme with Rick."

"Well, I can't promise anything there. Mantis Man is just the kind of gimmick that can really help a small town."

"I think you can find a better way to help Celosia."

He grinned and straightened his tie. "Let's start by bringing some library criminals to justice."

I FIGURED SOMEONE WHO kept a spaghetti cookbook for six months would be large and sloppy. James World was a short, trim man. When he answered the door, I said the most ridiculous thing I've ever said.

"Mister World, I'm Madeline Maclin and this is Jerry Fairweather. We're from the Public Library, and we're here for *101 Ways to Cook Spaghetti*."

"Oh, my," he said. "I've been meaning to get that back. One moment, please."

He handed over the book without a fight. Jerry looked disappointed.

"I was hoping for more drama," he said, as we drove on to Mazie Hurwitz's house.

Mazie was not, as her name suggested, a little old lady. She was an exotic gypsy type with dark hair down to her knees. She also handed over her book without any trouble. She smiled at Jerry.

"Are you the one who holds séances?"

"Yes, I am," he said.

"I may call you sometime."

"Anytime."

I steered him back to the car.

"Now, that's more like it," he said.

Bruce *The Complete Works of Emily Dickinson* Seldon looked like a member of a motorcycle gang, and Pat *Stories From Great Operas* Fenner was a female Pat, pale and wispy. Bruce dug around in his garage and tossed his overdue book to Jerry.

"Ever read any of them poems? They're damn good."

Pat Fenner had apologized over and over for her tardiness.

"I just got so caught up in the stories. They're so complex, so moving."

"I'm sure you can buy your own copy at Georgia's Books," I said.

"Really? Do you think they'd have it there?"

"If not, they can order it for you."

"I just never thought of that."

"Success!" Jerry said as we drove back to the library, all four books secured. "Score one for Madeline Maclin Investigations."

"Now if I could just find Patricia's umbrella."

Jerry leafed through *Stories From Great Operas.* "I think the Parkland Civic Opera is doing *Faust.* Want to go?"

I'm not the opera fan Jerry is, but I'm not passing on any chance to be with him. "Sure."

"Seattle's doing the Ring Cycle this season. Wish I could afford to go see that."

"Well, if you had a job you could afford it."

"There's always Mantis Man merchandise."

I knew a giant insect was too intriguing. "You'd have to have a bankroll first."

"Maybe." He closed the book. "I know you don't like Rick."

"He's much worse than any of your other partners. He's just so slick. I'm afraid he's going to slide right into jail and take you with him."

"He's not doing anything illegal."

I'd given up trying to explain the finer points of fraud to Jerry. "Just don't let him talk you into anything."

"I'm not. I've got my séances. The Eberlin house is set to star in a major motion picture. I'm happy."

"Good." Maybe this time, he'd stay out of Rick's schemes. "Now, what about Tucker's wedding?"

"Can't go."

"Why not?"

"I'm busy that day."

"All day? The wedding's just an hour, maybe less."

"You can tell me all about it."

I don't usually go for the low blow, but I know he loves Tucker. "Jerry, this is your little brother we're talking about."

"I know."

"The wedding's not even going to be in the house."

Thunderclouds gathered in his eyes. "I'm not going."

"What about Harriet? Have you gotten in touch with her yet?" I took out my cell phone. "What's her number? I'll call her."

For a moment, I didn't think he was going to answer. Then he told me Harriet's number, and I punched it in. After three rings, Harriet answered. Her voice, as usual, was harsh, her tone suspicious.

"Who is it?"

"Good morning, Harriet. It's Madeline Maclin."

"What do you want?"

"Jerry and I would like to come visit. We have something to discuss with you."

"What on earth would you have to discuss with me?"

"When would be a good time?" I figured that no time was a good time for Harriet Fairweather. I was right.

"I'm very busy," she said.

"This won't take long. It's about the fire."

Jerry looked alarmed by my bluntness. I couldn't see Harriet's face, of course, but imagined she looked just as horrified. "That's none of your business."

"Well, here, talk to Jerry." I handed him the phone. "Tell her you have a few questions you'd like to ask."

He tried to hand the phone back to me, but I wouldn't let him. After a few minutes shoving the phone back and forth like a game of hot potato, he reluctantly put it to his ear.

"Hello, Harriet. Yes, I know she's pushy." He paused to listen. "I know it's none of her business, but I need to know what happened. Exactly what happened." He paused again, and I imagined Harriet repeating the "playing with matches" story. Then Jerry said, "Well, maybe I don't believe that any more."

There must have been shocked silence on the other end

of the line. Jerry looked at me in surprise, as if he hadn't expected to say that. "Harriet?"

She answered so forcefully, I could hear her voice. "Jeremyn Nicholas Fairweather, how dare you? After all I've done for you!"

"And I appreciate that," he said, "but—"

"Why are you dragging all this up now? Will it change things? Will it bring our parents back? No! Leave it alone!"

Jerry handed me the phone. "She hung up."

"Jerry," I said, "that was some reaction."

"Now you know why I don't call her."

"We'll try again later."

"What? Are you nuts?"

"To react that strongly after all these years? I think your sister is hiding something."

"You think she set the fire?"

"Why not?"

"And blamed me? That's crazy."

"Why did she take care of you and your brothers? Why does she still send you money?"

"Until we started this, I thought it was because she loved me."

"Or feels really guilty about something."

He shook his head. "I don't know."

"That's why you hired me, and I happen to know you can pay."

"I wouldn't be surprised if Harriet closed my account."

When we stopped by the library to return the books, Joan was thrilled.

"I can't believe you got all four! That's wonderful. Would you track down some more?"

"Sure," I said.

"Let me get the other list."

Jerry grinned at me. "Madeline Maclin, Library Detective. Check her out."

I looked around for Bernice Coleman, but she wasn't at the desk. I did see a newspaper rack, which gave me an idea.

"Joan," I said, when she returned with her list, "how far back do you keep newspapers?"

"I'm proud to say we have every issue of the *Celosia News* since it began in 1925. Of course, we've had them all put on disks."

"Any old issues of the *Parkland Herald?*"

"No, but you can access any one you want through our interlibrary website. I'll show you."

She led us to a computer station and clicked on the website. "Right up here under Reference."

"Thanks." I sat down.

Jerry pulled up a chair. "All the newspaper reports say the same thing, Mac. Mysterious house fire. Tragic accident. You've read it before."

"I just want to read it again."

After a few moments searching and arrowing up and down, I found the account of the fire. Around midnight, Harriet Fairweather, age eighteen, had frantically called for help. Firefighters responded promptly, but the downstairs was destroyed, and the bodies of Victor and Lillian Fairweather discovered in the ruins. Police determined several large candles had fallen over, setting fire to the chairs and draperies in the living room.

I looked up from my reading. Jerry had taken a dictionary from the shelf and was leafing through the thin pages, avoiding the lines of print on the screen.

"Jerry, this says Harriet called for help around midnight."

"Yes."

"If you caused the fire by playing with matches, what were you doing up at midnight?"

"I don't know. I was just six years old when this happened."

"Exactly. If you were six years old, I think you would've

been in bed asleep. Didn't you tell me you remember Harriet pulling you out of the house? She got you and your brothers out of bed, didn't she? Why would you have been downstairs in the living room, lighting candles?"

He frowned. "That doesn't make a lot of sense, does it?"

"Why would anybody have been downstairs at midnight lighting candles?"

"Maybe Mom and Dad were having a séance?"

I read the account again. It was possible that someone in the family could've left candles unattended. There had to be someone else besides Harriet who knew what had happened.

"Let's stop by the bookstore," I said. "Maybe Georgia or Hayden know of another write-up of this story."

"I REMEMBER READING about it years ago," Georgia said, as she carried a stack of books to the back of the store. "There was an article in the paper. That's it."

"No one wrote a book about it?"

"Not that I know of."

Hayden was up front at the counter. "I'm sorry," he said when we asked him about the Fairweather tragedy. "I really don't know anything about it. My apologies, Jerry."

"That's okay," Jerry said. "But what about you? Mac said something about another ghost."

Hayden, as usual, was intensely serious. "I need you to hold a séance here. I think the store's haunted."

"What's up?"

"When I'm here by myself, I hear strange noises. Footsteps, whispers, strange cries."

This is business as usual for Hayden.

"And I find things rearranged or knocked over."

Jerry listened very seriously. He didn't say what I would've said, such as, "Are you sure it's not kids?" or "Have you been taking your medication?"

"Sounds like a poltergeist."

"Oh, my God. I knew it."

"Now, don't panic. They're usually more mischievous than harmful."

"Can you get rid of it?"

"Sure. Where did you find things rearranged?"

"I'll show you."

Hayden led us to the children's section. Between the bookshelves was an open space with child-size chairs and a little table. On the table was an empty plate.

"Georgia and I had some cookies for the kids. They're all gone. And the other day when we had special treats for a book club meeting, those disappeared, too." He pointed to the shelves. "And up there, I had a whole row of new books. Every single one was on the floor this morning."

"Stacked in a pile?"

"No, just scattered."

Jerry nodded. "It's a poltergeist, all right. No problem."

Hayden relaxed. "I knew you could take care of it. I was afraid it might have something to do with all this Mantis Man trouble."

"What trouble?" I asked.

"The movie they plan to make. It's really stirring up some resentment in town. I just hope it isn't stirring up the creature."

"Hayden, I seriously doubt that."

But he wasn't listening to me. "It's like digging up a grave. You have to leave these things alone. No wonder a poltergeist is in the store."

"What does Georgia's Books have to do with Mantis Man?"

"I don't know."

He looked so troubled, Jerry said, "I'm sure it's nothing. I'll take care of it."

Once outside, I frowned at Jerry. "Why in the world would you encourage him like that?"

Jerry shrugged. "He's already decided it's a ghost. Nothing's going to change his mind. Might as well go with the flow."

"But you don't honestly believe there's a poltergeist haunting the store."

"Well, there could be."

"No, there couldn't."

"Not gonna argue with you on this one, Mac. We'll just see."

When we got home, there was a message from Patricia on Jerry's answering machine to call her right away. The director of Voltage Films was in town and interested in seeing the house.

Jerry returned her call. "Tell him to come out anytime." He listened, nodding, and then said, "That would be great, thanks." He hung up. "They're on their way."

I have to admit the Eberlin house looks haunted. Although Nell's done wonders with the inside, the outside of the house still looks the same as it did the first day Jerry and I saw it. The porch still sags, the roof needs repair, shutters hang loose, and the gray paint is flaked and cracked, giving the house a scabby appearance.

We had to wait only twenty minutes before a dark blue van and a black Lincoln town car came slowly up the winding driveway and parked beside the house. A dark, bearded man in a black tee shirt, black jeans, and a black baseball cap got out of the van, followed by a thin girl, also in black, and another man. A lanky man I recognized as Lance Henderson got out of the Lincoln.

Lance Henderson looked impressive as long as he was in strong sunlight and a good distance away. Close up and in the shadows of the trees, I could see the fine network of lines around his eyes and mouth, the red-rimmed eyes and obvious hairpiece.

The dark man shook Jerry's hand. "You must be Jerry Fairweather. I'm Josh Gaskins. This is my assistant, Stephanie Harold, this is Flynn Davis, and of course you know Lance Henderson. Terrific house. Just what I was looking for." He walked back and forth in the front yard, holding his hands up in a square as if examining the house from different angles. "Can we have a look at the inside?"

"Sure," Jerry said.

Gaskins stood in the doorway and frowned at the living room. "Well, this is too nice for what I've got in mind, but the exterior's perfect."

Lance Henderson spoke up, his familiar bass voice echoing. "Perfect? What do you mean? The place looks leprous. What kind of setting is this for *Pastel Memoirs?*"

Gaskins exchanged a look with Stephanie. "Lance, I've explained to you. We're not doing *Pastel Memoirs.* We're doing *The Curse of the Mantis Man.*"

"I will not be seen in some cheap horror film."

"Could we talk about this later?" As he walked back to the porch, he said to Stephanie, "I want to create a feeling of dread, you know? A feeling that your very soul is in peril."

She made a note on her clipboard. "Okay."

Lance said, "I did not sign on this project to do a horror film."

"Face it, Lance, you're lucky to be signed on any film."

"*Pastel Memoirs* is my comeback film. It's a beautiful script. You promised you'd do it."

"I'll do it after we finish *Curse of the Mantis Man.* You've got a contract for two films with Voltage. Stephanie, where's my drink?"

Lance Henderson stalked to the van, folded his arms and took a dramatic stance, staring out across the fields.

"He seems a little upset," I said.

Gaskins wasn't concerned. "Oh, he's always throwing these little fits. He'll do it. He has to." Stephanie hurried up with a large plastic cup. Gaskins took a loud slurp through the straw. "He hasn't worked in months, unless you count appearances on game shows. Oh, this is our star, Flynn Davis."

Flynn Davis was an extremely handsome man with dark curly hair and blue eyes. He shook my hand. "Pleasure to meet you, Ms. Maclin. Is this your first film, too?"

"No, I live in this house. What part do you have in the movie?"

He stepped closer and lowered his voice. "I'm actually the lead, but I'm not supposed to say that. Lance thinks he's got the lead role, but his is really more of a character part."

"I see," I said, although I wasn't sure I did.

"I don't want to hurt the old boy's feelings, but his days of playing the hero are over. Got to clear the field for the rest of us. Oh, and Gaskins is bringing in Vivian Montrose for the heroine."

"Vivian Montrose?"

"She's the star of *Beach Island.*"

I'd seen exactly one episode of *Beach Island,* an overblown nighttime soap opera set on a tropical island and filled with overly endowed women in tiny bikinis.

Davis smiled. "She'll be a real asset to this picture. Nice to have met you, Ms. Maclin."

He sauntered off as if assured I was watching his rear. I was. It was a very nice rear, but I wasn't so sure about the rest of Flynn Davis.

While Gaskins and Jerry discussed what a few shots of the house were worth, I went over to Lance Henderson. He was still muttering about *Pastel Memoirs.*

"This was going to be my comeback film, a quality picture the whole family could enjoy. Now that upstart Gaskins wants me to be in some sort of low-budget shockfest."

"It might not be so bad," I said.

He eyed me. "Are you an actress?"

"I'm Madeline Maclin. I own a detective agency in town."

"Really? You look more like an actress."

He was trying what was left of his charm on me. "Thank you."

"I should hire you to find my career. I lost it somewhere in the eighties."

"You still have a lot of fans. People here are excited about seeing you."

It was pathetic how he brightened. "Really?"

"I don't think they'd care what kind of movie you were in."

"But this Mantis Man is just some silly local story, isn't it? There's no real facts."

"No, but it might be fun."

He sighed. "But I need a part with depth, with meaning."

"What part do you play in this movie?"

"We're still debating that." His dark look at Gaskins reminded me of the sheriff in *Red Canyon*. The bad guys hadn't stood a chance. "Excuse me, Ms. Maclin."

He went back to his car. Jerry and Gaskins were in conversation in the front yard.

"I'd like to come by tomorrow with my crew and film some establishing shots," Gaskins said. He took another loud slurp of soda. "There's supposed to be a full moon Thursday night, which will work in perfectly. Stephanie, make a note to have Davis and Vivian come out for some exterior scenes." Stephanie nodded and jotted down what he said. Gaskins shook hands with Jerry. "Okay, we're all set. Thanks very much. We'll see you tomorrow."

Gaskins and Stephanie got into the van with Davis and left.

"Did you settle on a price?" I asked Jerry.

"He made a generous offer. Can you drop me off at the theater? I've got a rehearsal in about ten minutes."

I have a slight problem with Jerry spending so much time at the theater. The director, Kenna Porter, is exactly Jerry's type, a small blonde with an attitude. Today, however, Kenna wasn't the problem. As we pulled up in the parking lot of the Baker Auditorium, I saw the Pageantoids. I groaned.

"What are they doing here?"

"Hoping to find a special souvenir sequin?"

"Get out of the car, quick."

Not quick enough. The Pageantoids saw me and rushed over to the car. Cathy's plaid shorts matched Mitch's plaid shirt. I couldn't move without hitting one of them. As tempting as this was, I had to restrain myself. I didn't want plaid all over the car.

Cathy's eyes brimmed with happy tears. "Great news, Madeline! You must hear this. We're going to organize another pageant for Celosia."

Mitch Hutton grinned. "We've already spoken to Mister James here at the theater, and he's thrilled."

Cathy clasped her hands together. "We're going to call it the Miss Celosia Summertime Pageant. Say you'll help us! It would be the very thing. This is the first time we've ever tried anything like this. We need your advice."

"I'd love to," I said, "but I'm right in the middle of a case. Evan James has done dozens of pageants. He can answer all your questions."

"But you have firsthand experience. You know what it's like to be a queen."

"And now I'm trying to find out what it's like to be a detective, so if you'll excuse me."

They reluctantly moved so I could drive away. Jerry waved good-by from the stage door. His grin faded when

Cathy and Mitch saw him and headed in his direction. It was my turn to grin as he ducked into the door to escape.

SHANA AMRY ARRIVED just as I was unlocking my office door. She had a big bouquet of flowers and a picnic basket.

"Congratulations on your new office."

"Thanks," I said. "Let me give you the grand tour."

I opened the door, and she went in.

"Madeline, this looks great! I'm so glad this all worked out." She put the flowers on my desk and began taking things out of the basket.

"What's all this?"

"An office-warming present. I've got tea and cookies, a pencil holder, some multicolored file folders, index cards and a stapler with your name on it." She held up the bright pink stapler. "I know, it's lurid, but no office is complete without one."

I laughed and reached for a cookie. When I came to Celosia, I never dreamed I'd find a good female friend. The pageant world is littered with the carcasses of friendships. Somehow, you just can't go for the crown and be a pal. But I'd found a real friend in Shana Amry. Shana's better known as Shana Fairbourne, author of such blazing historical romances as *Suppressed Desires, Flames* and *Passion's Mistress.* She could win any beauty pageant on earth by simply showing up, thanks to an abundance of red-gold hair, creamy skin and amazing golden eyes.

Now she fixed this tawny gaze on me. "Who's this guy Rick? If he were a character in one of my books, he'd be Sleazy Gambler Number Three."

"You've got that right. He's a gambler. He and Jerry ran quite a few scams back in college."

She passed me a plastic cup filled with iced tea and a straw. "Jerry's playing pet psychic, too?"

"No, I've managed to keep him too busy to play with Rick."

Shana's eyebrows rose. "Oh, ho. What kind of 'busy' are we talking about here?"

"Not what you're thinking. I'm trying to get him to find a job."

"Any luck?"

"Not yet."

Shana used her straw to swirl the ice cubes in her tea. "You're driving yourself crazy, you know that?"

Like me, Shana's not interested in having children. She tells me all her maternal instincts are centered on Hayden. It makes me wonder about my maternal instincts, such as they are. Until recently, I didn't think I had any. Now I'm constantly worrying about Jerry, as if he were eight years old instead of almost thirty.

Shana's gaze was sympathetic. "He'll figure it out. I just hope he isn't married to someone else when that happens."

I nodded. Shana let me sit in gloom for only a few minutes before changing the subject.

"I hear you're helping Evan with another pageant. That can't be true."

"Sort of."

"Who are those two odd people in charge?"

"Cathy Sloop and Mitch Hutton. The Pageantoids."

"Oh, that's good. Slightly obsessed, are they?"

"Just a bit, but Evan is, too, so they should work well together."

"Is Jerry going to play for the pageant?"

"Probably. He's over there a lot." Shana's frown made me say, "What?"

"Kenna Porter, that's what."

"I know, I know."

"Trouble in River City."

"I hope not."

"Remember your vow? 'Nothing is more important than my relationship with Jerry Fairweather.'"

"It's still important. I just need to approach things the right way. And Jerry keeps acting like he wants to tell me something."

Shana made a face and took another cookie from the basket. "Maybe somebody needs to talk to Mister Fairweather."

"I'd rather you didn't." It was my turn to change the subject. "What do you know about Kirby Willet?"

"In my book, he'd be Loser Number One. But I shouldn't be so judgmental. Hayden and I moved to Celosia only a few years ago. We're still considered upstart city folk. My impressions of Kirby Willet are completely from hearsay."

"Did anyone mention his interest in ghosts?"

"Don't talk to me about ghosts," she said. "That business with Juliet Lovelace was enough for me. Nell should be able to tell you everything, and if Nell doesn't know, try Denisha."

"What about Mantis Man? What do you know about that story?"

"Not a lot. I didn't grow up here, but I understand you haven't lived until you've stayed out on Lovers' Walk all night and seen the big red eyes coming at you. You can imagine what Hayden thinks of that."

"I personally think it would be really cool if Kirby Willet turns out to be Mantis Man."

"I suppose he could be. After all, has anyone seen him and Mantis Man together?"

"Seriously, is there anything to the Mantis Man stories? Has anybody actually been killed, or is it just another urban myth?"

"No, just scared. Now, there's a mystery for you," Shana said. "You could solve the Mystery of Mantis Man."

"Add it to the list."

"List?"

I nodded. "I'm not only searching for Kirby Willet, I'm searching for Patricia Hargrave's missing duck-head umbrella, as well as several overdue books from the public library."

"I had no idea Celosia was so full of crime." She fixed her golden gaze on my face. "Forgive my curiosity, Madeline, but as a writer, I'm always interested in peoples' motives. What made you decide to become an investigator?"

"That's a fair question," I said. "I wanted to do something useful, and it seemed to me that finding things people wanted was a lot more useful than standing around in an evening gown talking about world peace."

"So you don't really mind looking for umbrellas and library books?"

"No, because those things are just as important to their owners." I tried to think of some way to explain. "I guess I want everything to be in the right place."

As I said this, I thought, yes, that's it. That's the reason behind everything I do. Life's so disjointed and unpredictable, it's nice to know some things can be put in order.

"Plus I'm not judged by how I look," I said. "At least, not by a panel of judges."

Shana smiled. "I think I can relate to that."

"Does this mean I'll be a character in your next book?"

"No, you're not conflicted enough."

I feigned being insulted. "What? My angst-filled relationship isn't worthy?"

"Oh, you'll find a way around that."

Shana had another chapter of her latest Vixen and Slate saga to finish, so she said good-by. I had reached for another cookie when Chief of Police Gus Brenner tapped on my door and came in.

"Afternoon, Madeline. Got a minute?"

"Sure," I said. "Have a seat."

Nell's dad is big and square like his daughter. His hair is

a fuzz of blond on his large head. His small eyes, as shrewd and blue as Nell's, miss nothing.

"Need to talk to you about Rick Rialto."

I made a face. "I'll bet you do."

"I understand he's a friend of Jerry's."

"What's he done?"

"Just a few complaints." He took out a small pad and flipped through the pages. His brow wrinkled as he read. "Something about a cat not feeling wanted. A dog let loose because it said it needed some space." He glanced up. "You want to tell me what this is all about?"

"Rick says he's a pet psychic."

"Reading animals' minds, is he?"

"Pretending to."

The chief nodded. "That's a new one." He put the pad away. "What's he doing in Celosia? Seems there'd be more folks interested in this kind of thing in Parkland."

"He said something to Jerry about getting involved with the film company."

"What do you know about him?"

"I don't like him, and I don't trust him."

"All right. We'll both keep an eye on Mister Rialto."

"He also wants to exploit Mantis Man."

Chief Brenner shook his head. "That old thing. Every summer, I get at least one teenager who swears he's seen the Mantis. That's usually after too many beers at Kate's Beer and Bait Shop on Highway Forty-Five."

"How did that story get started?"

"Must have been about thirty years ago. Somebody saw something up in the woods by the covered bridge. Said it looked like a big insect with claws. Folks started calling it the Mantis Man. Now everybody's seen it, or they think they have. How's Mister Rialto planning to do anything with that?"

"He wants to sell Mantis Man tee shirts and coffee mugs."

"Well, that's no sillier than telling people what their cats are thinking." He scratched his head. "Hear you're on the lookout for Kirby Willet."

"I hope that doesn't interfere with any police business."

"Can't say that it does."

"No deep dark scandal to uncover?"

"Nope. Interesting thing about Voltage Films, though. Josh Gaskins used to live here when he was a teenager. I believe he and Kirby Willet knew each other, at least for a while."

I remembered Patricia Hargrave wondering aloud if Josh Gaskins was related to the Middleton Gaskins. "Gaskins lived in Celosia? Wonder why he didn't mention it."

Chief Brenner shrugged. "Too good for the town now, maybe. But why else would he choose Celosia? There's plenty of little towns closer to Los Angeles. Why come all the way to North Carolina?"

"To show his old pals how important he is now?"

"I've learned that spite can travel a long way."

"If he spent some time in Celosia, then he knew about the Eberlin house."

"Hard to overlook it."

If Gaskins has some sort of hidden agenda, what could it be? I thought. Even if he wants to spite his childhood buddy, Willet isn't here to spite.

"Thanks," I said. "This might be useful."

Chief Brenner touched his cap in a little salute. "Afternoon, Ms. Maclin."

Now I was even more curious to find what Kirby Willet had squirreled away at Frannie's house.

Frannie Thomas lived in a modest little brick home on May Avenue. I could see how she needed every inch of space. She met me at the door and led me down a short hallway to the back bedroom. Boxes were stacked everywhere.

"Which ones are Willet's?" I asked.

"All of them."

"Okay, let's start with this one."

Frannie stood by wringing her hands as I looked through Kirby Willet's stuff. Most of the boxes held clothes and shoes. One had soap, powder and shampoo. Another had paperback books and hunting magazines. I checked the magazines to see if any had an address label, but Willet must have bought them from a store. Another box was filled with model airplane kits and jigsaw puzzles.

"Nothing that personal," I said. I tried to assure her she wasn't breaking some privacy law, but she continued to clasp her hands nervously.

The next few boxes had socks and underwear, car manuals, pieces of wire, a flashlight, a hammer and some lightbulbs.

"See? No problem."

I opened the next box. It was full of money. A lot of money and a big jar of peanuts.

"Oh, my," Frannie said.

Oh, my, indeed.

THREE

CHIEF BRENNER LOOKED at the box of money and shook his head. "Now, I never would've guessed Kirby would have this much money."

After doing a rough count and finding over ten thousand dollars in the box, I'd called the police right away. Frannie stood in the doorway, still wringing her hands. "What do you think?" I asked Brenner. "Is it stolen money? Drug money?"

"I'll have to check," he said. He picked up the box and carried it out to his squad car. Frannie trailed anxiously behind.

"Chief Brenner, I had no idea, no idea at all! I thought he just had clothes and shoes and things like that."

"It's all right, Mrs. Thomas," he said. "No one's accusing you of anything. We're just going to put this in a safe place until Mister Willet comes to claim it."

"What about all his other stuff?" I asked.

He put the box in his trunk and closed the lid. "Tell you what. I'll send an officer by with a truck. We'll take it all down to the police station and Willet can settle with us later. How's that?"

Frannie sighed in relief. "That would be wonderful. I don't want any more surprises like this."

"Could've been a lot worse," Brenner said to me when Frannie had gone into her house.

"Drugs, you mean?" I knew even small, peaceful Celosia had drug problems.

He nodded. "Yep. We should be glad it's just good old cash."

"This makes me even more interested in finding Kirby."

"Maybe one of his inventions finally paid off."

Or maybe someone had murdered him for this money and was now looking for it. No need to mention this to Frannie.

Before driving to the theater to pick up Jerry, I stopped in at Georgia's Books and wandered around, alert for shoplifters. Everything seemed to be in order.

Georgia was checking a long list of magazines. "Madeline, I hate to waste your time. I'm not really sure we have a problem."

"I don't mind," I said.

"Well, you know how Hayden is. I thought if we took some sort of action, it would calm him down. I haven't found anything missing, and I know for a fact the store isn't haunted. It's old, but it isn't haunted."

"It's in very good shape."

"Yes, indeed." She tucked her pencil behind her ear. "You remember that rainstorm last week? That's the first time the roof has ever leaked, and fortunately, the water didn't do much damage. Hayden wanted to fix it himself, but I didn't let him. I had someone else do the repairs."

"You mean, Hayden isn't afraid of heights?"

"Not a bit. Strange, isn't it? He's terrified of things he can't see, but he'll climb way up on a ladder to change a lightbulb or brush away a spider web, which, by the way, I will not do! I suppose we all have our own phobias. Now, don't feel you have to hang around here all day, Madeline. I know you have things to do."

As I drove to the theater to pick up Jerry, I thought about what Georgia had said. I knew why Jerry had a phobia about returning to the family home. Would my reluctance to return to my artwork be considered a phobia? What exactly was I afraid of? My mother was no longer standing behind me, ready to give me a push or a last-minute instruction.

Keep your hand at your waist. Don't touch your hair. Remember to come in on the second chorus. If you don't sing out loud like I told you, you'll never win anything. Wave gracefully! And for God's sake, keep smiling!

I was so used to her harsh commands, her silent smirk at the failure of my one art exhibit had cut me to the core.

That was years ago, I told myself. Isn't it time you got over that? She's not standing behind you talking or smirking now, is she?

Evan James greeted me in the foyer by grasping both my hands in his. "Madeline, I can't thank you enough."

"Thank me?"

"For introducing me to your friends Cathy and Mitch. They're so enthusiastic and full of great ideas, I actually want to do another pageant."

Evan had been so upset by Juliet's murder, he'd sworn off pageants. Now he looked so pleased and excited, I didn't have the heart to discourage him.

"That's great, Evan, but I really can't help very much. I have several cases I'm working on."

He nodded. "Yes, of course. Frannie wants you to find Kirby Willet. I wouldn't dream of interfering with your work."

Celosia gives new meaning to the term "Heard it through the grapevine." Thank goodness news about the box of money hadn't quite made it to the vine yet.

"That shouldn't take all your time, though," Evan said. "You can stop by every now and then to give us some pointers."

"Aren't you busy with *Music Man?*"

"Kenna's in charge of that, which leaves me free to do the pageant. It's just what I needed, Madeline. I don't mind telling you I've been a little depressed. Working on a new show has been a godsend."

What could I say to that? "Oh, well, good, then."

Evan went upstairs to his office. I pushed open the double doors leading to the auditorium and went inside. The actors were attempting the "Marian the Librarian" song and dance. Donna Sanchez, one of the former Miss Celosia Pageant contestants, played Marian. She sat in the front row while the dancers worked on a tricky part of their choreography. She moved her pocketbook so I could sit down in the seat next to hers.

"Hello, Madeline."

"Hi, Donna. How's it going?"

She was still smarting from the pageant's cancellation. "Well, it's not as good as Miss Celosia was going to be, but I guess it's all right."

"I'm sorry Juliet got herself murdered. That was so inconvenient for you."

Donna missed the irony. "That's all right. There's a new pageant coming up."

"I hope it doesn't interfere with your debut as Marian."

"I've worked everything out with Kenna and Evan." She flipped back her hair. "I know I'll win. There's absolutely no competition."

"No one else has entered?"

More totally good irony wasted. "Well, Karen Mitman's mother made her, as usual. Then there's Jeanie Swain, Destiny Ray and a few others. None of them have a chance. They've never been in a pageant before."

"There's always beginner's luck."

She gave me a pitying look. "I don't think so."

Kenna called for Donna to come try her part of the dance.

When Donna went up on stage, Kenna came out into the auditorium to watch the dance. She had on a short leopard-print skirt and a black leotard. Large gold hoops hung from her ears. Her platinum-blond hair was decorated with pink-tipped spikes.

"Nice to see you, Madeline," she said as the dancers twirled and skipped through the library set. "I want Jerry in my next production. See if you can talk him into it."

At first, I heard only the "I want Jerry" of this sentence. Then I realized what she'd said. "I doubt he'll need much persuading."

"I think he'd be a natural on stage. We're planning to do *How To Succeed in Business Without Really Trying* next season. I think he'd make a perfect J. Pierpont Finch."

I'd seen the movie. "The scheming guy who works his way up through the company by sneaky tricks?"

"What do you think?"

"Oh, he could probably handle that. His singing voice is fair to medium, though."

"We can work on that. I'd rather teach an actor to sing than try to get a singer to act." She gave me a critical gaze. "What about you? I know you've had stage experience."

"Enough for a lifetime."

"You'd make a good Rosemary. Can you sing?"

"Not a bit."

Kenna wasn't discouraged. "Like I said, we can work on that." The dance ended. She raised her voice. "All right, everyone. We'll take a short break and run Act One." She turned back to me. "And I understand you're a painter?"

Jerry Fairweather, you are a dead man. "I used to paint a little."

"Portraits?"

"Some."

"Let me tell you what I have in mind. I'd love to have a

portrait of children in various costumes for the lobby. Do you think you could do something like that?"

"I haven't painted a portrait in a while."

Jerry strolled over in time to add to the conversation. "She plays the violin, too."

I couldn't believe he was bringing this up. "Jerry."

"Excuse me. I meant to say fiddle."

Kenna looked impressed. "You should be in our orchestra."

"I just know one song," I said. For my pageant talent, I had learned "Orange Blossom Special," a guaranteed crowd-pleaser, no matter how sloppily it's played. Since most of the other contestants belted out Broadway tunes or hopped about in character ballets, my not-so-perfect version of the fiddle tune was often enough to win the talent competition.

"Well, please think about the portrait," she said.

Two of the dancers came up to ask her about part of the dance, so she excused herself to demonstrate the move for the girls.

Jerry correctly interpreted the expression I leveled his way. "I think there's trouble in River City."

"You'd better believe it, bud. Why did you tell Kenna I was an artist?"

"That may have slipped out."

"And then to bring up the violin?"

"Now what's the harm in that?"

"I am definitely never sawing through 'Orange Blossom Special' again, and you know it. I pawned that fiddle years ago."

"Okay, okay," he said. "But look me in the eye and tell me you're giving up on your art."

As much as I enjoy looking him in the eye, I couldn't do it.

He slumped comfortably in the seat beside me and stretched his legs. I noticed the flamingo tie glowed faintly pink in the dim light of the auditorium. "Start out small, Mac. There are probably lots of people in town who'd like to have their portrait painted."

I didn't want to tell Jerry I wasn't sure I could still paint portraits. "I don't have the time."

"In between cases."

"I don't have any supplies."

He sat up straight. "Mac. Quit making excuses. You can start with me if you'd like to get back in practice."

I honestly felt my heart squeeze. I'd wanted to paint him forever, to see if I could capture his impish smile and the light in his clear gray eyes.

"You can't sit still that long."

"More excuses. I happen to know you can work from photographs."

"Damn."

He grinned. "You cannot escape your fate. What sort of brushes and stuff do you need?"

"I can buy my own."

"And you can use the parlor."

Ever since Jerry had mentioned turning the upstairs parlor into a studio, my imagination had been decorating the room. I'd have my easel by the window, my extra canvases stacked in that corner and rows of oils and acrylics arranged by color—

But another part of me cringed at the idea, the foolishly idealistic part that had been crushed by criticism and seared by my mother's silent smirk that broadcast "I told you so" louder than anything she'd ever spoken.

Jerry said, "It's worth a try, isn't it?"

"I'll think about it." I'll think about it. I'd been able to do nothing but think about it ever since he'd suggested using the parlor.

I could tell Jerry didn't quite understand my reluctance. "It's not like you have to put on a show," he said.

"That's never going to happen again."

"So paint some portraits. Earn a little extra dough for Madeline Maclin Investigations."

This time I did look him in the eye. "On one condition."

"This is going to cost me, isn't it?"

"You look for a real job."

He slumped back again. "Oh, man."

"Not feeling walls, or listening to spirits, or wandering around with a dowsing rod. A real job."

He groaned. "You're killing me. Okay. I'll look."

"You will look and you will find."

"In other words, something dull and predictable."

On stage, Kenna called for places. "Jerry, we're going to try the dance again."

He hopped up and went back to the piano. This time, the dancers were all on the right beat, and Kenna was pleased with the results.

"Much better. Do it once more, and we'll call it a night."

Other cast members came out into the auditorium to watch. I recognized two of the older women, Agnes Forsythe and Billie Lee Danbury, the same two ladies who "didn't know beans," as Austin had so charmingly described them. Somewhere there's an assembly line stamping out Small Square Grannies. Both women are short and squat with gray hair and glasses. They're often in Georgia's, flirting with Hayden. They looked through a box of large feathered hats the costume crew had left by the stage steps.

"This pink one will go with your costume," Agnes told Billie Lee. "I think I'll use the yellow one."

Billie Lee tried on the pink hat. "What do you think?"

"That's fine. What about this one on me?"

"I don't know. It's awfully big."

"It's supposed to be."

Agnes looked around, saw me and came over, trailing ribbons and artificial flowers. "Madeline, you know about these things. Doesn't this hat suit me? I'm playing the mayor's wife. I really should have the biggest hat."

"I don't know about hats of the nineteen hundreds, Agnes."

"But surely your pageant experience includes costumes of all kinds."

"I never wore a period costume, just fancy dresses. Ask Kenna."

She took off the hat and turned it around in her hands as if measuring the hat's circumference. "My hat really needs to be the biggest."

"I'm sure it will be," I said.

"Do you know the show? The mayor's wife is actually a very large part."

I honestly couldn't remember the mayor's wife. "I've seen the movie."

"It's not the same. The stage production has much more depth." She glanced up to the dancers. "That's coming along very well, isn't it? This is going to be a great show."

"Jerry's enjoyed it so far."

"Oh," she said. "A word in your ear, Madeline." She sat down beside me and lowered her voice. "All the young ladies have been flirting with him. I thought you might like to know."

And all the old ladies, too, I'll bet. "Thanks," I said, "but that's okay. He probably flirts right back."

Agnes blinked a few times. "Your relationship must be very secure."

"We're good friends, that's all."

"Well, still, I'd look out for that Donna Sanchez if I were you. I don't like to speak ill of anyone, but she is the closest thing to a tramp I've seen in this town."

"Thank you, Agnes."

Billie Lee came over to us, tying the ribbons of a blue

hat. She twirled around to give us the full effect. "I like this one the best."

Agnes sighed. "But your dress is pink! A blue hat would look ridiculous."

"I'll put some pink flowers on this one."

"Billie Lee, there is a perfectly good pink hat for you to wear."

Billie Lee ignored her. "Madeline, I'm glad you're here because I have so many questions. How many extras will this movie need? I am so excited! My neighbor says she saw Lance Henderson's car today at the Stop 'N' Shop. Is he as handsome as he is on TV?"

How to put this tactfully? "He's a little older."

"Well, that's all right. So are we! Are all the actors staying with you, or just the big stars?"

"They're all staying at the Wayfarer Motel," I answered.

"Oh, did you hear that, Agnes? After rehearsal, let's go over there and see if we can get Lance's autograph."

Agnes gave her a look. "Take that hat off first."

Agnes and Billie Lee left, babbling excitedly about the possibility of seeing their idol. Kenna thanked the dancers and reminded everyone of the rehearsal schedule.

Jerry tucked his music book under his arm. "Okay, Mac, we can stop by the employment office on our way home and see what's available."

"It's closed, and you know it."

"Gee, that's too bad."

We said good-night to Kenna and the dancers and walked up the aisle.

"If it's any consolation, you were psychic the other day," I told Jerry.

"Oh, yeah?"

"One of the boxes Kirby Willet left at Frannie Thomas's house is full of money."

"Mister Willet doesn't trust banks?"

"Maybe Mister Willet robs banks. This was stacks of hundred dollar bills."

"Counterfeit, maybe?"

"I brought a bill along to take to Warwick."

"You'll make his day. Mind if I tag along?"

I was pretty sure I could handle Milton Warwick alone, but I never turn down an opportunity to be with Jerry. "I think you'd make a good chaperone."

"If you want me to see you spooning with Milton, think again. I have shopping to do."

"Shopping?"

"I'm out of ectoplasm."

"What about flying trumpets? Don't you need a couple of those?"

His look was of mock scorn. "That's so old fashioned. You watch me tonight. I'll show you how it's done."

I've seen Jerry do dozens of séances. I'm always astounded that people take his otherworldly pronouncements seriously. Tonight, one of his regular customers, a thin, intense older woman named Flossie Mae Snyder, had brought along her round, jolly thirty-year-old niece, Sylvie. They came into the parlor and took seats at the round table. Jerry dimmed the lights, sat down, and they all took hands. After a few minutes of humming and making odd noises, he went into his fake trance and told them everyone on the Other Side was well and happy.

"Ask about Uncle Henry," Sylvie said.

"Uncle Henry says, 'Hello, Sylvie.'"

"Ask him if I'm going to marry Elbert Dooley."

"He says, 'Elbert is a good boy.'"

I would've said "You can do better," but it wasn't my séance.

Flossie Mae wanted to know if Aunt Marge and Aunt Marie had settled their differences and if there was any news about the gold watch. She'd been coming for several weeks, trying to find this important piece of jewelry. I was curious to see how Jerry was going to handle this problem.

"Marge and Marie are at peace," he said in his faraway voice. "The watch is very faint. Yet I sense its presence. It will be found when it wants to be found."

This answer satisfied Flossie Mae. She and Sylvie asked a few more questions. Then Jerry came out of his "trance."

"How did it go?" he asked them. "Did Henry come through?"

"And Marge and Marie," Flossie Mae said, smiling. "We're very close to finding the watch. An excellent reading, Jerry, thank you."

She paid for herself and Sylvie. They said they'd see him next week. He escorted them to the door. When they'd gone, he turned back to me. I was standing in the parlor doorway, my arms folded, shaking my head.

"What?" he said. "That was a very successful séance, thank you very much."

"You have no idea where that watch is."

"So? Neither do they."

"How can you lead people on like that?"

"I'm not leading them on. I'm giving them hope. Didn't you see how Sylvie's face lit up when Uncle Henry told her to marry Elbert Dooley?"

"Sylvie would be happy to marry anybody. You're such a fraud."

"But I'm a very good fraud."

Is there any chance of reforming him? I wondered. What am I thinking? I can't even tell him how I feel, much less convince him to give up these ridiculous séances. "These pretend séances aren't part of our bargain."

"They'll have to be for a while. You have to give me time to find another job."

"A legal job."

"A dull job. You're asking a lot, Mac."

"Finding a real job shouldn't be difficult for someone who talks to the dead."

He decided to go on the defense. "What about your studio? Have you set up shop yet?"

"I have to buy supplies, remember?"

"Great," he said, triumph in his eyes. "You can do that tomorrow after your visit to Warwick."

THE NEXT MORNING, we drove to Parkland. I dropped Jerry off at Transformation and Company, a magic shop in Commerce Circle Mall, and drove to Warwick's studio.

Milton Warwick is a long thin man with a domed head and shiny eyes, a real-life Mantis Man. He's also quite good with the tiniest scraps of evidence. If I can tolerate his unhealthy fascination with me, I can usually get some helpful information.

He held the hundred dollar bill up to the light and turned it around in his thin fingers. "This is a very real bill, Madeline. Couldn't be realer."

"Thanks."

He handed the bill back to me. "Bring me anything else today?"

"No. This is the only clue I have."

"Please, have a seat. I haven't seen you in weeks."

I had other stops to make, but thought it would be rude to rush off. I sat down in one of the white plastic chairs in what Warwick calls his waiting room. As far as I can tell, he lives and works within three small rooms—his lab, his bedroom and this room, furnished in Early Dentist. He sat down across from me.

"How's life in Celosia?"

"Getting more complicated by the minute."

"How so?"

"Well, for one thing, the Pageantoids are in town."

He gave a dry chuckle. "Your groupies."

"Fortunately, they've found something to keep them busy. Another thing happening is a movie about the Mantis Man. Ever hear of him?"

"Just a silly story. I wouldn't think there'd be enough material for a movie. You're not in the movie, are you?"

"No, but Jerry's house is."

Warwick steepled his long fingers. "Ah, yes, the haunted house. Are you still living there?"

"Just until I can find an apartment."

His eyes gleamed with hope. "How are things with you and Jerry?"

"About the same."

"You're wasting your time there, Madeline. You need to be with someone who appreciates you."

I didn't like the direction of this conversation. "I'm also investigating the disappearance of one of Celosia's mysterious citizens, Kirby Willet."

Warwick looked surprised. "Wrong Way Willet?"

"You know him?"

"The inventor, right? Eats tons of peanuts?"

"That's the guy. Why do you call him Wrong Way Willet?"

Warwick laughed. "Oh, my goodness. I hadn't thought of him in years! Some of his wackier inventions made the issues of *Astounding Nonsense*."

"Back up and give me all the details," I said.

"Well, as you know, I belong to several scientific organizations, legitimate organizations. The Parkland Science Club publishes their own magazine called *Astounding Nonsense*. Wait a minute. I think I may have a copy." He reached over to a white plastic table and looked through a stack of magazines until he found a thin magazine he passed to me. The cover declared, "Scientist Proves Moon Made of Cheese." Warwick sat back. "In the magazine, we discuss discoveries and inventions that are too ludicrous to be believed. Willet made the cover twice, as I recall. He used to be a regular."

I looked through the magazine. "Did he know you were mocking him?"

"Mocking might be too strong a word, Madeline. Refuting his evidence. Calling into question the usefulness of his inventions."

Astounding Nonsense contained articles about teaching ducks to swim, the supposed benefits of actually counting real sheep to combat insomnia, and the mathematical probability of there being more red than yellow M&Ms in the average pack.

"What else do you know about him?"

"Just that he lived in Celosia. Something of a hermit, I believe. You look very serious. Is he wanted for a crime of some sort?"

I was wondering how much ridicule Willet could take. "No, he's missing."

"And what would that perfectly good bill have to do with his disappearance?"

"He left about ten thousand dollars just like that in a box. That would buy a lot of peanuts."

"Unless someone knew about the money and has done away with Wrong Way."

"Yes, that occurred to me, too."

"You need to be careful, Madeline."

"Thanks." I stood. "I've got a few more errands to run. Thanks for your help."

Warwick unfolded his long length from his chair. "Sure you can't stay for lunch?"

"No, thank you. Maybe some other time. I'm heading out to the Fairweather place to see Tucker."

"He's getting married soon, isn't he? Tell him congratulations from me."

"I will." I paused at the door. "Warwick, do you know what happened to Jerry's parents?"

He shook his head. "Just some tragedy involving a fire."

"Would there be a record of that anywhere?"

"You might try that friend of Des's. What's his name? Jack?"

"Jake." I had almost forgotten. Jake Banner worked for the *Galaxy News Weekly,* Parkland's premiere tabloid. A mysterious fire was just the type of news item the *Galaxy* liked to exploit. "Yes, that's a great idea, Warwick. Thank you."

He leaned forward, a mantis about to grasp an unwary bug. "I'm always available if you need me."

This bug made her escape.

I STOPPED BY THE *GALAXY* office, sidestepping a man on a unicycle and a woman carrying something in a jar that had way too many eyes. Jake Banner looked up from his desk. Des's sometime partner is a small, energetic man with bright blue eyes and a toothy smile that could light up a coal mine.

"Whoo-ee, to what do I owe the honor of a visitation from Miss Parkland?"

I came right to the point. "I need to know what happened to Des and Jerry's parents."

Jake's eyes gleamed. "Oh, yeah, double death. Blue flames. Trappings of the occult. Must have been at least twenty years ago."

"Closer to twenty-four if Jerry was six."

"Mysterious stuff, Madeline. I'm not sure Des would want me to tell."

I moved a stack of old *Galaxy* photos off the folding chair and sat down. "All the more reason you'd tell me, right?"

Jake grinned, laugh lines radiating. "Yeah, you got me. Plus you could look it up yourself. Didn't you work here for a while?"

"Just for a few months." When I left the pageant circuit, a secretary's position at the *Galaxy* had been the only job I could find. I rarely saw Jake then because he was always out chasing phantoms and having lunch with Elvis.

"Then you know that's why we call this place Zombie Central. Old stories live again, just change the names, dates and locales."

"Well, I want to hear the original old story, not the *Galaxy* version."

Jake leaned back in his chair and propped his feet on his desk. "Seems Mister Fairweather was crazy about anything paranormal and was always rooting around in old books, trying out spells and things. So one day he tries this spell and it backfired in a major way. Killed him and his wife right there in the house."

"Killed how?"

"Here's where the spooky part comes in. Des says he remembers seeing these blue flames shooting everywhere. Mom and Dad are pretty well fried by this bizarre fire, but Des and Jerry both get hit with the blue flames and survive."

"Hit with blue flames?"

"I always thought that's why Des could attract anything supernatural. Don't know what it did to Jerry."

I'd never known Jerry to talk about being burned. And I'd seen most of him, and there weren't any scars. "Didn't it hurt them?"

"Nah, the flames went right inside." Jake spread his hands. "Poof!"

"What about Tucker?"

"Oh, yeah, I forgot. He probably got a shot of pyro power, too. The only one who missed out was the sister. She was somewhere else and came in when she heard the mother screaming. Couldn't have been a pretty sight."

I was thinking about what Jake had mentioned earlier.

"You said you thought that's why Des could attract super-natural things. What do you mean?"

"Well, now that he's got this big concert career, he doesn't get to come investigate with me as much as he used to, but whenever there was something spooky in the neighborhood, it would come right on up to Des and say howdy. 'Course, he always tried to find some logical explanation."

I couldn't figure this out. If Jerry's parents had been killed by some sort of spell, then why would he want to have anything to do with magic, or paranormal events, or anything "spooky," as Jake said? "Seems to me Jerry would be trying to avoid anything supernatural."

"Yeah, well, you never know what sets people off. Maybe he's trying to reverse the spell."

"Reverse the spell?"

"Sure. That way, the accident would never have happened."

This conversation was making me very uneasy. "Jake, are you trying to suggest that Jerry wants to find a way to bring his parents back?"

Jake shrugged. "I've known stranger obsessions."

"I don't believe any of this."

"Whatever he's doing, it's not a good idea to mess with the occult," Jake said. "Take it from me, things can get nasty."

Aside from irate people not happy to have been cheated out of their money, Jerry hadn't had a close encounter with anything really evil. "The only thing Jerry has to worry about is being able to outrun his marks."

Jake laughed. "You're just as bad as Des. True skeptics, the both of you."

"Somebody has to be. You know I don't believe in any of that stuff."

"Well, something's happened to make Des a happier person. Guess he's excited about his music. It's like he's found himself."

"I wish Jerry could."

Jake's eyebrows went up. "He's got you, hasn't he? That ought to make him a happy man."

"Not exactly."

"Oh. Man, when is he gonna come to his senses?"

"Thanks, Jake."

He grinned. "You really oughta be with me. Dealing with these Fairweathers gives us a lot in common, you know?"

I turned down Jake's generous offer of a cheeseburger and quickie marriage in Vegas. The *Galaxy* story was wilder than I had imagined. I couldn't picture Jerry's father as the kind of person who'd play with the occult. As for bizarre blue flames, well, that sounded exactly like the kind of spin the *Galaxy* would put on a mysterious tragedy, especially a tragedy involving the wealthier citizens of Parkland.

I was walking down the sidewalk outside the *Galaxy* office when whom should I see but my ex-husband, Bill, and his new wife.

"Madeline, hello," he said. "You've met Tina, haven't you?"

Bill's tall and good-looking, the kind of man you'd see on TV playing a CEO or a general. He has the commanding manner of someone who's always gotten his way. Tina, his new wife, was small, blonde and very pregnant. Bill always wanted a big family. This would be baby number three.

"Hello, Tina," I said. "I believe I should say congratulations."

Bill put his arm around Tina's shoulders. "Thanks. It's a girl."

"That's great."

"I hear you've moved to Celosia," he said. "How's that working out for you?"

"I like it."

"Staying with Jerry?"

"For now."

He nodded. He'd never seen Jerry as a threat. "Still doing that detective thing?"

"Yes."

In the awkward silence that followed, Tina glanced up anxiously at Bill. He gave her another encouraging squeeze. "Well, it was great seeing you, Madeline."

"When's the baby due? I'd like to send a little something for her."

"Oh, any day now, right, sugar?" Tina blushed and didn't reply. Bill hugged her shoulders. "We're shooting for next weekend."

"Then I hope everything goes well. Have you picked out a name?"

"We're going to call her Foster."

Foster? Good grief. What were the others called? Again, Tina blushed. I had the feeling she would've named her little girl something else.

Bill said, "Well, we've gotta run. Great to see you, Madeline. Keep in touch."

"Okay," I said.

I watched as Bill hustled Tina down the street. As usual, he'd gotten what he wanted: a timid, unprotesting little trophy wife who'd supplied him with children. That was fine. He had to live his life his way. I had to live mine. I just wondered if I knew what I wanted.

Right now, all I wanted to do was visit Jerry's younger brother and see if I could find some clues to the Fairweather mystery.

IT'S ALWAYS SOMETHING of a pleasant shock to see Tucker Fairweather, because he looks so much like Jerry. All the Fairweather men are blessed with slim figures and youthful looks, but Tucker is the shortest and the lightest. As usual, he was dressed in his gardening clothes, jeans, sneakers and an old shirt with the sleeves rolled up.

"Hello, Madeline. I'll be right with you as soon as I trim this hedge."

I couldn't see that the hedge needed a trim, but Tucker set to it with determined precision. Unlike Jerry, Tucker has found his purpose in life and is single-mindedly devoted to his garden. He's certainly created a showplace. Past a rolling lawn of velvet green, roses of every variety grow in perfectly arranged rows. Fountains are filled with water lilies and surrounded by sculptures of leaping dolphins. Trellises drip with flowering vines.

I paused to admire a fat yellow rose trimmed with red. "This is nice."

"That's American Sunset." He gestured with his gardening shears. "Take a look at Ivory Princess."

Ivory Princess was a snowy white rose with just a hint of pink. "Wow. That's beautiful." Just beyond the white rose, an oddly colored bud was unfolding. "Is that a purple one over there?"

He beamed with pride. "Twilight Dreams. They're very hard to grow."

"The garden looks fantastic," I said.

He gave the hedge another minuscule clip. "It has to look perfect for the wedding."

"That's one reason I'm here."

He stopped his work, straightened, and pushed his light brown hair out of his eyes. "Couldn't convince him, huh?"

"Not yet."

Tucker's eyes are exactly like Jerry's, wide, gray and expressive. "Don't worry about it, Madeline. I understand."

"Well, I don't," I said. "I never have." I sat down on the nearest garden bench. "What happened here to make him so adamant about never coming home?"

Tucker clipped off a fat yellow rose and handed it to me. "Harriet always told us that something evil had happened, and we weren't ever going to talk about it. Took me a while

and a couple of good psychiatrists to sort through that one."
He looked out across the peaceful sea of blossoms. "I was
only two years old. I have nothing but good memories of
this house. It's different for Des and Jerry."

"There was a fire, right?"

"Yes, I do know that much."

"You don't know how it started."

"All I remember is a lot of light and noise and Harriet
pulling me through the hallway." His grin was wry. "I was
way more interested in the fire trucks."

"And Harriet told you what? That there'd been an accident?"

He sighed and clipped a few more dead blossoms from
the rose bush. "She said something evil had happened, our
parents were gone and we weren't going to talk about it. So
we didn't."

The yellow rose smelled like the world's most expensive
perfume. "Do you mind if I look around the house, Tucker?
There might be something that'll help me figure this out."

"Go ahead. I'll finish up here and join you."

The Fairweather mansion is full of light from the open
foyer to the sunny side porch to the kitchen that runs the
length of the back. The color scheme is mainly yellow with
lots of white trim and touches of gold. I couldn't imagine anything evil happening here. I wandered upstairs and
looked into the large bedroom that was obviously Tucker's
from the stacks of gardening magazines. I checked out the
guest bedrooms and the elegant parlor with its curved bal-
cony overlooking the garden. Then I came down the wide
staircase to the living room. Here, modern slingback chairs
share space with an ornate Chinese screen, and oddly shaped
vases perch on delicate end tables. It's a nice mix of styles,
but the portrait over the mantel always intrigues me, a portrait of the three Fairweather boys painted just before the
family tragedy. Des stands with his hand on Jerry's shoul-

der. Jerry sits with baby Tucker in his lap. I've always wondered why Harriet isn't in this picture.

Tucker came in, drying his hands on a dishtowel. "Care for a drink?"

"No, thanks," I said. "Who painted this, do you know?"

"No."

"Do you remember sitting for the portrait?"

He shook his head. "I doubt any of us could've sat still for that long."

I leaned closer, trying to see a signature. "The artist probably worked from photographs. May I take it down?"

"Sure."

He helped me lift the painting from its hooks. I turned it around, hoping for a clue. A tiny gold label said, "Parkland Studios."

"What exactly are you looking for?" Tucker asked.

"I don't know. Why isn't Harriet in this picture?"

He shrugged.

I turned the painting back around and squinted at the bottom. "It isn't signed. Maybe someone at Parkland Studios will know."

We put the painting back where it belonged. The three boys smiled serenely from the past. "Tucker," I said, "if the living room was destroyed in the fire, why wasn't this painting burned?"

"I found it in Harriet's old bedroom," he said.

"Do you know how to get in touch with Des?"

"Des won't want to talk about it, either," Tucker said.

"What about Harriet, Tucker? What's she so angry about?"

"I have no idea. She's been angry all her life."

I had to agree this summed up her character. "Is she coming to the wedding?"

"Actually, yes. She's met Selene and likes her."

"I just wish Jerry would reconsider. I think he needs to come back here and see that it's not some nightmare place."

"It's okay." He smiled. "I understand, Madeline, I really do. Tell him not to worry about it."

But I worried about it. When was Jerry ever going to face this? And what exactly did he need to face?

THE FRONT WINDOWS OF Parkland Studios were filled with oversized portraits of happy families, children in meadows of daisies, babies in funny costumes, brides, anniversary couples and beaming graduates. Inside, frames of all sizes hung from gold hooks. A smiling salesman greeted me from behind a desk surrounded by more portraits.

"Welcome to Parkland Studios. How may I help you?"

"I'm interested in a portrait that was done several years ago for the Fairweather family," I said. "The artist did such a great job, I'd love to commission him or her for my own portrait, but unfortunately, there isn't a signature on the painting."

The salesman turned to his computer. "Let me see if I have that on file. Fairweather, you said?"

"Yes, it's a picture of three boys."

"All right, one moment, please." He typed and clicked for a while. "Well, it looks like that one was done by either Fredricka Spirtus or Monroe McKittrick. There seems to be some confusion in the records. Hmm, yes. McKittrick worked for us for several years, and then Ms. Spirtus took over for him when he left. I would say McKittrick is the artist."

"He left, you said. When was this?"

"Looks like about twenty years ago. He found employment elsewhere." He peered at the screen. "I'm afraid I don't have an address, but Fredricka Spirtus is excellent. I'm sure you'd be very happy with her work."

"I'll think about it," I said.

"If you particularly want McKittrick, you could try asking Chance Baseford at the *Herald*. He's well up on the art scene in this area."

I felt my smile freeze and hoped I didn't look as startled as I felt. "Thank you."

I managed to get out of the store and back into my car before I let myself relax.

Chance Baseford was the last man on earth I'd ask for a favor. There had to be another way.

TRANSFORMATION AND COMPANY isn't your typical dark, cramped magic shop. It's a huge, bright store with wide aisles, sort of like a supermarket for magicians. Jerry had filled a cart with boxes and bottles. He was chatting with one of the clerks, a lanky fellow with prominent teeth and a green top hat.

"Yeah, I really think Super-Glo works best when you don't have a lot of time, and it's much easier to get out of the rug than Ever-Gleam. Oh, Mac, this is Barney O'Hara, better known as the Mystic Leprechaun. Barney, Madeline Maclin."

Barney O'Hara tipped his hat. "Pleased to meet you."

Jerry picked up one of the bottles in his cart. "Barney and I were just debating the merits of different brands of ectoplasm."

"Don't go in for séances much myself," Barney said. "Are you a magician, Ms. Maclin?"

"Private investigator."

"Really? That's too bad."

I must have looked surprised because he added hastily, "Oh, not that there's anything wrong with that. I'm just looking for an assistant, and you'd be terrific, all dark and mysterious."

"Thanks," I said.

"You're not interested in the stage, perhaps?"

"I've done enough stage time in my life. Pageants."

Barney O'Hara grinned at Jerry. "What's she doing with you, then?"

"Old college pal."

"If you say so." O'Hara smiled at me. "Well, if you ever change your mind, look me up. I think we'd make a great team. See you later, Jerry."

O'Hara went up the aisle. "That's the tallest leprechaun I've ever seen," I said.

"How'd it go with Warwick?" Jerry asked.

"It's real money." I didn't tell Jerry I'd been to see Tucker, or that I'd snooped around at the *Galaxy*. "Have you finished shopping?"

"Yeah, I was just hanging around."

"Want to swing by Baxter's before we go home?"

"You bet."

Jerry paid for his supplies. We drove to Baxter's Barbecue, sat down at our favorite table near the windows and ordered sandwiches and fries. The dessert of the day was strawberry shortcake, so we ordered that, too. While we waited, Jerry practiced his sleight of hand with the sugar packets. Today he was wearing his brown tie with the yellow pineapples.

"Barney's getting together a show for the Magic Club," he said. "He's a mentalist."

I would've said he's mental, but I knew Jerry meant O'Hara did a fake mind reading act. "Didn't you and Rick play that game?"

"We had a pretty good run for a while."

"And then you had to run pretty good for a while."

He grinned. "Can I help it if Rick's microphone started going off?" He covered his mouth to approximate the sound of a radio. "'Breaker, breaker, one nine oh four. We've got a possible four eleven and a sixteen twenty with Smokey in the bushes. That's a big ten-four, good buddy.'"

"Have you ever considered a legitimate job?"

He put his hand down. "Well, I have to now, don't I? I haven't forgotten our bargain."

The waitress brought our order. For the next several minutes, we were in silent barbecue bliss. Jerry took a drink of his soda.

"You spend all this time at Warwick's?"

"No, I had a few errands. I ran into Bill."

"That must have been a treat."

I trailed a french fry through a pool of ketchup. "It doesn't really bother me to see him. I feel sorry for his wife, though, the baby machine. He's up to three now. Babies, I mean."

I know Jerry doesn't understand my reluctance to have children, but he never questions me about it. Oddly enough, today, for the first time, I wondered what our children would be like—assuming we ever got out of the friendship stage and into baby making. Would our children be tall and dark, like me, or fair, like Jerry, with his wonderful gray eyes? Would our little girl want to be in beauty pageants? Would our little boy want to talk to the dead? Knowing how fate likes to joke around, the boy would probably be the pageant winner and the girl a TV psychic selling the future for three ninety-nine a minute.

As I chuckled over this vision, Jerry asked, "What's so funny?"

"Just thinking about all those babies."

"You like Austin and Denisha."

"Because I'm not responsible for them. They go home."

"I'm not sure how I feel about having kids," he said. "I guess with the right person, it's different."

I'm the right person, I wanted to say. Me. We're sitting in Baxter's Barbecue, our favorite place, talking about kids and family and the future. What could be more perfect?

To my surprise, Jerry got that serious look again and reached across the table for my hand. "Mac," he started to say, when a very unwelcome voice said, "Madeline! Well, well. What's new?"

Jerry and I sat back as Reid Kent strode across the restaurant, pulled up a chair from a nearby table and sat down with us as if we were thrilled to have him interrupt our lunch. My former boss had the same self-satisfied smile, the same mocking tone.

"Business must be good in Celosia if you can afford to eat in such splendid surroundings."

"It was splendid till you showed up," I said. "What are you doing here?"

He gave me a wink. "Keeping an eye on you. My spies tell me when you're in town. Thought I'd just see if you'd reconsidered my offer."

"I'm doing just fine without you, Reid, as hard as that may be for you to believe."

"Oh, I'm sure you are," he said, his tone implying the opposite. "But I've got a big case coming up. I could use your help."

What sort of game was he playing now? When I worked for Reid Kent, he considered me just decoration. When I moved out and set up my own office next door, he was constantly harassing me. I gave Jerry an incredulous look. He shrugged. Times like this, I wish Jerry really were psychic. Maybe he'd be able to figure out what characters like Reid Kent want.

"Sorry," I said. "I'm busy."

"Don't you want to know what the case is?"

"If it'll get rid of you, yes. Tell me."

"Got a pageant suing a big computer corporation. Seems the corporation entered a CGI as one of the contestants, and she won the crown. Nobody could tell the difference!" He roared with laughter.

"That's real funny. Thanks for stopping by."

"So you don't want the case?"

"Go away."

He put both hands flat on the table and pushed himself up. "Okay. Your loss."

Jerry got up, too. "Let me see you out," he said.

Kent sneered. "I'd like to see you try."

"Guys," I said. "This isn't necessary. Kent, would you just leave?"

I'm not sure what would've happened if the waitress hadn't arrived with our strawberry shortcakes. There was a brief moment of confusion and bumping into each other as she maneuvered around the extra chair. Jerry sat down. Reid Kent made another snide remark and left.

"Did he want to order?" the waitress asked.

"No," I said. When she left, I asked Jerry, "What was that macho moment all about? I appreciate the heroics, but Kent could've mangled you."

He was grinning. "Oh, I just wanted to try something."

"Getting a black eye?"

He held up Kent's wallet. "Picking a pocket."

I couldn't help myself. I burst into laughter. "Jerry!"

"I'm a little out of practice."

"Damn it, put that away! He'll be livid."

"So what? He oughta pay for his crude remarks. In fact, he oughta pay for lunch." He started looking through Kent's cash.

"No," I said. "We'll leave the wallet at the register."

Jerry was disappointed. "Not even a fat tip?"

"No. But thank you."

"Next time I'll get his watch, too." He checked his own watch. "We'd better get going. The film crew's coming pretty soon."

Whatever Jerry had planned to say was gone. Still another reason to hate Reid Kent.

"We've got a couple more stops to make first," I said.

"More snacks?"

"Art supplies, remember? I'm keeping my end of the bargain."

"Uh-oh," he said. "She's serious."

We stopped at a craft shop, and I bought paints, brushes and cleaning solutions. Jerry pointed to a display of easels.

"You'll need one of these."

"I know where I can find a cheaper one," I said.

FOUR

WHEN WE RETURNED TO THE Eberlin house, the film crew had arrived and was unpacking the vans. Austin and Denisha met us as we got out of my car.

"Isn't this cool?" Austin said. "We've been waiting for almost an hour for them to show up."

"Just don't get in their way," I said. The crew had unpacked miles of cable and some expensive-looking equipment. I didn't see Lance Henderson, but Flynn Davis was getting his makeup retouched by an assistant. He smiled and waved. Josh Gaskins saw Jerry and came over with Stephanie in tow.

"We'll get some exterior and establishing shots today, Jerry. Shouldn't take more than a couple of hours."

Filming exterior shots took three hours, and by then the kids were completely disillusioned. They had stationed themselves under one of the big oak trees in the front yard and watched the crew's every move, but soon they were sitting in the grass tossing rocks at each other.

"This is so boring," Denisha said. "They took about a million pictures of the house, and then they filmed people walking up to the door and running around the side. There wasn't any Mantis Man or anything."

"Denisha, I told you," Austin said. "It's called 'exteriors.' That means the outside. That's all they want the house for."

"Well, they could've had him jump out or something."

"They'll do that somewhere else, and then they'll put it all together so it looks like it was here."

Josh Gaskins and Jerry strolled up in time to hear this. "You got it, buddy," Gaskins said to Austin. "You've got the makings of a director."

Denisha nodded. "He sure likes to boss people around."

"Got some great shots," Gaskins said. "We're just about finished here. We'll do the interiors at Voltage."

Austin gave Denisha a look that said "See?" The two of them didn't have time to start another quarrel. Twenty drove up, screeched to a stop and charged out of her car, every orange curl quivering.

"Josh Gaskins, I want a word with you."

He did a double take, the usual reaction to Twenty in one of her original outfits. In her red leather miniskirt, frilly yellow blouse and odd-looking white boots she reminded me of a hot dog, ketchup and mustard included.

"Do I know you?" he asked.

"I should say you do! We went to Celosia High together." He looked again. "Delores?"

"Yes, it's me."

"I didn't recognize you."

She stabbed a finger at his chest. "You can dress yourself up like Steven Spielberg, but you're still Josh Gaskins, skinny little Josh Gaskins who never could pass algebra, and I can't believe you'd do this to Celosia."

Gaskins started to say, "This will be a good thing," but Twenty rolled on.

"Do you want Celosia to become a circus? You know how crazy people can get."

"I don't know why you're so riled up," he said. "This movie could be a real boost to Celosia's economy."

"Mantis Man tee shirts and key rings? It's trash! Cheap junk!"

"Do tourists care?"

She spread her arms wide, bracelets sliding and clacking

together. "I care! And I'm not the only one. We'll find some way to stop you, Josh Gaskins."

I didn't like the way this sounded. "Twenty, you really need to calm down."

"But I've seen what can happen! Take Dixley, for instance. A perfectly lovely little town, and now they have the Annual Squash and Radish Festival, and people dressed like giant vegetables overrun the place!"

"I'd like to see that," Jerry said sotto voce.

I elbowed him in the ribs. "You're not helping."

"Look, Delores," Gaskins said. "At the risk of sounding cliché, this is only a movie. I don't think it's going to turn Celosia into a hotbed of Mantis activity. With any luck, the film will make a little money."

She folded her arms over the yellow frills of her blouse. "I still resent you coming back to do something like this."

"Well, I'm sorry, but that's the way it is."

Twenty gave him another glare and stalked back to her car. She stood there, still quivering with indignation.

Gaskins seemed unconcerned. Stephanie handed him his cup, and he took another slurp of soda.

"Think she'll raise a real stink?" Stephanie asked.

He smirked. "I hope she does. You can't buy publicity like that. If she says this film's gonna ruin Celosia, everybody'll have to come see how." He handed the cup back to Stephanie. "Jerry, thanks for everything. We'll be back tomorrow night when the moon is full, take a few more shots, and we'll be done." He gave me a nod, and he and Stephanie went to his car.

As soon as he was gone, Twenty charged over.

"Jerry, I cannot believe you had any dealings with that man."

"I'm sorry if you're upset," he said.

Twenty let her breath out in an exasperated sigh that made

the yellow frills bob. "It's just so frustrating getting people to take this seriously."

"I really think the whole thing will blow over very soon," I said.

"I've been talking with Lance Henderson, and he thinks it's a crime the way everyone's been treated. He's behind me and my committee one hundred percent."

"What committee's that?"

"S.T.O.M.P., Stop The Opening of the Mantis Picture. I organized it yesterday. Do you want to join?"

"I'm going to stay out of this," I said.

"Fine. I didn't expect you to understand, anyway."

She gave another huff of breath and left. Denisha and Austin, who had been listening, didn't seem too concerned that their town was split over the Mantis issue.

Austin voiced an opinion. "I think a Mantis Man tee shirt would be cool."

"Me, too," Jerry said.

I had a question for Denisha. "Denisha, have you ever heard of a man named Kirby Willet?"

"Yeah, I know him," she said.

"You do not," Austin said.

"I do, too. He's that nutty inventor."

Austin always had to be specific. "But you don't *know* him."

"I know *of* him, okay? He's like that scientist in the movie about the stuff that bounces and makes cars fly. One time, he made this invention that was supposed to pick up cans in the road, only it was too strong and it pulled everybody's mailbox out of the ground. My aunt was mad about that."

"Any idea where he might be?" I asked.

She shook her head. "I haven't seen him in a long time."

"Where did you last see him?"

"He was working at the Super Food, washing vegetables with a big sprayer."

"Oh, yeah," Austin said. "He fixed it so the sprayer was like this jet-powered water gun and all the vegetables got torn up."

Denisha swung around as if she couldn't believe he knew something she didn't know. "You're making that up!"

"No, I'm not. You ask my cousin. That's how come Mister Willet got fired from the grocery store. There was tomatoes in the next county."

AFTER THE KIDS HAD GONE, I took my painting supplies and the Goodwill easel up to the parlor. I'm not ready for this, I thought. I'll just put everything down and walk away.

No, I told myself. You made a deal. If Jerry sees you're serious about painting, maybe he'll honor his part of the bargain and try to find a job.

As I unfolded the easel and tacked on a piece of white paper, my stomach clenched. Relax, I told it. The least you can do is try. If it doesn't work out, you can stop.

I laid the pencils and brushes in a neat row on the low coffee table and stood back. All right. Everything's ready. Go get some photographs and just do it.

I heard a metallic tapping sound and found Nell opening a paint can in the bedroom next door.

"They told me to go ahead," she said. "Wouldn't bother the filming." She chuckled. "Tickled me to see Josh Gaskins strutting around like a big shot. He was kinda puny last time I saw him."

"What can you tell me about him?" I asked.

She shrugged. "Not much to tell. He wasn't from around here. Came to the high school his junior year. Didn't make much of an impact. Guess he's found his calling."

"Twenty wasn't happy with him."

"Yeah, I could hear her fussing all the way up here. She needs to calm down."

I thought the soft green shade she was painting looked great and told her so. "What color is this?"

Nell looked at the paint can. "Seafoam. I'd call it light green, myself."

"Nell, can you tell me anything about Kirby Willet?"

"Wrong Way Willet. Never did get the hang of anything."

"So he'd be the type of person to leave a lot of personal items and never come back for them?"

She dipped her roller in the paint tray. "I wouldn't exactly say he's absentminded. Probably holed up somewhere working on another invention."

"Anywhere around here?"

More light green paint covered the gray walls. "We'd know it. There'd be broken water pipes and downed power lines."

"Did he have any enemies?"

"Nah. People used to get annoyed with his gadgets, but everybody knew he was harmless."

"Was he likely to have earned a lot of money?"

Her little eyes crinkled as she grinned. "Like, say, ten thousand dollars?"

When was I going to learn it was impossible to keep anything a secret in this town?

"Where did you hear that?"

She stopped painting and turned to me. "Don't get your tail in a crack. I ain't spreading it around. Frannie's been babbling about it. We're all a bit puzzled about where Willet got that much money. Guess he's been saving up all his life. You can do that if you just eat peanuts."

"Yeah, I'm puzzled, too."

"I wouldn't worry. It's not like he killed somebody."

"I'm afraid somebody's killed him."

She gave me a look I couldn't quite interpret. "Nice of you to be concerned. I wouldn't say Willet had many friends in town."

"What about Bernice Coleman?"

Nell made a face. "Old sourpuss."

"Why would she suggest Frannie's house as a storage place?"

"Maybe Willet was going to invent a personality for her." She continued rolling paint on the wall. "He was in the library a lot, looking up how to make things, that's all I can figure."

I thanked Nell for the information and was about to leave when she said, "What about the parlor? You gonna paint it yourself, or you want me to slap a coat of green in there, too?"

I paused in the doorway. "It can stay like it is for now."

"You still thinking of using it for your pictures?"

"Still thinking about it."

"Still thinking about telling junior how you feel?"

I gave Nell my darkest look, but her attention was on her painting. Even though her back was to me, I knew she was grinning.

When I came back downstairs, Jerry was in the séance parlor slash music room hunting through the bookshelf. Most of his uncle's books are leather-bound copies of the classics, but we'd found some odd titles, as well.

"Mac, have you seen that old *Farmer's Almanac?*"

"I thought it was with the dictionary."

"I wonder what I did with it."

"Do you need to check the phases of the moon or something?"

He put the dictionary on the floor and stacked other books on top. "Gwen Macmillan asked me to conjure up some prizewinning tomatoes, remember? Wouldn't hurt to see when the best growing time is."

"That almanac's outdated, isn't it?"

He thought this over. "You're right. It would be better to

get a new one. I'll check at Georgia's the next time we're in there."

"You want any supper? I'm still full of barbecue."

"I think I'll wait and make a sandwich later." He handed me a large brown book. "This is a good one. *Winged Insectivores of the Mid-Atlantic States.*"

Val Eberlin had studied bats. I thumbed through *Winged Insectivores,* grimacing at the sepia photos of gargoylelike bat faces. "Guess you have to know your insectivores."

"Just a little light reading. Oh, how about this? *Bats and Their Relation to History; A Theoretical Musing.* A theoretical musing, you understand, not a real musing." He pulled more books off the shelf. "*The Myth and Legend of the Bat. Common Bats of the Carolinas.* If I'm going to live here, I need a bat tie."

"I'm shocked you don't already have one." I returned the book to the stack. "Do you have a rehearsal tonight?"

"Kenna's reworking some dances. She usually uses a CD for that."

"I want to stop by the theater. I need pictures of some kids for the portrait."

He paused, another book in hand. "So you're really going to do it?"

"I'm going to give it a try."

"Uh-oh," he said. "This means I'd better update my résumé."

"Have you made any progress in your job search?"

"I've ruled out welder and air traffic controller."

"Are you going to leave all these books on the floor?"

He looked at the untidy stack. "I think all the bat books can go out—unless you want them."

"No, thanks."

"Can we swing by Georgia's?"

"Sure."

GEORGIA WAS GLAD to find an almanac for Jerry. We were at the counter paying Hayden for the book when Gregory Prill swept in. "Swept" is the accurate word. Prill's a large, overly dramatic man who wears a gray cape with his suit and enjoys making an entrance. His springy hair bobbed, and he bulged out his eyes as he made his announcement.

"Congratulate me! My poem, 'Dust of Latter Years,' has been accepted for the December issue of *Soul's Crossing!* My career is coming to fruition! My future is assured!"

We applauded and made all the right noises.

"Clear out the front window now, Hayden. I want 'Dust' displayed with all proper elegance."

"I think we can wait until December," Hayden said.

"Philistine." He turned to me. "Madeline, what on earth is all this about you finding thousands of dollars in a box? Why haven't you contacted me? Don't you know a starving poet who could use a loan?"

I laughed. Prill's far from starving. He lives in a beautiful house and collects Art Nouveau furniture and jewelry. "If it had been my money, I would've given you some. The money belongs to Kirby Willet."

Prill made a dismissive sound. "Willet. The consummate loser. He can't have amassed thousands of dollars. He must have robbed a bank."

"If I could find him, I'd ask him. Do you have any idea where he could be?"

"Not I. I never associated with the likes of Kirby Willet." He flipped back his cape and leaned one elbow on the counter. "My dear Jerry, whatever do you want with the *Farmer's Almanac?* You're not going rural, are you? I just can't see you in overalls and a straw hat."

"A little research for one of my clients."

"Ah, your paranormal nonsense. And Madeline, can't you do something about the proliferation of pageants in these parts? Everywhere I look, a queen is springing up. Those wretched friends of yours! They must be stopped. What do you call them? Pageantitis? Pageantniks? Idiots, I say, idiots!"

As usual, Prill didn't wait for a reply, but plowed on to the next subject. "I do, however, wish to hear of your latest exploits."

"Can you help any of my cases?"

"Name them, and we shall see."

"The Mystery of the Missing Umbrella."

"I have no desire to track down someone's misplaced parasol."

"The Mystery of the Overdue Library Books."

"Tantalizing, but no."

"The only case left is the Mystery of the Missing Inventor, and you've already said you don't know where Willet is."

"Well, I don't, my dear, but should I hear anything, I will alert you posthaste."

"There's the Mystery of the Haunted Bookstore," Hayden said.

Prill rounded on him. "For heaven's sake, don't start that again! You're cured, do you hear? No more ghosts! Do I have to come back there and smack you around the head and shoulders?"

Hayden held his ground. "No."

"Then shut up." He smiled at me. "Is there something I should know?"

"I'm investigating some strange noises here in the store," I said.

"That would be the cries of long-suffering poets such as myself who wish to be displayed in the front window. What do you think it is, Hayden?"

"Jerry and I think it's a poltergeist."

Prill gave Jerry a scornful look. "What have I told you about leading him on? Do I have to smack you, as well?"

Like Hayden, Jerry wasn't intimidated by Prill's overbearing manner. "Prill, what do you know about Mantis Man?"

"A blatant attempt to frighten the feebleminded."

"Don't look at me," Hayden said.

"You're the very one to look at. I'm surprised you aren't cowering under your bed at the thought of some giant insect knocking at your door. This ridiculous movie should put an end to the Mantis myth."

"Do you know Josh Gaskins?" I asked. Prill was older than Twenty; I wasn't sure when he'd been in high school.

"I've never met him, but I applaud him for working to his strengths. The movie will go straight to video, and we can go on about our lives." He brushed his sleeves and readjusted his diamond tie clasp. "I merely stepped in to tell you of my success. I have spent enough time here amongst you." He gave Hayden a warning glance. "Hayden."

"It's under control, I promise."

"You need to quit this job and devote more time to your work. We've discussed this. I expect you to give the matter serious thought. Madeline, you look ravishing, as always. Georgia, my dear, and Jerry, farewell."

Without waiting for an answer, he swept out.

Georgia shook her head. "A day without Prill—"

Hayden finished her sentence. "—is really, really quiet."

Georgia picked up a stack of magazines from the counter. "So what is the real story about the money, Madeline? Did you really find thousands of dollars?"

"About ten thousand dollars."

"I can't imagine Kirby Willet having that amount of cash."

"Maybe he sold one of his inventions."

"But they never worked."

"I guess we won't know the answer until I find him," I said.

She started toward the shelves and turned back. "Jerry, I

put that *Music Man* poster in the front window next to the one about the gospel sing at First Methodist."

"Thank you."

"How's the show coming along?"

"Very well."

"I was a little surprised to see that Donna Sanchez was in it. I didn't know she could sing."

"She's doing a good job."

"And you like playing the piano? You know, Light of Heaven Evangelical is looking for an organist, but I bet they'd take someone who plays piano."

I nudged Jerry. "A job."

"Thank you, Georgia," he said. "I'll check into that."

We said good-by to Georgia and Hayden and went out. Jerry was shaking his head. "I'm not going to get tied down to playing for church every Sunday."

"You could at least call them and see what they want."

"Nope. I'm holding out for an executive position."

"You may have to work your way up."

We'd reached the car when an unwelcome voice called, "J!" and Rick Rialto came up the sidewalk.

"Whoo, glad I caught you," he said. "Gotta talk to you about something. Excuse us, Mac."

He pulled Jerry over by the shoe store and spoke in a low, excited whisper. I couldn't hear what he was saying, but from the way Jerry brightened, I knew Rick had some scheme going. Then Jerry said, "Are you sure?" Rick grinned and nodded and whispered some more.

"I don't know," Jerry said. "I don't think there's enough money in Celosia to pull that off."

Rick shrugged. "Won't know till we try. Is it worth a shot?"

"Yeah, sure."

"I'll set things up. Talk to you later."

Jerry came back to the car. When he saw my expression, he slowed his steps. "Just a little business with Rick."

"A little illegal business."

"Not exactly."

"Jerry, it's either illegal or it isn't."

"It's nothing," he said. "It won't work here, anyway."

I opened my door. "Whatever it is, it better not."

He got in the passenger side. "You told me to get a job."

"A job, not a con. If you don't get a real job, then I don't have to paint real pictures."

He grinned. "Does that mean you'll paint clown pictures?"

Despite being very annoyed with him, I couldn't help but chuckle. "No."

"Clown pictures on velvet? Dogs playing poker? Bug-eyed children clutching flowers?"

"Shut up."

He gave me examples of bad art all the way to the theater.

"When are you going to be useful? What are your job prospects so far?"

He gazed up as if thinking hard. "Hmm, sheepherder? No. Health inspector? Too risky. Trapeze artist? Too dull. How about a possum farmer?"

I laughed. "Possum farmer?"

"You just round them up and keep them away from the major highways."

"That would be perfect for you."

We parked in the theater lot and got out into the sticky heat of early evening. It was a relief to step into the cool theater. The foyer walls were covered with framed photographs from past productions. I'd never paid too much attention to the photographs. Pictures of children remind me of Bill's photos. He'd hung them all over our house as if to inspire me.

"What are you looking for?" Jerry asked.

"Kenna said I could take whatever I needed. Find some kids in cute costumes."

"I'll start over here."

Jerry looked along the right wall. I took the left. I found a good picture of several children in animal costumes and one of some little girls all dressed as Dorothy from *The Wizard of Oz*. Jerry handed me a picture of a little boy dressed as Tom Sawyer and one of an older boy and girl in a production of *Our Town*.

"Yes, these are good," I said. "I think one or two more ought to do it."

On the back wall was a large framed set of plaques indicating donor contributions to the theater. Next to this was another framed document listing recipients of theater grants. A name caught my eye.

Kirby Willet.

Also listed was a Josh Gaskins. Gaskins had won the grant. Willet was runner-up.

"Jerry, look at this."

He came over, and I pointed to the names. "Willet and Gaskins both tried out for the Samuel Baker Scholarship."

"What's it for?"

"We'll have to ask Kenna or Evan."

Evan was upstairs in his office. As we entered, he looked up and smiled. "Madeline, I was just thinking about you. We have finalized nearly all the details for the Miss Celosia Summertime Pageant. I'd love for you to look over them for us."

"I'd be glad to," I said, "if you'll answer a question for me. Josh Gaskins won the Samuel Baker Scholarship. What's that for?"

"We award that every year to the most promising young director. They submit a theater or film project. I believe Gaskins won when he was a senior in high school."

"Over Kirby Willet."

"Yes. As I recall, it was a very close vote."

"Do you have copies of these projects they submitted?"

"They should be on file in the library. Does this have something to do with Willet's disappearance?"

"I'm not sure. It may help, though."

"Good." He handed me a fat folder. "Here are the plans for the new pageant. I'd appreciate any and all suggestions. And Madeline, later on, would you mind coming and saying a few words to the girls? Just encourage them and maybe give them some helpful tips? It would mean a great deal to them and to me."

I started to say no, but I couldn't. Evan was back to his old self, confident and excited about a new pageant. I just couldn't refuse to help.

"Maybe for just a few minutes, Evan."

"Thank you so much."

I thought Jerry and I could make a clean getaway, but when we came back downstairs, the Pageantoids were lurking in the foyer. They were bursting with news.

Cathy spoke first. "We saw your car. Have you been talking with Evan? Did he give you the information? I hope we have everything in order."

I patted the folder. "I'm sure you haven't missed a thing."

They exchanged a look. "Well, we have another project we think is even more spectacular," Mitch said.

"More spectacular than Miss Celosia Summertime?"

"What do you think about this? Miss Mantis!"

Somewhere behind me, Jerry choked on a laugh.

"It would be the very thing for Celosia!"

Cathy spread her hands wide, as if indicating open curtains. "Can't you just see the opening number? We'll have a huge backdrop of flowers. The girls could all be dressed as butterflies and other attractive insects."

"Just the attractive insects," I said.

"Oh, yes, no earwigs or anything like that."

Jerry's voice behind me said, "Watch out for insectivores."

"Cathy," I said, "this might not be the best idea. You have heard that a lot of people in town oppose anything with Mantis Man?"

"This will change their minds," Cathy said. "The movie's the best thing that could have happened for the pageant."

Mitch agreed. "You should be in the movie, Madeline. Vivian Montrose only came in second in the Miss California Pageant."

"Can we come out and watch the filming?" Cathy asked.

"They've finished except for a few more exterior shots."

"We'd love to see the movie crew in action."

"Yes, it might inspire us," Mitch said.

Not that they needed any more encouragement. I started to say that would be all right when Cathy grasped my arm. "You know there's been another sighting."

Now Jerry was interested. "Of Mantis Man?"

"Three people saw him last night. We heard them talking about it in that hamburger place."

"Where and when?"

"Down by the covered bridge around midnight."

I could almost see Jerry's mind at work, planning a way to trap the Mantis. "Okay, thanks," he said. He didn't say anything else until we were in the car. "Mac, if we could get a picture of this thing, or better yet, catch it, it would be the best *Galaxy* story ever."

"You can stay out all night if you want to."

"Don't you want to come with me?"

"Jerry, it's nothing. You know how these rumors get started and grow."

"But what if it's real? It could be worth a lot of money."

"This wasn't what I had in mind when I said get a job."

"You didn't say I couldn't be a Mantis catcher."

I sighed and drove to the Celosia Public Library. We found Joan in the back, knee-deep in books. Torn and bulging cardboard boxes sat on the tables and floor. Slippery stacks of magazines, dusty rolls of posters and maps, and ancient sets of encyclopedias filled the corner.

Joan laughed as she pulled an old sneaker out of a box. "People forget what they have in these boxes. They see books on top and haul the boxes over here without checking."

"Looks like someone cleaned out their attic," I said.

"Stuff for our used-book sale," she said.

Jerry grinned. "Have we got a collection for you."

"Really?" she said.

"Val's bat books. You want them?"

"Sure. If we can't use them in the library, we'll put them in the sale. We usually make a lot of money." She wiped her hands on her jeans. "You have good news, I hope."

Jerry bumped into a stack of paperbacks and managed to catch them before they crashed. "Hope these weren't in any sort of order."

"Just set them on the floor."

I helped Jerry find a space to put the paperbacks. "I haven't tracked down any more books, Joan. I'd like to see the student films, the ones that won the Baker Scholarship. Can they be checked out?"

"Yes. Which ones?"

"The ones Josh Gaskins and Kirby Willet submitted."

"All right. I'll be just a moment."

Jerry nudged me. "Who's the dragon?"

His gaze indicated Bernice Coleman, who radiated hostility from her computer station. "That's Bernice. She thinks I'm up to no good."

"Wonder how she stands on the Mantis Man issue?"

"Why don't you ask her?"

"Okay."

He strolled over to the main desk.

Joan returned with two videotapes. "Here you are. They'll need to be back in two days."

"Looks like you could use some help with all this," I said.

"Oh, we've got everything under control. Have you been to our sale before? It's a really big deal. Everything's under a dollar. We'll have refreshments and prizes. Bernice makes wonderful cookies."

I could see Jerry trying to engage the dour Bernice in conversation. "Does she?"

"Yes, I leave all the snack management to her."

Bernice continued to give me daggerlike stares as Jerry and I left the library.

"What did you say to her?" I asked.

"I asked her if there were any books on Mantis Man. She said no."

"That's all?"

"She asked me if we were still living in the Eberlin house. I said yes. Then she glared at you. I believe she thinks we're living in sin." He found this highly amusing.

"Did you say anything else?"

"I asked if she'd heard about the Mantis Man movie, and she said that was complete nonsense."

"Which one, Mantis Man or the movie?"

"I get the feeling Bernice sees the entire world as nonsense. Anyway, my polite manner and charming smile had no effect. Did you get the movies?"

I held up the tapes. "Double feature."

WE TOOK THE VIDEOTAPES back to the house and set up camp in front of the giant-screen TV. Jerry made some sandwiches and some popcorn and sat down on the living-room sofa with the remote in hand. "I hope these movies are better than the last one we saw," he said.

Gaskins's movie was a predictable tale about a guy heading out to the big city for the first time. His luggage was stolen, he had to stay in a fleabag hotel and he ran afoul of some pimps and hookers. Willet's movie was quite different. The story was hard to follow, but at the same time, had a dreamy quality about it that made it intriguing. I think it was about a man finding his soul.

Jerry found both movies boring. "Doesn't anyone want to do a really good car chase anymore?"

"If you were a judge, wouldn't you give the prize to Willet?"

"I wouldn't give it to either of them. I'd be down at the drive-in watching Jackie Chan kicking the hell out of fifty evil minions."

I took a handful of popcorn. "But think about it. Here you have a typical coming-of-age tragedy versus something more original. I think Kirby Willet had real talent and was overlooked. That kind of thing tends to make one resentful."

"Are you looking at me in that particular tone of voice? You ought to know about being overlooked."

"But I don't have that much real talent."

Jerry almost upended the popcorn bowl. "Damn it, Mac, when are you going to get off that dead horse? You're a very talented artist. Just because your mother doesn't think so, you're going to throw away that part of yourself? It doesn't make sense."

"About as much sense as you wandering around playing with the occult and never wanting to settle down."

"I'm not playing with the occult. Don't ever say that."

"Is that what your parents were doing?"

He gave me a narrow-eyed stare for an uncomfortably long time. I knew he was thinking, what the hell?

"Okay," I said. "When I took the hundred-dollar bill to Warwick, I ran into Jake."

"Jake's not a reliable source."

"He's your brother's best friend."

"Des would argue with you about that."

I held up both hands. "Jerry, please. Be straight with me.

I said I would help you figure this out. What's all this about blue flames?"

"It's just some stupid story the *Galaxy* made up."

"Are you sure?"

"Yes, I'm sure. It bugs the heck out of Des because Jake believes the blue flames make Des a real ghost magnet."

"Well, I wish you'd come back to the house and help me look for clues."

"You're perfectly capable of finding clues all by yourself."

"The house is not at all scary. It looks terrific."

I shouldn't have said that. His look told me I'd made a serious slip.

"You went there, didn't you? You talked with Tucker."

"Yes, I did."

I could tell by his expression he was torn between being annoyed and being curious. Curiosity won. "So did you find out anything?"

"I want to know more about the artist who painted the portrait of you and your brothers. I can't help wondering why Harriet isn't in the picture."

"Maybe my parents wanted a separate picture of her."

"Maybe. It just seems odd to me."

"Okay. Who's the artist and what does he remember after twenty years?"

"I'm still tracking him down. There's going to be a problem, though."

"He's dead? Had a sex change? Moved to Borneo?"

"I don't know a thing about him except his name. But there's someone who can tell me more. Chance Baseford."

Jerry sat back. "Oh, brother."

"Think he'll remember me?"

"Mac, you don't have to do this."

"It's okay," I said, despite the shudder I managed to repress. "I can handle it."

"I'll come with you."

"Thanks, but this is something I should do alone. If I don't, I'll never get over it. Besides, he doesn't know I've started painting again. And I don't care if he does."

Just saying Baseford's name conjured up his sneering face and the way he looked at my paintings with such disdain, as if I had no right to even exist. I'd been told Chance Baseford was a harsh critic, but I never believed he could make his remarks so personal.

"What do you expect from a beauty queen? Did you draw this with mascara? A waste of perfectly good makeup, if you ask me. Stick to the runway, girl. The art world doesn't need another poser."

His acid comments, combined with my mother's "I told you so" look, had ruined my first and only art show. But, damn it, if Baseford had information that would solve the Fairweather mystery, I was going to get it from him. He could make all the stupid remarks he liked.

I must have looked fierce, because Jerry said, "I think you can take him, Mac."

"Thank you."

"He's bound to be eighty years old by now."

"He's sixty and works for the *Herald*."

The telephone rang.

Jerry answered. "Hello? Okay, okay, calm down. Tell me again." He covered the receiver and whispered to me, "It's Hayden." Then he spoke into the phone. "It's okay. We'll be right there." He hung up. His eyes were shining. "'Curse of the Poltergeist.' Let's go get it."

HAYDEN MET US AT THE DOOR of Georgia's Books. "I have some news."

I thought maybe he'd caught the poltergeist himself, or perhaps now there was more than one.

"What's up?" Jerry asked.

Hayden's eyes were wide with apprehension. "You know Georgia suspected Terrance and Clarence Yates of shoplifting."

Georgia had told me she didn't feel the Yates boys were a threat. "Did you catch them in the act?"

"They've been in the juvenile home for weeks. Do you know what that means?"

I knew where this line of reasoning was headed, but couldn't resist saying, "Somebody else caught them?"

Hayden shook his head. "It means they haven't been anywhere near the store. We definitely have a poltergeist."

Jerry rolled up his sleeves. "And I'm going to get in touch with her."

"Her? You think it's a female spirit?"

"More than likely. Where's the site of the latest activity?"

"The children's section."

He led Jerry to the children's section. Jerry sat down on the floor, closed his eyes and asked for quiet.

"Okay," he said. "I'm getting a strong vibration here. You two let me alone for a while. I'll straighten her out."

Hayden lowered his voice as he followed me back to the counter. "Thank goodness Jerry has experience with this kind of thing. As much as I like working here, I can't stay if there's a vengeful spirit."

"Maybe she's a nice spirit," I said. "Just a little playful."

He wasn't convinced. "If she's a book lover, she wouldn't throw them on the floor."

Hayden was too nervous to sit down, so I hopped up on one of the stools behind the counter. "I want to apologize for not checking on your shoplifters."

"That's all right. As I said, the Yates boys aren't the problem." He glanced toward the children's section. "I hope Jerry isn't putting himself in danger."

"That's the last thing you have to worry about." From my perch, I could see Jerry's head. He was sitting very still. Probably gone to sleep, I thought. "How's your writing coming along?"

Since I exposed Juliet Lovelace as the ghost haunting his house, Hayden had been able to concentrate on his poetry.

"I've finished twelve poems," he said.

"That's great."

"I can't thank you enough, Madeline."

"Just don't let this poltergeist thing disturb you. I'm sure it's nothing."

About that time, a weird howling came from somewhere over our heads. The sound was like a child's angry cry.

Hayden turned white. "Oh, my God."

Jerry stood up. I saw him frown. He hurried up the aisle until he was under one of the air conditioning vents. To Hayden's horror and my amusement, a sudden shower of large insects fell on Jerry's head. He spluttered and shook the bugs out of his hair.

"Yuck!" Seeing Hayden's expression, he added, "It's okay. They're all dead."

I laughed. "I think the poltergeist is trying to tell you something."

"Yeah. 'Bug off.'"

Hayden grasped the edge of the counter. "Wh-what are they?"

Jerry plucked more bugs from his hair. "I don't know."

"Are they—? Do they look like m-mantises?"

I picked one off the floor. "I'm not sure what they are." I knew how this unexpected landslide of dried creatures appeared to Hayden, so I wasn't surprised when he swallowed hard.

"It's the curse."

"Hayden," I said, "it's just some dead bugs. They tend to die and accumulate in vents."

He gulped again. "We've never had a problem with bugs before."

"Have you got a broom and a dust pan? Let's get this cleaned up."

He didn't move. "Something made them fall. Something disturbed them."

"This is an old building, right? The roof probably settled a little and tipped them out."

"Or it's the poltergeist playing another joke," Jerry said.

I gave him one of my fiercest looks. He grinned.

"We should never have started anything about the Mantis Man," Hayden said. "Those kinds of things should be left alone."

Jerry brought one of the bugs to the counter. "This isn't a mantis. I think it's a katydid."

Hayden backed away. "Just get them out of here."

I found the broom and dust pan in the closet. I swept up the bugs while Jerry cleaned off the top of the bookshelf. By then, Hayden was ready to lock the store and go home, but not before he asked Jerry to come back and try another exorcism.

"I'll be here bright and early tomorrow morning," Jerry said.

Once we were in the car, I said, "I'm going to smack you if you don't stop."

"Stop what?"

"Telling Hayden the store has a poltergeist."

"Well, now I'm pretty sure it does."

"A shower of dead bugs doesn't mean the store's haunted."

"Looked spooky to me, all the little ghostly remains." He held up one of the dead insects. "Doesn't this look like a shed skin of some kind?"

Now I recognized the insects. "That's a locust skin."

"Those bugs that come out every twenty years?"

"Every seventeen years. Nothing mysterious about a bunch of old locust skins."

"How do you explain that weird sound, then?"

"It was probably Locust Man."

Jerry intoned in a horror movie voice, "Locust Man! Every seventeen years the terror beings anew!"

"That's just as stupid as Mantis Man."

"Yeah, why not Locust Man, or Mosquito Man?"

"Or Weevilman."

"No, I've got it: Chigger Man! Horror that really gets under your skin."

"Or Gnatman."

"Gnatman!" Jerry was delighted. I had to wait until he finished singing the *Batman* theme song before I could get his attention.

"Just please stop feeding Hayden's worst fantasies. The poor guy's going to have another nervous breakdown."

"Oh, he'll be okay. Shana will take care of him." He rolled down the window and tossed the locust skin out. "She's great, you know? Not only is she fantastic looking, she supports him in everything he does. That's what marriage is all about."

Good grief, where was he going with this conversation? "They seem to have a pretty good marriage."

"Here's Hayden, working at a stressful job in Parkland that almost kills him, so he leaves the company where he was making this huge salary, and does she nag him to go back? Does she complain because there isn't enough money? Does she give up on him? No, she finds Celosia, a nice little town where he can do what he really loves doing."

Before I could say that Shana wasn't the only one who did things like this, he said, "I know we have a deal, Mac. I'll find something."

I wasn't going to be the one who nagged him into something he didn't want to do. "I'm going to start painting again, anyway. I won't hold you to your part of the bargain."

"No, I'll find something."

"What about the B&B?"

"I don't know. It seemed like a good idea at the time."

He was looking at me with such warmth, I wondered if I dared hope for something more. Was he going to get all serious again? Was he going to say let's explore another facet of our relationship? Or let's go home and go upstairs?

But what he said was, "So what do you say we go find Mantis Man?"

So we went to find Mantis Man.

THE COVERED BRIDGE ON A summer evening could have been a romantic spot, had Jerry not been shouting "Ya-ha!" and leaping into the bushes. Fireflies sparkled in the darkening woods. The river gurgled over smooth white stones. Jerry smacked at harmless grasshoppers.

I looked at my watch. "I'm giving Mantis Man fifteen more minutes."

"Is it midnight?"

"Almost."

He came and sat by me on the bench next to the river. We'd brought flashlights, but out here under the moon, we didn't need them.

"Nice view, huh?" Jerry said.

His face was half in shadow, his clear eyes like silver. I could see the portrait already: *Jerry By Moonlight*. It would be my masterpiece.

Shana was right. This was too much. I couldn't go on like this.

"Jerry."

He turned to me, his expression expectant.

"A few times before, there's been something you wanted to tell me."

"Oh, yes."

My heart was pounding so hard I knew he could hear it. "This might be a good time."

He took a deep breath. "Yes, it is."

I waited, hardly able to breathe, myself. I knew whatever he was going to say would forever alter our friendship, our future.

"Mac," he began. Then he turned his head. "Hang on. Did you hear that?"

"What?"

"That rustling sound."

"It's just the wind."

He stood up. "It's the Mantis."

"You know what kind of sound a giant mantis makes?" A giant mantis with a damned crummy sense of timing, I wanted to add.

He clicked on his flashlight. "Come on."

He ran into the covered bridge. It swallowed him like the dark mouth of a whale. I followed his flashlight, a small spot of brightness that bounced erratically on the walls. To my horror, a large stick figure jumped at him from a crouched position. In the beam of my flashlight, I saw red alien eyes and a set of evil-looking claws.

"Jerry, look out!"

He ran right into it, fell and rolled in a tangle of long limbs and muffled cursing. I rushed up and grabbed his arm. As I pulled him free, my flashlight revealed one red mantis eye on the ground and the other still attached to what looked like a bike helmet on the head of a very real person. The mantis staggered up and started laughing.

"Didn't think you'd be suckered in, too, J."

Jerry was trying to catch his breath. I couldn't tell if he was angry or amused. "Damn it, Rick. What do you think you're doing?"

"Adding fuel to the fire, pal, and fanning the flames."

I kept my light in Rick's eyes. He had on a brown tur-
tleneck shirt and brown pants. The claws were cardboard.
The eyes were the kind of red reflectors used on bikes and
driveway markers. I could've killed him. "You're pathetic,
you know that?"

"Fooled you, didn't it?" He took off the helmet. "Hell, J,
you knocked my eye off."

"This is crazy," Jerry said. "Are you actually scaring anybody?"

"You should hear them yell."

"And nobody comes after you?"

"So far, you've been the only one brave enough to tackle
the Mantis and live to tell the tale—if you want to call that
collision a tackle." He grinned at me. "I like the way Mac
came screaming to your rescue."

My heartbeat had finally returned to normal. "I did not
scream."

"Like a banshee."

Jerry used his flashlight to locate Rick's reflector eye.
"Are you out here every night?"

"Nah, just when I feel like it. I try to pop out of the woods
on the other side of the lake, too, for a little variety. People
expect the Mantis, they see the Mantis. It's classic." He put
the reflector in his pocket. "Took you long enough to come
looking."

Jerry laughed. "You must be pretty desperate for customers."

"Nah, just bored."

I'd had enough, and I certainly didn't want Rick to en-
list Jerry in this scheme. I could just see the two of them:
Mantis Man and Mantis Man, Junior. "Come on, Jerry. You
found Mantis Man, and he's a bigger fake than I could've
imagined."

Rick's grin never faltered. "I may be a fake, but I'm going
to be a rich fake."

I switched off my flashlight so I wouldn't have to look at that grin. "You might sell a few tee shirts to some kids, but you're not going to get rich."

"But Mac, old girl, this isn't the only thing I've got cooking in town."

"Okay, so you've swindled a few old ladies out of their life savings. You should be very proud. And stop calling me Mac."

He put on his helmet and adjusted the strap. "The pet-psychic project has run its course. Want to hear my latest?"

"No," I said, "and Jerry doesn't, either." I grabbed Jerry by the arm and pulled him away. "Good night, Rick."

Jerry was still chuckling as we got into the car. "Gotta hand it to him, that Rick's a pro."

"A pro jerk, you mean."

"You aren't going to tell people he's the Mantis, are you?"

"No, I think anyone who's taken in by cardboard and bike reflectors deserves a good scare."

We drove in silence for a few minutes. I wanted to ask Jerry what he was going to tell me before the Mantis attacked, but I knew that, thanks to Rick, another special moment had bitten the dust.

Jerry said, "You look awfully grim. Did you think it was a real Mantis Man?"

"It's late. I'm tired, that's all."

Jerry was unusually quiet the rest of the way home. Just before he went upstairs, he startled me by kissing my cheek. "Rick was right about one thing. Thanks for screaming to the rescue."

All I could think to say was, "I didn't scream."

"Yes, you did. It was blood curdling. Any self-respecting mantis would drop to its knees and pray for mercy."

I had to push him away. It was either that or grab him and hold on forever. "Good night, Jerry."

FIVE

THE NEXT MORNING, I dropped Jerry off at the bookstore so he could continue his exorcism, or extermination, and went to Parkland. At the *Herald* office, I asked to see Chance Baseford. The secretary checked to see if he was available and told me Baseford could give me a few minutes. I went down the hallway to the last door on the left and tapped on the door.

"Enter," a deep voice said.

Chance Baseford looked the same. The same broad pinkish face, the same mane of silvery hair, the same pompous attitude. "I'm very busy, Ms. Maclin, was it? This had better be important."

I didn't think he remembered me. "It's a question only you can answer," I said.

This approach worked. His manner changed. "Please sit down." He smoothed back his hair. "How may I be of assistance?"

"I'm looking for the artist who painted a portrait of Desmond, Jeremyn and Tucker Fairweather. I was told his name is McKittrick."

Baseford put his fingertips together. "Ah, yes. McKittrick. Not a bad portrait painter if you want something ordinary. Sad to say, he left town years ago. Why are you looking for him?"

"I'm hoping he can tell me more about the fire that killed Victor and Lillian Fairweather."

Baseford's white brows drew together. I thought he was

pondering the mystery, but abruptly, he sat back and pointed both first fingers at me as if shooting a gun. "Miss Parkland."

I sighed. "Yes."

"I knew I'd seen you before. I hope you took my advice and never picked up a paintbrush again."

"Mister Baseford, if we could get back to my original question."

"Did you continue with a so-called art career?"

"That has nothing to do with this."

"Why in the world are you interested in a twenty-year-old tragedy? Not hoping to solve the mystery, are you?"

"As a matter of fact, I am."

He rolled his eyes. "Oh, my God. Don't tell me you've become one of those annoying female detectives. Aren't there enough of them cluttering the fiction shelves?"

"Mister Baseford, what I've done with my life is not your concern. I just want to know if you have any information that might help the Fairweather family."

"What's left of it."

"Yes."

"With your looks, you should be doing just one thing."

"With your looks, what should you be doing?"

I didn't let the old bastard stare me down. I held his gaze until he gave a snort that might have been a laugh.

"Well, you've toughened up, I can see that."

"Thank you."

"Yes, it is thanks to me."

I'd let him go on believing that. "What can you tell me about the fire?"

He steepled his fingers again. "It happened late at night. Some candles overturned and caught the living room on fire. The older girl got the children out, but the parents weren't as lucky."

"You know something else, though, don't you?"

"Why do you say that?"

"Because you keep glancing to something behind me."

"That would be the clock. Your time is almost over."

"Why glance at the clock when you've got a very expensive watch on your wrist?"

He snorted again. "That picture behind you. It's by McKittrick."

I turned around in my chair. Baseford's back wall was covered with framed newspaper articles, plaques, awards, photographs and pictures. The picture he pointed to was of a much younger Baseford. His hair was brown, but his face was still pink and his expression still superior.

"I'm surprised you kept such an ordinary painting," I said.

"Take a closer look."

I got up and examined the painting. An inscription at the bottom read, "To my dear friend and most exacting critic, sincere thanks, Monroe McKittrick." Further down was the name "Jackson Frye."

"Who's Jackson Frye?" I asked.

"His assistant. He never did anything worthwhile. Always running around with the ladies. Come to think of it, I believe he was enamored of young Harriet Fairweather. Probably after her fortune, although she was tolerably good-looking."

This was news. "Did he assist with the Fairweather portrait?"

"Most likely."

"Do you know where he is?"

"You'd have to ask McKittrick."

"Do you know where McKittrick is?"

"I know where he went. He may not be there now."

I waited. Either the old bully would tell me or not. I wasn't going to beg. Looking at Baseford now, I realized I'd built him into a monster when he was actually just a grumpy old man. "Do you paint, Mister Baseford?"

"No. Waste of time."

You probably don't know how, I thought. So you have to tear down those who can. I was too young to see that before.

Baseford said, "You might try the artists' colony in Riverdale."

"Thank you."

"Now I really must get back to work." He picked up some papers on his desk and made a great show of looking through them. "Good day."

I went out and shut the door behind me. I stood in the hallway for a few moments and took some deep breaths. Wait till Jerry hears about this. Baseford's nothing but a crusty old coot. On second thought, I might not tell Jerry. He'll say now there's nothing standing in the way of my art.

Only, I had to admit that nothing was ever standing in the way. I put up all the roadblocks myself. I let other people talk me out of something I loved. This was not going to happen again.

Riverdale was several hours away. I decided to save that road trip for later and get back to my office in Celosia. When I got there, several extra cars sat in the parking lot. At first, I thought Ted must have a lot of clients. Then I recognized the people standing at the front door. When I first met Ted, he and a group of concerned women were protesting the Miss Celosia Pageant. Here were the same protestors, only now they had a new cause and a new leader.

Twenty waved from the pack. "Good morning, Madeline! We're organizing the members of S.T.O.M.P."

I knew most of the members of Twenty's anti-Mantis group. Samantha Terrell is Austin's mother. The other women are local soccer moms and members of Twenty's garden club.

"Are you in with them?" I asked Ted.

"I agreed to listen to their side of the story."

Twenty didn't let him get away with this. In her bright blue sundress with silver trim, she looked like a bolt of electricity. "Ted Stacy, you know where you stand. Anything that harms the town has to go. Do you want us to become like Dixley, saddled with that awful Squash Festival? I suppose you'd want a Slug Festival or maybe Black Widow Spider Days?"

Ted tried to calm her down. "I still think you need to wait and see the movie."

Her round silver earrings swung like little wrecking balls. "What about that creepy Mister Rialto and all his ideas about merchandising?"

"Those ideas have to pass through the Chamber of Commerce, and I doubt the mayor's going to agree."

"But it's a free country, Ted! Rialto can set up his stuff by the roadside."

"Chief Brenner can take care of that."

Twenty sighed. "It's just so tacky."

Samantha Terrell agreed. "I don't want Austin running through the woods trying to find the Mantis Man. He's wild enough as he is. If he sees a movie about this creature, I know he's going to want to see the real thing."

"There is no real thing," Twenty said. "It's just a stupid story. If I could get my hands on the idiot that invented Mantis Man, I'd squash him like a bug. Madeline, when is Gaskins coming back to the Eberlin house?"

"The night of the full moon."

"That's tonight. We'll be there. Ted, are you coming tonight?"

"I wouldn't miss it," he said.

"Samantha, I want you and Esme to make signs. Patty

and Janie, you need to start the petition. No Mantis movie. No Mantis merchandise. Ted, what are you going to do?"

"I'd really like to see the movie first before I make a decision."

"Madeline?"

"I'm sort of neutral on this issue, Twenty."

She put her hands on her hips, and for a moment, I thought she was going to blast off like a rocket. "Well, sometimes you just have to take a stand. If S.T.O.M.P. has anything to do with it, there won't be a movie. Come on, girls."

The group moved on, Twenty giving us several dark looks over her shoulder.

"I can't believe she's so upset over this," I said.

We watched as Twenty gave the women some last-minute instructions before they got into their cars. Ted gave Twenty a wave. She didn't wave back.

"Neutral is probably the way to go, Madeline."

"I hope I don't lose her friendship."

"I don't think it's that serious." He rubbed his neck. "It's too hot to stand out here worrying about the Mantis."

As we went down the hallway to our offices, Ted said, "Speaking of Mantis Man, I heard a couple saw him last night. Guess the old legends die hard."

I started to tell Ted that it wasn't an old legend but an old con man when Ted's phone rang.

"That's my client," he said. "Talk to you later."

I went back to my office and sat down at my desk. I had my second list of overdue books to track down, and I'd promised Evan I'd look through the Miss Celosia Summertime Pageant materials. Might as well get the pageant stuff out of the way first. Cathy and Mitch had put together an official-looking brochure with all the rules for Miss Celosia Summertime, a mission statement and an application form. "A New Chance to Show the World What You Can Do!"

the headline proclaimed. "The Miss Celosia Summertime Pageant is all about Girl Power! Everyone's a Winner!"

I sighed and read on. Miss Celosia Summertime was created "to bring out the best in every young woman." The pageant offered cash prizes and an exciting trip to New York City. I wondered how they managed that and then remembered Mitch had connections in New York. A modest twenty-five dollar registration fee was required. Contestants were encouraged to bring in canned foods for Celosia's United Community Can Drive.

I was reading about Poise and Personality when Shana knocked on the door.

"I hear you and Mantis Man went a couple of rounds last night."

I closed the folder. "Something like that. How did you know?"

She came in and sat down in the chair. "High-school kids were making out on the other side of the bridge. They said they heard a rustling noise and a terrific scream."

"It wasn't a scream. It was a battle cry. I thought that thing had Jerry."

"So there really was a Mantis Man?"

I was still so disgusted with Rick I didn't care what I'd promised Jerry. "It was Rick Rialto."

"Rialto's the Mantis? He must be older than he looks. People have been seeing this thing since the thirties."

"He's trying to create interest—as if people aren't Mantis-mad already."

"Well, the kids were really frightened."

"Tell them the Mantis is just a two-bit con man who'll do anything for the almighty dollar."

"Did Jerry know this?"

"No, he was just as surprised as I was."

Shana indicated the folder. "That looks like an important case."

"Rules and regulations for Miss Celosia Summertime. I promised I'd have a look."

"And?"

"There's nothing wrong with it. I just can't seem to escape the pageant world. That part of my life is so over." I set the folder aside. "For some teenage girls, it's a good opportunity. They really can learn poise and self-confidence. But when you come right down to it, a pageant is a beauty contest. Why else would you parade around in a bathing suit and an evening gown?"

Shana picked up the folder and looked inside. "You have to admit, your pageant experience has come in handy."

"But it's not something I want to depend on to solve mysteries."

"That's unlikely, isn't it?"

"Oh, here's the best part. Cathy and Mitch want to have a Miss Mantis Pageant."

Shana almost fell out of the chair laughing. When she could speak, she said, "You can't be serious!"

"Coming soon to a theater near you."

"If I put something like that in one of my books, no one would believe me." She wiped her eyes. "I'm imagining the talent competition."

"My mind won't go that far."

"Shiniest Carapace. Best Antennae. Healthiest Spiracles. I want in on this. Do the Pageantoids need a consultant?"

"Please don't encourage them."

Shana dug in her pocketbook for her notebook. "You don't mind if I write this down, do you? I'll have to use it somewhere."

"I didn't know you wrote comedies."

"You never know." She jotted some notes. "On a different topic, I appreciate Jerry's help with Hayden's latest ghost."

"I can't see that he's helping very much. He keeps adding to the stories."

"Hayden needs someone to talk to. He knows I've heard enough of it." She looked up from her writing. "How's the Fairweather campaign coming along?"

"It's taken a very odd turn. Jerry keeps wanting to tell me something."

Her eyebrows stayed up. "Really? What kind of something?"

"Something serious. But we keep getting interrupted. Last night, for instance. It was the perfect setting. Jerry and I were alone by the bridge. The moon was shining on the river." I held up my thumb and first finger a few inches apart. "We were this close."

"And?"

"And Rick decided to play Mantis Man."

"So now you know how Twenty feels."

"Yes, I could gladly kill him." I shook my head. "She's too serious about all this."

"Celosia's her home."

"Parkland's my home, but I don't panic if someone wants to make changes."

"Small-town life is different."

"I believe that," I said. "I also believe there's more to this than Twenty wanting to keep Celosia Mantis free."

Shana's eyes gleamed with humor. "Then we'd better not tell her about Miss Mantis."

I SPENT THE REST OF THE morning tracking down library books. While shaking down Reverend Dobbs at the Presbyterian Church, I caught sight of a red umbrella in his umbrella stand, but it didn't have a duck head. Dobbs handed over *Journeys With Paul,* grinning sheepishly.

"I thought it was my copy."

"No problem."

My next stop was the television and radio station. Benjy Goins, local DJ, grinned from his booth and held up *Make*

Your Ads Count where I could see it. When he had a commercial break, he came out and handed me the book.

"I knew you were on the trail, Madeline. The word is out. Madeline Maclin, Watchdog of the Library."

"I'm letting you off easy because this is your first offense."

"What can I say? I'm a hardened criminal." Benjy actually looks like the scruffy dog from the *Benji* movies. He scratched his beard. "You know I'm judging Miss Celosia Summertime for those nutty friends of yours."

"Yes, and they're not my friends. They're more like remoras."

"I've got Chuck on board, too."

"I'm sure you'll have a great time. What do you know about Josh Gaskins and Kirby Willet?"

"Don't know Gaskins, but Willet's always been a town character."

"Any idea where I might find him?"

"Wayfarer Motel."

"Nope. Not any more."

"Then I don't know." He looked at the clock in his studio. "Can you wait till my next break?"

I sat in one of the fake leather chairs and thumbed through *Make Your Ads Count* while Benjy played three more of "Benjy's Big Hits." Then I heard something that made me slap the book shut.

"So come on in to Deely's, home of the Mantis Man Burger. So much meat, it'll make your eyes bug out!"

"What the hell was that?" I asked Benjy when he came out.

"New ad for Deely's."

"Mantis Man Burger?"

"Kinda catchy, huh?"

"You know Twenty's launched a protest group against Mantis Man merchandising."

He made a dismissive gesture. "She's wound too tight. This Mantis Man stuff could be a lot of fun, bring in a lot of tourists. I figure, we're gonna have a movie about it, why not cash in on the publicity? But forget that. What I wanted to tell you was Kirby's probably gone to Riverdale."

Riverdale. Boy, that was convenient.

"He always talked about a cousin who lived there and how the two of them were going to work on inventions together. He should've moved to California. California's the perfect place for him, if you ask me."

"As far as you know, none of his inventions ever worked?"

"Not a one."

"Do you know the cousin's name?"

"He never said."

My cell phone beeped. It was Jerry.

"Mac, I just heard about Mantis Man Burgers on the radio. If we don't try one, we'll regret it the rest of our lives."

"I'll meet you there," I said. When I put my phone away, Benjy grinned at me.

"The power of the media."

DEELY'S WAS MORE CROWDED than usual, but we found places at the end of the counter and ordered a cheeseburger.

"No flies," Jerry said.

Deely got the joke and grinned. "No problem."

"Nonsense," the man next to me said. "Absolute codswallop."

Lance Henderson peered out from under a false beard and moustache.

"Lance?" I said. "What's with the disguise?"

He shushed me. "It's the only way I can move about your rustic little town. Otherwise, I'm swamped with requests for autographs. The people at your sorry excuse for a motel have been hounding me mercilessly."

He couldn't keep the pride from his voice. Another fine performance, I thought.

"Are you enjoying your Mantis Burger?"

He glared at his sandwich. "A ridiculous name for such a delicious hamburger. You see how the madness has already taken hold?"

Alicia Fields, one of Deely's waitresses, brought me a Coke and Jerry a glass of tea. "Need a refill, Mister Du-Bois?" she asked Henderson.

"No, thank you," he said.

"You just take your time."

"Thank you, my dear."

Alicia moved down the counter. Henderson wiped his hands on his napkin. "There is one ray of light in all this. Vivian Montrose is unable to join our merry band."

"Will Gaskins cancel the project?"

"No, he'll just corral some other mindless starlet."

"She'll have to be here by tonight, won't she?"

He spoke with satisfaction. "That's his problem."

Alicia brought our cheeseburgers.

"Are you eating two of those massive creations?" Henderson asked.

"No, one's for my friend Jerry Fairweather." I leaned back so the men could see each other. "May I reveal your true identity?"

Henderson gave a gracious wave of his hand. "Yes, of course."

"Jerry, this is Lance Henderson."

Jerry shook hands with Lance. "I never would've recognized you," he said with a perfectly straight face.

"Well, one learns the tricks of the trade early on, young man. It's your house Gaskins intends to use for his schlock-fest, isn't it? Can you honestly believe such a picture can succeed?"

"It has possibilities. Nothing like *Wings of Power.*"

Henderson brightened. "Ah, my World-War-I epic. Kind of you to remember, Mister Fairweather. Do you have a favorite episode?"

"I think the prison escape was my favorite."

"An excellent show. I was able to explore the full range of my talents in that one."

Of course Jerry would know about any TV show. He and Lance talked about *Wings of Power* for a while. As I ate, Henderson kept giving me glances, as if he couldn't believe I was immune to his charms.

"What did you think of the spy episode, Mister Fairweather? I was never happy with the results. We had a writer who would not budge from his storyline, even though I had many excellent suggestions."

"I can't say I recall that one."

Henderson gave the counter a slap. "I knew it! My ideas would have made that show memorable! Award winning!"

"Did you write any of the episodes?" Jerry asked.

"Just one, and our producer failed to recognize its significance." He wiped his mouth on his napkin. "As for our current conflict of interest, Ms. Maclin, I'm hoping for rain tonight. A good thunderstorm. Lots of clouds and interference."

"It'll only add to the spooky atmosphere."

He growled down in his false beard. "I'd do anything to ruin this movie's chances. Gaskins promised me a decent, award-winning film. I have no patience with his quirks." He put his money on the counter. "Good day to you, my dear. Mister Fairweather. A pleasure talking with you."

For someone trying to be incognito, he made a big production of leaving the diner, waving and calling to the waitress and commenting loudly about the blast of heat as he went out. I wondered if Henderson was always all talk and no action. I swung around on my stool. "Henderson doesn't want the movie to happen, either."

"I noticed that."

"His glory days are over, and he's having a hard time letting go."

Alice stopped by to refill our drinks. To Jerry's amusement, she confirmed my opinion by asking, "Who was that old geezer, and why did he want me to call him Mister DuBois?"

"Lance Henderson," I said. "He used to be famous."

"Never heard of him."

"You're too young," Jerry said.

She gave him the kind of twinkly smile most women in town give Jerry. "Thank you, Jerry. Is this Henderson in the Mantis Man movie?"

"That's right."

"Does he play the Mantis? He looks too old."

Jerry and I shrugged. "We're not sure," I said.

"Have you seen that other man, the real good-looking one with the black curly hair? I'll bet he plays the hero, and the old guy plays his grandfather or something."

Thank goodness Henderson wasn't around to hear this. "We'll have to wait and see."

She set the iced tea pitcher down, flipped through her pad until she found our orders, tore them out and placed them on the counter. "Can I come out and watch the filming? Deely says they're doing some shots tonight on account of the full moon."

"I think that would be okay," I said.

Alice picked up the pitcher and moved on down to her other customers.

"So, how was your morning?" Jerry asked.

"I found two more library books."

"Good."

"And I talked to Chance Baseford."

Jerry had taken a drink of tea and almost did a spit take. He swallowed and wiped his mouth. "You did what?"

"Talked to Chance Baseford. I'm pleased to report he no longer has any control over me."

"What did you say? What did he say?"

"McKittrick had an assistant, Jackson Frye. Do you remember another man at the house? Somebody standing by to hand McKittrick his brushes?"

"I just remember trying to hold Tucker. He was a wiggly little guy. Did Baseford recognize you?"

"Yes, and he was a complete ass about it. I don't think he's used to people standing up for themselves. I couldn't do it back then, but I sure as hell could do it now. He told me to try the artists' colony in Riverdale. McKittrick might be living there. And, just because I'm living right, Riverdale's where Kirby Willet's cousin lives. Maybe I can solve two mysteries in one day."

"Heading up there now? I'd like to go with you, but I promised Hayden I'd do a full-spectral analysis of the store, and the movie crew's filming tonight."

I checked my watch. It was almost one. By the time I got to Riverdale, it would be four or five. "I'll probably wait till in the morning."

AFTER LEAVING DEELY'S, we stopped by the bookstore to see if any more spectral insects had fallen from above. While Jerry and Hayden went to the back to check on celestial vibes, I talked with Georgia. She was rearranging the children's books.

"Madeline, I hate to say this, but I laughed like a fool when Hayden told me about Jerry's close encounter. Imagine the ceiling being full of dead bugs! I'm glad there weren't any customers in the store."

"I hope all this nonsense isn't bothering you."

"Oh, I'm not upset," she said. "Hayden actually saw the humor in it this morning. Even with all the séance nonsense, Jerry's the best thing that's happened to him." She glanced toward the front of the store. "Isn't that one of the movie actors?"

Flynn Davis wasn't in disguise like Henderson, but he scowled just as fiercely.

"Can you believe this?" he said. "Not only does Vivian have another commitment, that washed-up Henderson has convinced Gaskins to let him narrate the movie! That's so old-fashioned! How are we going to establish a mood with his ancient voice muttering through the soundtrack?"

"Give the guy a break," I said. "Didn't you tell me Henderson thought he had the lead? Gaskins is probably trying to soften the blow. You'll have more screen time, right?"

"There's no telling what that old crackpot will say."

"Gaskins has final edit, doesn't he?"

Davis stopped griping and looked at me. "I thought you said you weren't an actress."

"I'm not."

"'Screen time.' 'Final edit.' You sound like one."

I shrugged. "Everybody in America knows about the movies."

Now his stare was on full power. "You'd be perfect for Vivian's part."

I put both hands up. "Hold on. Don't even think about that."

"All she does is run around and scream. You can do that, can't you?" He clutched my hands. "Please say you'll do it. You'll save the picture."

I pulled free. "That's crazy. I can't act."

"Have you ever seen Vivian act? She just stands there and looks gorgeous. You can do that."

Just like being in a pageant. Good lord, is there no escape?

"Davis—"

"Please," he said. "You don't know what this movie means to me. It's my first big break, my first starring role.

If Gaskins has to fold because of Vivian, it's back to the soaps for me. Plus, I'll have to listen to Henderson gloat. At least say you'll try."

Besides Georgia, who was listening avidly, we had attracted a small crowd of interested shoppers.

Davis took advantage of his audience. "Don't you think she'd be perfect in *Curse of the Mantis Man?* Don't you think she'd make a beautiful heroine?"

Georgia beamed. "Madeline! A chance to be in a movie!"

"I'd take it," one of the shoppers said.

"Me, too," another said.

A third shopper nodded. "Everybody in town's been wanting to get in. You'd be silly to turn it down."

I took Davis's arm and pulled him out the front door. "Could we talk about this somewhere else?"

He gave me what I'm sure he thought was a winning smile. "How about my motel room?"

"How about the dark side of the moon?" I said and walked away.

He called after me. "Make that a full moon, Madeline. That's tonight, you know."

I thought I'd had my share of idiots for the day, but I caught sight of the premiere idiot, Rick Rialto, unloading boxes of tee shirts into an empty store just two doors down from Georgia's. He saw me and held up one of the shirts.

"Hey, Mac. What do you think of this?"

A garish red-and-black mantis waved three of its six legs. Letters above its head proclaimed just as Twenty had feared: "Greetings From Celosia, Home of Mantis Man!"

"Charming."

He folded the shirt and replaced it on the stack. "I knew you'd like it."

I came into the empty store and looked around. Traces

of cedar shavings and musty scents hung in the air. "Wasn't this a pet shop?"

"Went out of business a couple of days ago. Wasn't that lucky?"

"How did you get it, Rick?"

"The owners were anxious to rent."

"No, I mean where did you get the money?"

He grinned that shit-eating grin I hate so much. My heart sank.

"Hey, you know J and me are tight. We used to be partners. My old buddy's not likely to refuse a request, especially for something so important. Want to see the hats? They turned out great." He dug in another box and brought out a baseball cap with the same Mantis Man design. "Cool, huh? And I've got bumper stickers and key rings and Christmas cards. You haven't lived till you've seen old Mantis Man in a Santa suit."

I knew if I stayed one more minute I'd smack that grin so hard it would come out the back of his head. As I left, I heard him call, "Thanks for shopping Mantis Man Merchandise. Come back soon."

I decided to let Hayden bring Jerry home so I'd have time to calm down. I went up to the second floor parlor. I stared at the blank piece of white paper on the easel for a long moment. Then, using the photographs I'd brought from the theater, I started sketching the first child's face, a pale oval peering out of a rabbit costume. I was surprised by how easily I was able to capture the little boy's expression. The next boy, dressed as a bear, was making a humorous grimace I'm sure he imagined as a fierce face. A few quick strokes, and his dark features grinned from the paper. Relief eased my shoulders down. I could do this.

When Jerry called, "Mac, want some pizza?" I glanced at my watch and then stared. I'd been working for over two hours. I washed my hands and hurried down the stairs. Jerry had the lid up on one of three takeout pizza boxes.

"Pepperoni, sausage, or Super Combo?"

"A slice of each, thanks." I sat down at the table and reached for one of the plastic cups of cola. "I didn't realize it was so late."

"It must be coming along okay, then."

"Better than I thought. Did you rid the bookstore of evil spirits?"

He slid a large piece of sausage pizza out of the box. "Yep. It's nice to have a second job to fall back on."

"You don't have a first job," I said.

"Can I wait until *Music Man* is over?"

"I've started painting."

"Can't I just be your sidekick?"

As appealing as this sounded, I had to keep him on track. "We have a deal."

"I promise as soon as the show is over, I'm circling the want ads in the paper."

"Maybe you could work in Rick's store."

Jerry paused, the piece of pizza halfway to his mouth. He set the piece down.

"He's got the stuff already?"

"He said you paid the rent. I thought you weren't going to have anything to do with him any more."

"He just needed a loan."

I didn't know what else to say. Jerry must have sensed my frustration.

"Rick and I go way back, Mac. I'd do the same for you."

I really liked being lumped in the same category as Rick Rialto. "That's good to know."

"I don't know why you're pissed. I'm not the one selling the stuff."

"Never mind," I said.

We ate in silence for a while. Then I said, "I'm going to work on the picture a little more."

"The music won't bother you, will it?"

"No."

I thought he was going to practice *Music Man* tunes, but after a while, some operatic singing filtered up the stairs. I didn't recognize this one, but nearly all opera sounds the same to me. I became so involved in getting the children's expressions correct, I didn't hear anything for another hour.

When I came downstairs, Jerry was lounging on the sofa, listening to a tape. I made him move his feet so I could sit down. "What's this one?"

"*Faust*," he said.

"That's the one about the devil, right?"

"Mephistopheles."

"And Faust makes a bargain and they sing about it for three hours."

"Oh, it takes much longer than that."

The tenor voice throbbed with emotion. "What's he singing about?"

"'Let me gaze on your face, lost in wonder, as the pale moon above shines through the dark of night.'"

I had an instant memory of his face in the moonlight. "That's pretty romantic."

"It gets better. 'Do you know what happiness means? To love, to know the flame that will bind two souls together and brings ecstatic joy to our hearts, never ending.' Or something like that."

Now a soprano's voice joined the tenor. The music soared around us, the two voices declaring undying love, joy and ecstasy.

"Jerry, you started to tell me something last night."

A chorus of car horns blared over the singing.

Jerry hopped up. "Movie time!"

I sighed and then followed him out to the porch. Despite

Lance Henderson's hopes, the night was clear. A huge full moon made its way up past the trees. Down the driveway, I saw a row of headlights.

"Jerry, did you invite the whole town to the filming?"

He paused on the steps. "Looks like it, doesn't it?"

"That's Twenty's car and Ted's. Oh, hell, that's Cathy and Mitch."

Gaskins's van arrived first, followed by Henderson's car. As the crew set up, Twenty and the other protesters formed a line. Ted stood a little away from them. Cathy and Mitch huddled nearby, taking notes. I saw Rick get out of his Buick. Nell and her dad arrived in the chief's police car. Pretty soon, the front yard was filled with spectators.

Gaskins looked unconcerned. When he had his cameras and lights ready, he called for Davis and Henderson. Then he called for me.

"Davis tells me you're interested in standing in for Vivian."

"That's Davis's idea, not mine," I said.

"It would help considerably if you'd just be in a few exterior shots. We'll shoot in shadow and substitute another actress later."

Jerry was delighted. "Go for it, Mac."

Gaskins called for quiet. "All right, let's get started. Davis, you and Madeline come around the side of the house."

Davis grabbed my hand and pulled me with him. We ran around the side of the house about thirty times before Gaskins was satisfied.

"All right, I want one more here in front of the house. Stephanie, where's my drink?"

Stephanie handed him his cup. He took a noisy slurp and said, "Lance, come out the front door, look around and go back in."

Henderson did this until Gaskins had the shot he wanted.

"Now I want everyone out here around the tree looking

back at the house." Gaskins took another annoying slurp of soda. "Just stare at it like it's the worst thing you've ever—"

I'm sure he meant to say "seen," but he never finished his sentence. He shook his head as if to clear it and fell over.

Davis said, "What the hell?"

Stephanie screamed "Josh!" and knelt down. She looked up, her face ghastly white in the moonlight. "Get a doctor!"

A woman I didn't know hurried up from the crowd to examine Gaskins. I heard Chief Brenner call for assistance on his radio. Then he pushed through the crowd. "Everyone stand back." He and the woman had a brief conversation. Using his pen, he carefully lifted Gaskins's paper cup from the grass. "Who fixed this drink for Mister Gaskins?"

Stephanie got to her feet. She held her arms tight around her. "I did. I always do."

"Where do you keep the cola?"

"In the van."

"Who has access to the van?"

"Everyone in the crew." She looked around and pointed a shaking finger at Rick. "That man was hanging around in the back."

Rick took several steps back. "I was just looking around."

Chief Brenner's gaze took in the crowd. "Any one of these people could have gone to the van while we were watching the action." He raised his voice. "No one is to leave until I talk to you. Nell, make sure of that. Jerry, I'll be using your living room."

I watched the faces of the people. The movie crew was stunned. Stephanie continued to cry. Cathy and Mitch clutched each other. Ted looked shocked. The other protestors looked grim, their gaudy S.T.O.M.P. signs down by their sides. Henderson and Davis sat on the porch steps, heads down. The only expression I couldn't read was Twenty's. She stood apart from the protestors, arms folded, gazing across the moonlit fields. She stayed that way, even when the police cars and ambulance rolled into the yard, even when the EMS team told us what had happened to Gaskins.

Poisoned.

The word went through the crowd like an evil whisper. Gaskins was put into the ambulance, and the woman, Doctor Chapman, Nell told me, got inside with him. The ambulance raced off into the night, followed by a police car. Everyone else was instructed to come into the Eberlin house living room one by one to be questioned.

I was the last person in. I sat down on the living-room sofa while Chief Brenner stood by the coffee table. He turned another page of his notepad.

"Was it Mister Gaskins's habit to have a large soda during filming?"

"Yes, Stephanie always brought him one."

"And he always used a straw?"

"Yes. Do you suspect Stephanie?"

He rubbed his short blond hair and consulted his list. "I have plenty of suspects: Ms. Harold, Lance Henderson, Davis, the protest group, the entire movie crew, Cathy Sloop, Mitch Hutton, yourself, Jerry, Ted and Twenty. And let's not forget Mister Rialto."

"Cathy and Mitch are harmless. They're just here to watch the filming."

"I'll determine how harmless they are."

"You don't really suspect Ted, do you?" I didn't even want to mention Twenty.

He put his pad away. "We've had this talk about you getting involved with police business."

"It worked last time, didn't it?"

His eyes narrowed. "Last time, you got lucky. Very lucky. You need to leave this to me." His phone beeped. He answered. "Yes?" He listened a few moments and then put the phone back on his belt. "Now you definitely need to leave this to me, Madeline. Gaskins is dead."

The other officers had finished with the crime scene. Chief Brenner told the crew to pack up but not to leave town. Another officer drove the van. Everyone else got into cars and left. I wanted to speak to Twenty, but she had already left. Rick, however, was still there. I noticed his face was pale and he was shaking.

"Come inside," Jerry told him.

"Man, I can't believe this," Rick said. "The guy took a sip and just keeled over. Who do you suppose poisoned that drink?"

"That's what the police will find out."

We went into the kitchen. Jerry offered Rick some of the leftover pizza. Rick sat down and waved him away.

"I couldn't eat after that. That Brenner's tough, you know? I thought he really wanted to pin this on me."

"Why would he think that?" I asked. "Did you even know Gaskins?"

Rick shifted his gaze to Jerry and back to me. "Sort of."

"You want to tell me what's going on?"

Jerry said, "I think you'd better tell her. She's solved one murder in town."

The threat of being a murder suspect must have been too strong. Rick grimaced. "Gaskins owes me money."

Things fell into place. "So you came to Celosia to see him."

"No crime in that."

"You knew Voltage Films would be here."

He shrugged. "A lucky break."

I was tired of his attitude. "If you want me to help you, you'd better tell me everything."

He thought it over and must have decided I was his one good chance. "The thing is, I've been looking for Gaskins for months. He owes me from a pyramid scheme we had going in Pineville."

"Jerry, did you know about this?"

Rick answered, "Hell, yeah. I mean, he knew I was look-ing for Gaskins. But he wasn't part of the pyramid deal, if that's what you're worried about. Gaskins and I set it up. Then Gaskins takes the money. I knew he'd lived in some small town near Parkland for a while. Then I heard J had moved here and figured he could help me. Then this movie company arrives, and Gaskins happens to be the director. I figured my luck was running pretty good—until now, that is."

"Have you talked to Gaskins since you've been in town?" I asked.

"You bet I talked to him. I wanted my money."

"Did anyone hear you demanding your money from him?"

Rick looked troubled. "Yeah, I guess quite a few people heard me. That Davis guy and the old actor and the assis-tant."

"You didn't threaten him, or anything like that?"

He gulped. "I may have. I didn't threaten to kill him, though."

"What did he say?"

"He said I'd get it back out of the movie profits, but I couldn't see how a dinky horror film could make any se-rious dough. That's one reason I wanted to drum up more interest."

"Do you know Kirby Willet?"

"No."

I wanted Rick to stay on track. "You've got bigger prob-lems, Rick. What were you doing in Gaskins's van?"

"Looking for the money, of course." He glared at us. "The both of you quit looking at me as if I'm some kind of crim-inal. That daffy woman in the Day-Glo clothes is the one who did it. She's been hollering about Gaskins ever since he came to town."

I was very much afraid he was right, but I wasn't going to agree.

A pleading look came into his shifty little eyes. "Mac, I didn't do it. If you can prove that, I'll be your friend for life."

"If I can prove it," I said, "you'll leave town, taking all your Mantis Man crap with you, and you'll never come back."

He stuck out his hand. "Deal."

I gave his hand one shake and told him to get out. As soon as he was gone, Jerry said, "Thanks, Mac. He's a con man, but he's not a murderer."

"I hope not," I said. "And thanks so much for telling me about his connection with Gaskins."

Jerry looked uncomfortable. "I didn't think it was important."

"You swear to me you knew nothing of this pyramid scheme?"

"Rick told me Gaskins owed him some money, that's all. I figured the two of them would settle things and Rick would leave."

"Well, Gaskins is permanently settled, and if you're so sure your pal Rick isn't a murderer, then who did it?"

"Lance Henderson's been unhappy with Gaskins. So has Flynn Davis."

"So has Twenty."

"It can't be her," Jerry said. "I can't believe it. Maybe a member of the crew has a grudge."

"I still think Willet has some connection to Gaskins. All that money in the box. Maybe some of that was from the pyramid scheme. Unfortunately, I can't ask Gaskins what was going on."

"Maybe Willet killed him."

"What, with one of his inventions? Long-distance poison? Poison dart from a blowgun somewhere in the woods? Now more than ever I need to find Kirby Willet."

"Didn't you say he might be in Riverdale?"

"That's a possibility."

"Well, let's go."

"I appreciate your enthusiasm, but we can wait until morning."

We were too unsettled by Gaskins's death to tuck in, so we stayed up late planning our road trip. I finally slept a few hours. By the time I was up and dressed, Jerry had breakfast ready. By eight o'clock, we were on our way. We arrived in Riverdale around ten.

Riverdale's a tiny mountain community specializing in artsy shops and galleries. No cars are allowed on Main Street, so shoppers can browse and then have coffee or tea at one of the many little outdoor cafés. Along with the paintings and sculptures on display, we saw pottery, jewelry, wind chimes, mobiles and other things I didn't recognize.

We stopped at the largest café in the center of town. I asked the owner if he knew Kirby Willet or Monroe McKittrick.

"Never heard of Willet," he said. "McKittrick, however, has a studio on Fourth Street, just two blocks down."

Two blocks down, we found a large dark house surrounded by a dull wooden fence. The lawn was filled with long weeds, and patches of grass pushed between the cracks in the walkway.

"This looks more like a haunted house than a studio," Jerry said.

The doorbell didn't work, so I knocked. We heard the sound of shuffling feet and an odd tapping sound. The door opened, and there stood an elderly stoop-shouldered man with a cane. His dim eyes peered up at us.

"Yes? Who is it? What do you want?"

"Monroe McKittrick?" I asked.

"Yes."

"I'm Madeline Maclin, and this is Jerry Fairweather." I

started to tell him the reason for our visit, but at the mention of Jerry's name, he flinched.

"Fairweather. That was years ago. I had nothing to do with it."

"Sir, we're not accusing you of anything. We just have a few questions."

He steadied himself with his cane. "Questions! The police bombarded me with questions. They called me to say the Fairweathers were dead. Said it was a fire and they wanted to know where Frye was."

"Frye? Your assistant?"

"The police tried to blame me for what happened! Ruined my reputation in Parkland. I had to leave." He fumbled for the door. "Now I have to ask you to leave."

I already had my foot in the door, but I didn't need to force my way in. Inside the dark hallway, I caught a glimpse of paintings. "We were considering buying one of your paintings."

He stopped. "What's that you say?"

Jerry took up my lead. "The painting you did of me and my brothers is wonderful. I was hoping to have another for my new house."

McKittrick paused, clearly torn between our unwanted presence and the possibility of a sale. "I may have something." He stepped aside to let us enter. "But just in the hallway, mind you."

The house smelled musty. At the end of the hall, I could see a small room with a chair and a lamp where McKittrick no doubt spent his days. Leaning on his cane, he gestured with a shaky hand to the paintings on the wall.

"Here are some nice landscapes. There should be one of Natural Bridge. Some fall scenes of the Blue Ridge near the end here, if I recall."

Jerry stopped in front of a landscape of woods. "I like this one. How much?"

"One hundred fifty."

"All right."

For once, Jerry's money was going to pay for something useful. As he counted out the money into the old man's hand, McKittrick squinted at him. "Yes, I remember you. You were the one who could never sit still. Or were you the baby? There were two of you who looked very much alike."

"I'm the one in the middle," Jerry said. "I'd really appreciate it if you could tell us more about your assistant."

"That happened a long time ago. What difference does it make now?"

"Because I need to know exactly what happened."

I felt sorry for this frail old man. "And wouldn't it be worth something to you to finally be cleared of any suspicion?"

He nodded. "Yes. It still bothers me to this day, those little boys losing their parents like that." He put an unsteady hand on Jerry's arm. "It must have been rough for you, son."

"Can you help us, Mister McKittrick?"

"He was a student from the college. Jackson Frye."

"Why did you have an assistant?" I asked. "Was he learning your technique?"

"Even then, my eyesight wasn't the best. I relied on others to help me with the fine details. Frye was just one of the eager young artists I knew back then. I thought I was doing him a favor, but I didn't get much work out of him. Mainly, he wanted to hang around and flirt with the Fairweather girl. Hannah, was it?"

"Harriet," Jerry said. His voice was subdued.

"Harriet. Yes, that's it. I was to do her portrait next. Of course, that never happened."

"So it's possible Frye was at the house to see Harriet?"

"I don't know why he'd be there at midnight, but I imagine so."

"Do you know where Frye is now?"

"No. He ran off. I never saw him again. I suppose the police suspected him, too."

I was beginning to suspect him, myself. Jerry took the painting down. We thanked McKittrick and went out and stood for a moment at the car. Jerry looked abstracted.

"Jerry?"

"I remember something, Mac. I remember Harriet laughing and giggling over some boy. We thought it was sickening, of course, and made fun of her. But I'll bet it was this guy."

"It could've been, but Harriet probably had lots of boyfriends to giggle over."

"No, that's just it. That's why I remember. He was the only one. Harriet was dancing around the house. We'd never seen her like that."

"The only boyfriend she ever had? That's a little far-fetched, isn't it? After all, she was a very wealthy young lady, and Frye was an artist's assistant, so he may not have been so wealthy. Jerry, there may be something to this. Maybe Frye was flirting with Harriet because she was rich. Maybe he hoped to gain something from the relationship."

"Then he wouldn't burn down the house, would he?"

"No, but there may have been something in the house he wanted."

"And it wasn't Harriet."

"Sadly, no. This would explain why she's so grumpy. If Frye's innocent, if he really loved her, he would've stood by during the rough times, maybe even volunteered to help with you and your brothers, made himself useful. Instead, he disappears. We've got to talk to Harriet." I checked my watch. "And I've got to talk to a lot of people in Celosia."

We asked in several of the shops and cafés, but no one knew Kirby Willet or his cousin. Although this was frustrating, I was glad our trip had yielded some results in the Fairweather case. How serious had Harriet been about Jackson

Frye? Had they planned a secret midnight meeting in the hopes of eloping?

When we got back, I dropped Jerry off at the theater and started with Ted.

He sat back in his office chair. "My God, Madeline, that was horrible. I'll never be able to forget the look on Gaskins's face. What was in that drink? Why would anyone want to kill him?"

"That's what I'm trying to find out," I said. "Did you see anyone else besides Rick at the van last night?"

"I didn't pay any attention to that. I was watching you and the others run around the house."

"Where exactly were you and the members of S.T.O.M.P.?"

"We were all by the trees."

"Twenty was with you?"

He looked uncertain. "I thought she was. I really can't say for sure." He sat forward. "Dear God. You don't think she did it?"

"She's been awfully angry about anything having to do with Mantis Man."

"Yes, but—that's—that's just not— I can't imagine her killing anyone."

"Me, either, but it looks bad for her right now."

We sat in glum silence for a few minutes, and then Ted asked, "Have you talked to her?"

"I'm going to her house next."

"Madeline, the only person anywhere near the van was Rialto. Does he have a good excuse?"

"He says Gaskins owed him money."

"And he thought it would be in the van? That's a little suspicious, isn't it?"

I really wanted Rick to be the villain. "Everything about Rick is suspicious."

TWENTY WASN'T HOME. I caught up with her at Shana's. Shana and Hayden live in a large redwood house in a wooded area of Celosia called Autumn Fields. Twenty and Shana were sitting on the porch. Despite the heat, Shana looked cool in a white shirt and red shorts, her long hair pulled back in a smooth ponytail. Twenty had on a green blouse decorated with brown fishnet and orange shorts with lace trim. Her black and white curls stuck out at odd angles as if she'd slept on her head. Shana started to say hello when Twenty interrupted.

"I know why you're here, Madeline. You think I did it. Everyone thinks I did it."

"Well, did you?"

She looked taken aback. "No!"

"Just thought I'd ask."

"I hated what Gaskins was doing, but I didn't hate him. He was just a greedy, misguided man."

I sat down in one of the rocking chairs. "Exactly where were you last night when he took his last drink of soda?"

"With the other members of S.T.O.M.P."

"Ted doesn't remember seeing you."

She gasped at this betrayal. "Of course I was there! It was my idea to picket the production."

"So you were with the group the whole time?" Something in her expression made me push. "Twenty, I'm on your side. Please tell me the truth."

She glanced at Shana, seemed to gather some confidence, swallowed hard and said, "Not the whole time."

I waited.

"I wanted to disrupt the filming, so I went around behind the cameramen, hoping to see a cord I could unplug or something, but even with the moonlight, it was too dark. That's when I heard the woman scream."

"Did anyone see you?"

She shook her head. "Everyone ran to see what was wrong, including me."

Shana tried to lighten the conversation. "I told her she

should've had on one of her lime-green outfits. Then everyone would have seen her."

Twenty's curls bounced as she rubbed her forehead. "This is all so awful. I just wanted Celosia to stay the way it is. Now we've had another murder."

"That's my fault," I said. "People were safe till I moved to town."

Shana got the joke, but Twenty was too upset for any attempts at humor. "Madeline, you've got to solve this mystery, too. If someone's going around putting poison into drinks, you've got to stop them. That kind of news will ruin Celosia's reputation just as badly as a horror film."

"What about Lance Henderson?" Shana asked. "He's been very vocal about his dislike of Gaskins and the movie."

"I'll be talking to him, too."

EVERYONE INVOLVED WITH *Curse of the Mantis Man* was in the lobby of the Wayfarer Motel. They were having a community gripe session about having to stay in Celosia.

The minute Henderson saw me, he said, "I'm not sorry he's dead, but I didn't kill him."

"Take it easy," I said. "I'm not accusing you. I just want to ask everyone a few questions."

"Why should we talk to you?" one of the cameramen asked.

"She's a detective," Davis said. "Though we don't really need to say anything. I don't know why Henderson doesn't just confess." He turned to Lance. "We all know you hated him. Why don't you admit you got rid of him so we can all get out of this backward little town?"

Henderson snarled. "I'd just worked out a deal with him to narrate the stupid movie. You had an equal chance to kill him yourself."

Davis laughed a short laugh. "Why would I kill him? He was giving me my big break in show business."

"Oh, yes, your big break. *Curse of the Mantis Man.* Well, it turned out to be a curse, all right."

Davis poked his finger at Henderson's chest. "In case you've forgotten, old man, we were right out in front of everybody filming a scene when Gaskins died."

Henderson pushed Davis away. "And how did he die? We don't even know if he was murdered. He could've had a heart attack."

"He was poisoned," I said. "Anyone could've put the poison in his drink at any time."

Stephanie sat by herself, crying into a wad of Kleenex.

"Where did you keep his sodas?" I asked her.

"We have a little fridge in the van. I always bought the kind of cola he liked and kept at least six bottles in there."

"So you'd open one of the big bottles and keep his cup filled all day?"

"Yes. He always drank it up before it became flat, so buying big bottles was cheaper."

And easier to slip something in. "Who else knew about this?"

"Everyone in the cast and crew. It's a running joke how much soda he drinks—used to drink." She wiped her eyes. "I always put in just the right amount of ice. He liked the plastic straws with red and white stripes. He said they were much better than just plain straws." Her voice quit. She sobbed. "I really liked him. He never yelled like some directors."

"Were you happy as his assistant? You didn't want to be in the movies?" I thought Stephanie might harbor some desire to be in front of the camera, and Gaskins had refused her request.

She shook her head. "I was very happy with my job. I liked being the one he depended on. Now what am I going to do?"

"I'll tell you what you're going to do," Davis said. "You're going to do what the rest of us are doing, sit around wasting valuable time while that hick sheriff bumbles through the investigation, assisted by Miss Beauty Queen here."

How could I have ever thought this man was remotely handsome?

"You didn't seem very happy with Gaskins's decision to have Lance narrate the film," I said.

Davis's eyes narrowed. "Not a very solid motive to kill someone, is it?"

"Oh, I don't know. My last case involved a woman who wanted to be a porn star. I think people are capable of just about anything."

"Well, why was that other guy hanging around the van?"

"He says Gaskins owed him money." I turned to Stephanie. "How did Gaskins finance this film? Did he ever talk to you about that?"

She nodded. "I looked after the accounts, too. He had a backer."

"Who was it?"

"Some fellow he knew from here, a man named Kirby Willet."

Finally, a connection. "What can you tell me about him?"

"He and Josh went to high school together. Josh said Willet would advance him some money to get started. That's why we came to Celosia."

"Did you ever meet Willet?"

"Here's the odd thing. We were supposed to, but Willet never showed. Josh was very upset. I guess he thought Willet had backed out."

"So he didn't get his money?"

"No, and there isn't a record of it anywhere. We had to go ahead and start filming and hope Willet would show up with the money."

"Wait a minute," Davis said. "There isn't any money? How are you planning to pay us?"

Stephanie looked at him as if she couldn't believe he'd

be so crass. "There's enough money for your salary, Davis. Willet isn't the only backer."

"I'm looking for Willet, too," I told Stephanie. "If he gets in touch with you, let me know."

I WENT BACK TO THE THEATER to pick up Jerry. I also wanted to speak to Cathy and Mitch. They were thrilled to have been part of the drama, but even more thrilled I had agreed to speak to the contestants.

Cathy almost galloped down the aisle of the theater. "Madeline, we're so happy you changed your mind! Here we thought you were out of the pageant world, and Evan tells us you're coming to coach all our girls."

"No, I'm coming to speak to them and answer some questions," I said. "Nothing was said about coaching."

"It doesn't matter. We're so excited to have you on board."

I wanted to grab Cathy by the collar and shake her till her eyes rattled. I gave her a look that made her back up and clutch Mitch by the arm. "I don't want to talk about the pageant. I want to talk about what you saw last night. If either of you have any useful information, I'd appreciate hearing it."

Mitch said, "We saw that poor man fall over, that's all. We heard later that he'd died."

"Anything else? Anyone snooping around the van?"

They shook their heads. "I did see a woman creeping around behind the cameramen," Cathy said, "but I thought she'd lost something. She kept looking at the ground."

Twenty, trying to find a cord to unplug. Maybe Cathy could supply Twenty with an alibi. "Was this woman dressed in odd clothes?"

"Yes, I remember saying to Mitch she looked like she could use a good fashion consultant."

"Do you recall where she was when Gaskins fell?"

"I couldn't say. We really didn't pay much more attention to her."

"Was she anywhere near the van?"

"I don't think so. Do you think she killed him?"

"I'm trying to prove she didn't."

"Well, if you ask me, Lance Henderson's your prime suspect. Some of the people were getting his autograph before they started filming, and I've never heard such griping and complaining in my life. Not about the autographs. He was tickled by all the attention. He was complaining about his tiny role in the movie."

"What about that other fellow, though?" Mitch said. "The one running around the house with Madeline? He did a fair share of griping, too. I thought the whole crew was cranky."

These two were not much help. Cathy beamed. "All right, then," she said, as if she and Mitch had solved the mystery. "Can we expect you here at three?"

"I'll be here."

Cathy and Mitch hurried off. Jerry finished playing for the "Wells Fargo Wagon" number and came down the aisle to me.

"How's your investigation coming along?"

"Plenty of suspects, plenty of motives, and no clear leads, although I almost had an alibi for Twenty."

"Almost?"

"I thought Cathy Sloop could place Twenty away from the van."

"Can she? I guess the better question is will she?"

"She and Mitch were more excited about me dispensing words of wisdom to the pageant contestants."

"What about Ted?"

"What about him?"

"You said you were going to see him today."

There it was again, that odd impression that Jerry might

be jealous. "I needed to know if he saw anything that might help me."

"Was he helpful?"

I tried not to smile. "Not really. I talked to Twenty, also, and the whole cast of *Curse of the Mantis Man.* As I said, plenty of suspects, plenty of motives. It's been a long morning. Are you ready for lunch?"

"There's some pizza left."

"That sounds perfect."

Austin and Denisha were waiting on the porch and very happy to learn that Jerry had some leftover pizza. They were very unhappy they had missed all the excitement the night before.

"My mom wouldn't let me come," Austin said. "Something about her stupid S.Q.U.I.S.H. group."

"It's S.T.O.M.P., not S.Q.U.I.S.H.," Denisha said, "and my aunt said it was too late for me to be out. I told her it was summer and not a school night, but she says midnight's too late for anybody to be out."

I sat down in one of the rocking chairs and took a slice of pizza from the box. "It wasn't something you two really needed to see."

Austin was pleased to have the inside scoop. "My mom said Mister Gaskins fell over dead, and the police think he was poisoned."

For once, Denisha had nothing to add. She licked pizza sauce off her fingers and acted as if Austin's news was too boring to comment on.

"Yes, that's right," I said.

"So he was murdered, right here in front of everybody?"

"It looks that way." I gave the pizza box a doubtful look. "Isn't there anything else to eat besides pizza?"

"Peanut butter," Jerry said.

"We'll make a run to the grocery store." I wanted another look in room sixteen at the Wayfarer Motel, but that would have to wait. I didn't want to involve the kids. "What's up with you two today?"

Austin reached for another piece of pizza. "I want to buy a Mantis Man tee shirt, but my mom won't let me. She says it's tacky."

"That salesman's a friend of yours, isn't he?" Denisha asked Jerry.

"Yes."

"Somebody told me he dressed up like Mantis Man and scared some people last night at the bridge."

"Could be."

As much as I admired Jerry's sense of loyalty, in this case, it was unnecessary. "Can we be straight with the kids? Everybody knows everything in town before it happens, anyway."

Jerry thought it over for a minute. "I don't guess he'd really care. It was a publicity stunt," he told the kids. "To help drum up interest for his Mantis Man store."

"He didn't need to do that," Austin said. "There's lots of interest in Mantis Man."

Denisha wiped sauce off her mouth. "You was there, too, wasn't you, Madeline? With Jerry?"

As I hesitated, Jerry grinned. "Can we be straight with the kids?"

"Yes, Denisha," I said. "Jerry and I were there, but we were just investigating."

"People say they heard a really loud scream."

I sighed. "Yes, that was me."

She frowned. "But if you knew this Mantis Man was Jerry's friend, how come you screamed?"

"Because at the time, I didn't know it was Jerry's friend."

"Oh."

I thought the matter was settled. I should've known better. Denisha's frown deepened as she thought things over.

"So how come Jerry didn't tell you?"

"He didn't know, either."

"Oh." She turned to Jerry. "Was you scared?"

"A little. But then I decided to attack."

"I wish I'd been there," Austin said. "I would've given him a good smack!"

Denisha gave him a pitying look. "Austin Terrell, you would've run the other way."

He stuck his tongue out at her.

"Don't start," I said. I got up. "Peanut butter, anyone?"

I didn't have any takers, but Denisha followed me inside to the kitchen and sat down at the table while I made a sandwich. The smell of the peanut butter reminded me I hadn't followed up on the Blue Ribbon brand of peanuts Kirby Willet preferred.

Denisha had another question for me. "Madeline, when Jerry attacked Mantis Man, is that why you screamed?"

"Yes. I thought he might get hurt."

"I'd rescue Austin if Mantis Man was after him."

"Good for you."

"We need to keep an eye on the boys."

I laughed. "Denisha, sometimes I forget you're only ten."

"Auntie says I'm old for my age."

"What happened to your folks?"

"They died in a car crash when I was just a baby. I don't really remember them. Auntie is my mother's sister, so she took us in. She didn't have no children, so it worked out." She paused. "Jerry's sister had to look after him and his brothers, didn't she? It's almost the same."

I couldn't imagine Jerry sharing this information with her. "How do you know about Jerry's family?"

"Auntie read the wedding announcement in the paper about Jerry's brother getting married, and she told me their sister brought them up."

I brought my sandwich and sat down across from her. "What else did your aunt tell you?"

Denisha folded her hands in front of her on the table. "Well, I already knew Jerry had two brothers named Des and Tucker, but I didn't know he had a sister. Auntie says her name is Harriet and she's the oldest. She had to take care of all the little boys after their parents died in a fire. The reason I remember is because Jerry is an orphan, just like me."

"A fire. Your aunt didn't know anything more?"

She shook her head. "It sounds very sad."

"It is," I said, "and Jerry doesn't like to talk about it."

"Is that why he don't want to go to the wedding? I'd like to go. I'd like to see the mansion and all the jewels and stuff. Are there servants and carriages?"

"No, just Tucker. No jewels, either, just a big fancy house."

"Is it bigger than this house?"

"A little bigger." I was wondering how much more to tell Denisha when she figured it out for herself.

"So it makes him sad to go to his old house and his parents not be there."

"Yes." At least, I thought that was the reason.

She nodded. "I won't say anything."

"Thank you, Denisha. You're a good friend."

"I like Jerry very much," she said. "Not as much as I like Austin, you understand."

"Completely."

"Things are going pretty well between us. How about you and Jerry?"

"We're just friends. I've told you that."

"What about that other woman? Jerry don't seem too sad she's gone. Now's your chance."

I put my sandwich down. "Look. Stop playing Cupid."

"Didn't he like it when you rescued him from Mantis Man?"

"Yes, he did."

"Well, then."

I couldn't think of an answer for this. While I was struggling for one, Denisha leaned forward to give me a very adult look. "Then you'd better do like my Auntie says and make play while the sun shines." Before I could answer or correct her, she hopped up. "So that's what I'm going to do with Austin. Play while the sun shines."

Off she went, leaving me with a soggy peanut butter sandwich and the sinking feeling she was right.

SIX

After Denisha had gone off to play with Austin, I told Jerry I wanted to have another look in room sixteen of the Wayfarer Motel.

"Does this involve some major skulking?" he asked.

"And your special keys."

I may complain about Jerry's so-called psychic abilities, but he's a whiz when it comes to picking locks. How and why he learned this skill I'd rather not know. I just use this talent of his whenever I need it.

"You want to go now?" he asked.

"After a stop at the grocery store."

Like Parkland, Celosia has a large Super Food store that carries all kinds of snacks, including Blue Ribbon brand peanuts.

Jerry hefted a jar. "They look pretty good."

"Recommended by all missing inventors." I inspected another jar. "They're more expensive than the others."

"Are you going to leave a trail?"

"Not exactly." At the checkout counter, I asked the clerk if she recalled selling this brand of peanuts to anyone lately. "Anyone who might have bought the giant economy size?"

She didn't remember. I asked the other clerks, but no one had sold a large amount of Blue Ribbon peanuts in the past week.

"But we sold tons when they had that contest," another clerk said.

"What contest was this?" I asked.

"They wanted a new jingle, but you had to send in a label from a jar along with your entry. We sold a pile of jars."

"Any to Kirby Willet?"

She shrugged. "I really don't know who he is. County Maxwell bought a lot of jars, though."

"Does he live in town?"

"Yeah, near the school."

"Thank you."

"'County,'" Jerry said as we walked out. "Do you suppose his brothers are named 'City' and 'State'?"

"Too bad his last name isn't 'Line.'"

We put our groceries in the trunk of my car. "Maybe Willet doesn't buy his peanuts here," Jerry said. "Maybe he grabs a pack at the Seven-Eleven."

"Let's find out."

A quick check of the Seven-Eleven and other convenience stores killed that theory. The smaller stores didn't carry Blue Ribbon brand.

Jerry hopped back in the car. "Maybe he has a supplier in Columbia."

"Maybe he's got enough to get through the winter."

"Maybe he's had peanut overload and has switched to pretzels."

"Let's see what Mister Maxwell has to say."

I EXPECTED SOMEONE WITH a name like County Maxwell to be an old grizzled cowboy. Mister Maxwell was in his mid-thirties, tall and oddly familiar. It took me a few minutes to realize Maxwell had played the young man in Kirby Willet's movie.

When I mentioned this, he brightened and invited me and Jerry to sit on the front porch of his house, a small white building that showed signs of recent renovation. Maxwell had screwed hooks in the ceiling for a porch swing, and Jerry helped him hang the swing.

Maxwell slid the chains over the hooks. "Yes, I agreed to be in Kirby's film. I didn't have to do much except look pensive."

"Have you seen him lately?" I asked.

He stood back to check on the height of the swing. "I heard he moved to California. We weren't really friends. I think he picked me for his movie because everyone else said no. Knowing his reputation, I'm guessing they figured the movie would be filled with inventions going horribly wrong. Jerry, I think we need to go up three more links."

They rearranged the swing until Maxwell was satisfied. "Try it out, Miss Maclin. Can I offer you folks a drink?"

"No, thanks," I said. I sat down in the swing. Jerry perched on the porch railing. "Very nice."

Maxwell reached for one of the porch chairs. "Do you mind if I continue sanding? I want to get these chairs done before tomorrow."

"Please don't let us interfere with your work. I just have a few questions."

"Fire away."

I asked Maxwell when he'd last seen Willet.

"Several months ago."

"You share his interest in Blue Ribbon peanuts."

He scrubbed the chair arm with sandpaper. "We ate a lot of them during filming. I kidded him about being paid in peanuts." He squinted at me. "Do I know you from somewhere?"

"You may have seen me around town. I've just opened a detective agency."

"Were you ever in a beauty pageant?"

"Yes."

He snapped his fingers. "Miss Parkland. I knew I'd seen you before. My sister is Eleanor Dover, Miss Far Ridge. She was in that pageant the year you won. She sang 'My Way.'"

I recalled Miss Far Ridge and how the tendons in her neck

stood out as she reached for the glory notes. "I remember her. How is she?"

He finished one arm and turned the chair to reach the other. "She had enough of the pageant life. She's married now, got a couple of kids. Do you still compete?"

"I've had enough of the pageant life, too."

"A detective agency, you said. Is Willet involved in something shady?"

"I'm trying to find him, that's all."

He paused. "Wouldn't have anything to do with Josh Gaskins being poisoned the other night?"

"It might. Did you know him?"

At first I thought he wasn't going to answer. Then he rubbed his chin and sighed. "At Celosia High, Gaskins was a nasty little snot who enjoyed making everyone feel inferior. He transferred from Charlotte his junior year, and he thought we were all the simple rural characters he'd seen on the *Bingo Dingo* show. He wouldn't let anyone work on his film. We were not worthy."

"Is there anyone in particular he snubbed who'd hold a grudge?"

"The entire senior class."

"Would Willet hold a grudge for any reason?"

Maxwell brushed the shavings onto the porch floor. "Kirby lives in his own world. He always has. I doubt he noticed Gaskins that much."

"Yet he agreed to finance *Curse of the Mantis Man.*"

"Did he really? I don't know why he'd do that."

"That's one reason I need to find him."

"Well, like I said, I think he's gone to the West Coast. He has family out there, a cousin, maybe." He turned to Jerry. "I hear you're fixing up the Eberlin place. How's that coming along?"

"Nell Brenner's doing the work for me."

"Yeah? She's good. Have you thought about what you want to do to the outside?"

"Just paint it, I guess."

"I've got some great ideas for exteriors. Let me get my books. I'll show you."

Maxwell went into the house.

I stopped swinging. "The entire senior class."

Jerry wasn't concerned. "That's maybe, what, twelve people?"

"Twelve or twelve hundred, they all hated Gaskins. Too many suspects."

County Maxwell brought out three large books filled with pictures of remodeled homes. Jerry was impressed by the before and after pictures, but told Maxwell he was leaving the renovations up to Nell.

"I'm not much of a handyman, as Mac will tell you."

"Maybe I could come out and help."

"That's fine with me."

They exchanged phone numbers. Jerry and I got into the car.

I started the car. "As much as I'd like to continue the peanut hunt, it's almost three. The Pageantoids will be waiting. Come watch me bestow my secret pageant tips."

"Like, 'Run for your life,' and 'Get out while you can'?"

"'Sequins make you look fat.' 'You can go blind from too much eyeliner.'"

We continued to make up helpful pageant advice until I parked the car in the theater parking lot.

Jerry unhooked his seat belt. "Tell me again why you're doing this?"

"Because I agreed to help Evan. You were there. You heard me."

"Yes, but I didn't believe it."

I really didn't want to go in, but it was my own fault. "Sometimes, you just have to do things you don't want to do."

I didn't think I sounded meaningful, but Jerry said, "I know what you're getting at."

I frowned at him. "I'm not talking about you."

"You don't have to be so obvious."

"Well, now that you've brought it up."

He got out of the car and slammed the door. I sighed and followed him to the front of the theater. "Jerry, I just don't want this to be something you'll regret all your life."

"I'm not going."

"Maybe we could make a deal?"

"No. One hard bargain is enough."

"All right, all right."

When we entered the auditorium many pairs of eyes turned to stare. The room hummed with excitement. Jerry whistled softly as I walked down the aisle.

"Are you ready for the talent portion of this contest?"

I had no problem striding up to center stage. I'd walked through many a dressing room and backstage corridor filled with seething, jealous females. Speaking to a group of anxious young women wasn't a challenge. I would've liked to have wiped the self-satisfied smile off Cathy Sloop's face, however. She hurried up and shook my hand.

"Madeline, dear, thanks so much for coming! See, girls, I told you she'd show up."

The young women applauded. Karen Mitman looked unhappy, but I knew from past experience that Karen's mother had forced her into the pageant. I understood and sympathized. Destiny Ray, Jeanie Swain and Donna Sanchez had expectant expressions. Three young women I didn't recognize sat together on the front row with Evan James and Mitch Hutton.

"We have three more entries," Cathy said. "Isn't that exciting? This is Sharon Gray, Rose Farrington and Evelyn Chevis. Girls, this is Madeline Maclin, a former Miss Parkland, and she's here to answer all your questions."

"I'd like to say a few words first," I said.

"Oh, yes, please do." Cathy sat down in the auditorium and stared up in rapt attention.

I sat down on the edge of the stage. "Ladies, I hope you're here because you want to be here. I hope you know that being in a pageant won't solve your problems, or make you a better person. It won't always impress others. In fact, it may be a liability. I'm trying to establish a new career as an investigator, and a lot of people in town don't take me seriously because I was once Miss Parkland."

Cathy's smile began to droop. Mitch bit his lower lip. Evan, however, nodded in agreement.

I looked right at Donna Sanchez. "If you're here because you think you're prettier, smarter and more talented than anyone else, you're in for a rough time. There will always be someone prettier, smarter and more talented. You have to decide what you want to be and then work hard to improve yourself. Don't compare yourself with everyone else. You'll go crazy."

Donna gave me a smirk as if to say, I'll do what I want. I ignored her and continued.

"Now, here's what a pageant can do for you. Being in a pageant can help your self-confidence, it can help your social skills and it can bring you in contact with a lot of wonderful people. You might get a chance to travel. You might make some great friends. You might be discovered and become a huge star. But whatever happens, keep things in perspective. It's just a show. It's not life or death. If you don't win, the world won't end." There. That was a pretty good speech. Serious but not too preachy. Not the glittery welcoming speech Cathy and Mitch wanted, but Evan seemed pleased. "Okay, any questions?"

Jeanie Swain raised her hand. "Do we have to put Vaseline on our teeth?"

Jerry wasn't successful at covering a burst of laughter. Miss Swain turned to glare at him. "Well, I need to know," she said.

"Not if you don't want to," I told her.

Evelyn Chevis raised her hand. "Does it matter what kind of talent we have?"

"What were you planning to do?"

"I wrote a poem I want to recite."

"That's fine."

Evelyn gave Donna a look that suggested Donna had told her otherwise. "Thank you, Miss Maclin."

Destiny Ray wanted to know the best way to wear her hair, and Rose Farrington wasn't sure if yellow was her color. Sharon Gray asked if I could recommend a really quick diet.

"I thought about Diet Coke and lettuce, but I don't like lettuce that much. What do you think?"

Sharon was at least five nine with a very slim figure.

"I don't think you need to diet, at all," I said.

She poked her non-existent stomach. "But this flab is just hideous."

Another reminder why I got out of the pageant world.

"I think you look fine, Sharon. Remember, you're not comparing yourself to anyone else."

She looked doubtful but nodded. I answered a few more questions, wished everyone the best of luck, and they gave me another round of applause. Cathy and Mitch hustled the contestants backstage to begin the talent rehearsal. Evan came up to me, still smiling.

"Madeline, that was a wonderful speech. Thank you."

"I'm not sure I got through," I said.

"Of course you did. It's such an honor for these girls to have you here." He took out his handkerchief and wiped his forehead. "It just thrills me to be involved with another pageant. I honestly didn't think I could manage, but with your help and Cathy and Mitch being so supportive and creative, I can't tell you how good I feel about this whole project. We can finally get Celosia back to where it needs to be."

I wasn't certain exactly where Celosia needed to be, but what the heck. "I'm glad to hear that, Evan."

"I know this was a big sacrifice for you, since you're so busy with your agency. In return, I may have some information that will help you with one of your cases."

Hmm, I thought. Patricia Hargrave left her umbrella in the auditorium. Or maybe a lost library book was discovered in the light booth.

Evan put his handkerchief back in his pocket. "I've been talking to all our young ladies, of course, and I found out that Rose Farrington's mother, Poppy, a former Miss Celosia, used to go steady with Kirby Willet when they were in high school. She might know where he is."

A real clue! I almost didn't recognize it. "Thank you."

"No, thank you for coming today. These girls should treasure this moment."

"I treasure this moment," Jerry said as we walked back to my car. "I feel incredibly inspired."

"To find a job."

"To make the world a better place."

"Well, you can start by breaking into the Wayfarer Motel."

As IT TURNED OUT, I didn't need Jerry to pick the lock of room sixteen. Sue Ann had finished cleaning and let us in. We stepped inside the still-musty-smelling room.

"What are we looking for?" Jerry asked.

"I don't know."

"Okay."

We looked under the beds, behind the ugly pictures of bridges, in all the drawers, under the trashcan, under the table and two chairs, in the curtains, in the air conditioner and even inside the hanging lamp. Then I found something taped under the sink, a plastic bag full of a dry, brownish powder.

"This doesn't look like peanuts to me."

"You want to take it to Chief Brenner?" Jerry asked.

"First I'm taking it to Warwick."

"Two visits in one week? I'd better come with you."

WARWICK WAS INDEED delighted to have me show up on his doorstep again. He tried to hide his disappointment when Jerry came in, too.

"Madeline, I'm so pleased to see you. Hello, Jerry. What have you got for me this time?"

I handed him the plastic bag. "Poison, I think."

"Oh, my. We'll be extra careful."

While Jerry and I waited, I showed him the articles in *Astounding Nonsense*. He was still chuckling over a paper on "Where Numbers Go When Erased From the Chalkboard" when Warwick returned.

"Yes, it's poison. Digitalis, as a matter of fact."

"Undetected in soda?"

"Yes. Very toxic. Between seven drops and one teaspoon is a lethal dose. Has something happened to Kirby Willet?"

"I still haven't found him, but Josh Gaskins, the director of *Curse of the Mantis Man,* was murdered last night. He may have been poisoned by that substance."

"You think Willet may be the culprit?"

"He's on my list. A lot of people were angry with Gaskins, though, including a friend of mine."

He oozed over. "And you're trying to clear this friend's name? Admirable work, Madeline."

Jerry put down *Astounding Nonsense* and maneuvered his way between Warwick and me. "Ready to go, Mac?"

"Yes, we'd better go. Thanks so much, Milton."

"You're most welcome."

As WE GOT INTO the car, I said, "I owe you one."

Jerry grinned. "Not a problem. Most guys like to drool over you, I've noticed."

I tried to keep my tone light. "You've never felt the need to drool over me?"

"Fishing for compliments?"

"Not exactly."

He thought I was teasing. "I find you extremely drool-worthy. What do we do now?"

Well, we run off together and make hot monkey love all day long. "We try to find out who put the poison in Gaskins's soda. Lots of motive, not as much opportunity."

"Where did he get his drinks?"

"Stephanie was in charge of buying drinks."

"Then I'd start with Stephanie."

"I've already talked with her, but there are a few things I need to clear up." I stopped at the red light. "You know, while we're in town, we could stop by and see Tucker."

"Go right ahead."

"You could at least say hi and congratulations."

"I already have. When he called to tell me he was getting married."

"It would only take a minute."

He turned to face me. "Look. This is not part of our bargain. I get a job. You paint. There's nothing in the deal about going to that house, and if you don't shut up about it, I'm jumping out of the car."

"Okay. How about going to Harriet's house?"

"Mac."

"Would she be home?"

"She's always home."

"That makes it easy."

He stewed for a while and must have decided I wasn't going to leave Parkland without seeing one of his relatives. "Okay."

"You're afraid if you make her angry, she'll cut you off, aren't you? Then you really will have to find a job."

"I have many reliable scams to fall back on."

"I think she's hiding something about her relationship with McKittrick's assistant. I think he's the culprit, and for some reason, she feels she has to protect him at your expense. Does she still live on Bently Street?"

"Yes, but she won't come out."

"If she doesn't want to face you, maybe she'll talk to you through the door."

We drove to Bently Street and parked in front of the dark little house where Harriet lived. The shades were drawn. Jerry and I got out of the car and walked up the steps to the front door. We knocked and waited.

Jerry knocked again. "Harriet, it's Jerry. I'd like to talk to you."

No answer.

I couldn't see anything past the dark window shades. "Are you sure she's home?" I took out my cell phone and called her number. We could hear the phone ringing in the house. After a while, I put my phone back in my pocketbook. I knocked one more time and raised my voice. "Harriet, it's Madeline. Jerry and I need to know about you and McKittrick's assistant, Jackson Frye. If you're looking for someone to blame, you might blame him. Tell me if I'm wrong."

No answer.

Jerry looked at me and shrugged. "I told you."

"We'll come back another time. We'll keep trying." When we got back in the car, I said, "Harriet plans to be at the wedding, doesn't she? You could speak with her then."

"I could," he said. "If I were going."

"Think about it."

I could tell he'd reached his limit of family interaction for the day. "Let's go talk to Pansy or Peony or whatever her name was."

"Poppy."

"Poppy. Let's go talk to Poppy."

So I drove to Poppy Farrington's house.

Rose Farrington met us at the door. "I'm sorry, but Mom's not home. She went motorcycling with her boyfriend and won't be back till later."

We thanked her and were about to leave when she said, "Miss Maclin, what you said about people not taking you seriously. I want to be a doctor. Do you think people will hold it against me if I win beauty pageants?"

"Not at all," I said. "A pageant would be a good way for you to make some money for medical school."

She looked relieved. "That's what Mom said, but I wasn't sure, and since you've been there and everything, I thought I'd ask."

"Many successful career women have pageant experience. It's nothing to be ashamed of. Just don't let pageants rule your life. That's what I was trying to get across to everyone."

"Okay, thanks," she said.

JERRY AND I WENT BACK to the theater. During the evening rehearsal, I sat out at the picnic table under the trees and made a few phone calls. The first call was to Jake Banner at the *Galaxy*.

"Jake, who told you about Jerry's parents?"

I could picture him at his desk, feet up. "Story's been around forever," he said.

"But where did you hear it?"

"I guess Des told me. Come to think of it, I don't really know where I first heard it."

"If Des was eight, Jerry only six and Tucker barely two years old, who was there to see what happened? Harriet came running in from another room."

Jake chuckled. "Guess you'll have to talk to Harriet."

"I'm trying to."

"Bound to be somebody else who knew the Fairweathers."

I felt my heart sink. "I know somebody."

"Who?"

"My mother."

"Harriet doesn't sound so bad now, does she?"

I rarely talk to my mother. She's never forgiven me for giving up my pageant career. She's a plain pushy woman with an overwhelming desire to outdo her coven of friends, and having a beauty queen for a daughter gave her bragging rights for eighteen years. Her house is still a shrine to Former Me, from Most Beautiful Baby to Miss Parkland.

Mom didn't seem surprised to hear from me.

"So you're living in Celosia now. Have you met Evan James?"

Of course she would know any pageant connection. "Yes, he's very nice."

"Someone told me you helped with the Miss Celosia Pageant."

"It was cancelled."

"Really? That's a shame."

I could picture her sitting on the black living-room sofa. Despite all my efforts to add color to the house, Mom insisted on black and white furnishings, saying they were cleaner looking and less trouble to match. All the doors and windows would be shut so the air conditioner could keep the house about sixty degrees. She'd have on one of her white summer dresses, a black sweater and sandals. She was probably drinking some unsweetened tea and maybe eating a few carrot sticks. Mom was proud of her slim figure and determined to keep fit.

"What are they doing now?" she asked.

Maybe a little pageant news would help my cause. "Evan's planning a new pageant called Miss Celosia Summertime."

"Are you going to be in it?" The eagerness in her voice was pathetic.

"I'm too old, Mom."

"You're consulting, then."

"On a very limited basis."

"So what's the theme?"

"Summertime. I need to ask you about the Fairweathers."

She made an exasperated sound. "You're still seeing Jerry? I'd heard he'd given up the money."

"I need to know what happened to his parents."

"Everyone knows what happened. They died in a fire."

"Is there someone among your friends who knew them well?"

I could tell by the tone of her voice Mom was wondering why I was asking these questions. "I suppose the Deatons."

"The Deatons?"

"Hamilton and Alexandra. I know they ran with that rich set."

"Where do they live?"

"Deer Point Estates. They finally got their wish, living among the nouveau riche."

Mother always says "nouveau riche" in a snide tone of voice, but I know she would've given anything to live within the gates of Deer Point, Parkland's ritziest neighborhood.

"Why are you worrying with that old tragedy, Madeline? They weren't murdered. Aren't you poking around in murders now?"

"I'm solving murders," I said.

"You won't solve that one. It was an accident."

"I just need to ask the Deatons a few questions."

As usual, she wasn't interested in anything that didn't involve an evening-gown competition. "Tell me more about this Summertime Pageant."

I told her Cathy and Mitch were in charge, and she laughed.

"I had forgotten about those two! Are they still just as deranged?"

"They're a little intense."

"Oh, during Miss Little River Falls, I thought they'd never leave you alone. And you remember that time in Atlanta when they made those tacky posters that said 'We're Mad About Madeline' and stood out along the highway and waved them? I thought they'd be arrested!" She laughed some more. "Oh, oh, and the Junior Miss in Valdosta, remember that? They showed up in identical plaid outfits. So embarrassing!"

"I remember."

"They need to get lives."

There wasn't a safe answer to this. I decided to go with, "Yes, ma'am."

"When are you coming home? Am I going to see you any time soon?"

"Maybe when this case is solved."

"Well, honestly, Madeline, just remember you can't fix everything."

I said good-by and hung up. No, I couldn't fix everything, but I sure as hell could fix some things, no matter what my mother believed.

I called the Deatons and asked if I could stop by tomorrow. They said they'd be delighted to see me.

THE NEXT MORNING, at the entrance to Deer Point, I stopped at the gate and was admitted. I passed perfectly manicured lawns and vast flower beds, houses big enough to be hotels, columns and gates and ornamental trees. Hamilton and Alexandra Deaton lived in their own court, Deaton Circle. Three Eberlin houses could've fit into their mansion.

The Deatons met me at the front door. I didn't remember the Deatons but liked them immediately. Hamilton was a short, strutting little rooster of a man, and Alexandra reminded me of a rose just past full bloom. He had on khaki shorts and a yellow golf shirt. She was in layers of pink chiffon. A large, pink straw hat covered her wispy blond hair.

She grasped both my hands. "Madeline, it's so good to see you. Please come out back. We're sitting by the pool."

The pool was Olympic size, surrounded by exotic plants. Hamilton showed me to a deck chair. "Can we get you a drink?"

"Iced tea would be fine," I said.

"Get me one, too, Hamilton," Alexandra said. She draped herself into the chair next to mine. "We haven't seen you or your mother in ages. How is she?"

"She's doing well, thank you."

"And what are you up to these days?"

"I've opened my own detective agency in Celosia."

Her eyes widened. "Remarkable! So you're not doing pageants anymore?"

"No."

"That's too bad. You have quite a talent for it. But being a detective sounds like so much fun! Is that why you're here? Are you on a case?"

"Sort of," I said. "I need to know more about the Fairweather family."

"Oh, yes, we knew Lillian and Victor. Such a tragedy."

"Can you tell me what happened?"

"I wish I knew. The police called us, you see, because Harriet wanted us there. We'd always been like an aunt and uncle to the children, so it was natural for her to want us. We went right over, but by then, it was much too late to do anything for their parents."

"Tell me what you know about the fire."

Hamilton returned with the tea in time to answer. "The firemen said it was caused by some candles."

"Did anyone mention blue flames?"

He handed me a glass of tea and gave one to his wife. "That's all nonsense."

"So there wasn't anything supernatural associated with the accident?"

He laughed and sat down in another chair. "You've been reading those old tabloid stories. They went crazy with theories about avenging ghosts and evil spirits."

Besides the mysterious fire, I'd never heard any strange tales about Jerry's family. "Were there ghost stories associated with the Fairweathers?"

"Lillian had some very odd relatives, didn't she, Alex? What was that brother of hers studying? Bats? That's probably where the spooky stories came from."

"Val Eberlin," I said. "I'm staying in his house."

"Well, he was an odd duck. Why are you staying in his house?"

"He left it to Jerry."

"Really? I don't think he ever met the boys."

Alexandra patted my hand. "We were very close to the children. If it had been possible, we would've taken them in, but we had four of our own to raise, and Harriet insisted on taking care of the boys herself."

"Wasn't she too young?"

"Almost eighteen. She had plans to go to law school, too, didn't she, Hamilton? Had to put all that on hold. We helped out as much as we could, but she took over the family."

"Had her hands full," Hamilton said.

"Oh, the boys were precious. Des was always very shy except when he was playing the piano. You know, even when he was little, he'd hop right up and play. Tucker was the cutest baby. As for Jerry, well, he was just plain rowdy. Always up to something, playing pranks, trying to get attention, I'm sure. It's hard being the middle child."

Hamilton brushed away a bee that tried to take a drink of his tea. "Is there some reason you need to know about this, Madeline? It was a long time ago."

"I'm just trying to understand why Jerry won't go back to the house."

"He's coming to the wedding, isn't he?"

"I don't think so."

"I wouldn't have thought the accident would affect him that strongly. Seems to me Des took things a lot harder than his brothers did. Of course, he was oldest. He realized what had really happened."

And what had really happened? I wondered. "So no one else was there? What about the artist who painted the boys' portrait, McKittrick? What do you know about him? And his assistant, Jackson Frye?"

"I don't know anything about an assistant. I know the McKittrick fellow was a suspect for a while. There were some things missing, weren't there, Alex?"

"Oh, yes. First we thought they'd been destroyed in the fire, but come to find out, they were gone. McKittrick didn't have them, though."

I was beginning to get an idea what might have happened. McKittrick and Frye are in the house every day working on the portrait. Let's say something bright catches Frye's eye. He comes back for it at night and accidentally knocks over some candles. Or was it an accident? A house fire would be the perfect cover for his crime.

"I'm sorry we can't be of more help," Alexandra said, "but you know about as much as we do. Have you spoken with Harriet?"

"Not yet."

"She's a little more approachable than she used to be," Hamilton said. "I'm not sure why. Maybe with Des established and Tucker getting married, she can finally relax."

I stayed and chatted with the Deatons for about an hour, thanked them for their help and hospitality and then drove back toward Celosia. I pulled over in a church parking lot and punched in Harriet's number. I was surprised when she answered.

"Yes?"

"It's Madeline, Harriet. Sorry Jerry and I missed you yesterday."

I heard her take a deep breath. "Just stop, Madeline. Nothing you or anyone can do will bring them back."

"I'm sorry you lost your parents in such a horrible way, but I can't believe Jerry is to blame. Is your family name so important that you have to cover up what really happened?"

Silence.

"I want to know about Jackson Frye," I said. "I want to know about the things missing from your home."

"You don't know what you're talking about."

"I'm just trying to help Jerry."

"You can help Jeremyn by leaving him alone. Good-by."

Hamilton Deaton was right. Harriet had mellowed a bit. In the past, she wouldn't have said good-by.

I DECIDED TO SWING BY the Farrington house and see if Poppy was home. Rose Farrington was tall and dark-haired, but her mother was short and blonde, her round figure packed into short denim overalls. Her frizzy hair was tied in two pigtails, and she had the rough, sunburned features of someone who no longer gave a damn about her complexion. Her legs were skinny and slightly bowed. She was in her flower garden, a hose in one hand and a cigarette in the other. She waved me over.

"You must be Madeline. Rose said you'd stopped by earlier."

"Yes, nice to meet you," I said.

She stuck the cigarette in her mouth, wiped her hand on her shorts and shook hands. "Pleasure. You don't mind if I continue my watering, do you? This weather sure is hard on the impatiens."

"Please go ahead," I said. "I won't take but a few minutes.

I'm looking for Kirby Willet, and I was hoping you might be able to help me."

She hitched up one overall strap. I caught a glimpse of a flower tattoo on her shoulder. "Well, I last seen Kirby about three months ago, up at his hideout. He's got a place up in the woods. He holes up there every now and then, tinkering on those contraptions of his like any one of 'em's ever gonna work. Used to drive me nuts."

"Would you give me directions to this place?"

"Well, I might. Depends."

"Depends on what?"

"Whether or not you think my little Rosie has a shot at Miss Celosia Summertime."

Did everyone in town want to deal? "I'm not judging the pageant, Mrs. Farrington."

She took one last drag on the cigarette and tossed it into the flowerbed. "Hell, I'm not asking you to fix the pageant. You're the expert. I just want your honest opinion."

"I think Rose has as good a chance as anyone."

She gave a snort that might have been laughter. "As good as that Donna Sanchez? She's a tramp. Ask anybody. I was once Miss Celosia, did you know that? I told Rose she had to do the family name proud, keep the tradition going."

So did that mean in another ten years Rose Farrington would be squat and sunburned, chain-smoking in the garden?

"I'm not really a pageant expert," I told Poppy. "I have a new job now, and part of that job is finding Kirby Willet."

Poppy lit another cigarette. "All right, about Willet's secret place. Trouble is, he keeps moving it. Thinks somebody's gonna come mess with his stuff or steal his ideas. That's a laugh." She turned the hose on a clump of daylilies. "You go up past the covered bridge about half a mile. You'll see a wooden sign for Lucky Lakes, only there ain't no such place. Some fella thought he'd build a development up there, but the deal fell through, so all that's left is the sign. Wasn't very lucky, if you ask me. Go past the sign, you'll come to some big rocks. If Kirby's camp ain't there, it's nearby. Like I said, he keeps moving it."

"I understand you dated Willet once."

"Yeah, once was about it. He was hopeless when it came to women. Too busy thinking about inventing things." She chuckled. "Some of the girls kept on trying, though, poor souls. That Bernice Coleman thought she'd have him for sure."

"The same Bernice Coleman who works at the library?"

"Yep. She thought old Kirby was a catch, but then, she was lucky to have any boy pay attention to her."

Bernice said Kirby Willet was a friend. She hadn't mentioned what kind of friend. "Was Willet interested in Bernice?"

Poppy made a face that suggested I was crazy. "You ain't been listening, have you? Kirby's only interested in his inventions. I coulda walked around stark naked in front of him, and he wouldn't look up. Did it, too, a couple of times."

Way too much information. "Thank you, Mrs. Farrington."

"No problem. You find the old boy, tell him I said hey."

I went back to my car and jotted down the directions to Willet's hideout. Despite some disturbing mental imagery, Poppy had given me my best lead yet. I was anxious to get back to the Eberlin House and share my findings with Jerry.

SEVEN

WHEN I GOT OUT OF MY CAR at the Eberlin house, I could hear the piano. Since I'd been hearing songs from *The Music Man* for weeks, I recognized the tune, "Good Night, My Someone." I paused at the parlor door to listen. When Jerry finished, I said, "That's really nice."

He turned around on the bench. "Thanks. How'd it go with the Deatons?"

"They didn't know about Frye, but they said some things were missing from your house after the fire. So now I think the fire was a cover for a robbery."

"And this Frye guy planned it all?"

"Looks that way. I managed to get Harriet to answer the phone, but she wasn't very helpful."

"What did you say, 'Hello, Harriet. By the way, did your boyfriend set fire to the house so he could steal the candlesticks?'"

"But I think that's exactly what happened. I think Jackson Frye came back to the house that night to steal something he'd seen earlier, knocked over the candles either by accident or on purpose and then ran like hell."

"Then why would Harriet have me believe I was responsible?"

"That's the main question she needs to answer."

"Did you get to see Petunia?"

"Poppy. Yes, I did, and she gave me directions to Willet's secret hideout. Want to go?"

"I sure do. We've got a dress rehearsal tonight, but it should be through by ten."

"I'd like to see the show," I said. "Don't you need a page turner or something?"

"Yeah, come on down in the pit. That's where the action is. Have you had lunch?"

"Not yet."

"The kids are coming over. I promised them we'd roast some hot dogs outside."

It wasn't long before I heard Austin and Denisha as they argued their way across the meadow. They tossed their bikes on the grass and ran into the house. Austin had a bag of hot dog buns. Denisha had a bag of marshmallows.

"Jerry! Can we toast marshmallows, too?"

"You can toast whatever you like."

"Where's our campfire?"

"We'll make it in the backyard."

Austin volunteered to gather the wood, which made Denisha toss the marshmallows on the nearest chair. "Me, too!"

Jerry grinned as they dashed out. "Do you feel the urge to gather wood, Mac?"

"I'll get the drinks."

"I'll make the fire. I'm good at that."

Austin and Denisha had a battle to see who could find the most sticks, rushing up and throwing the twigs and branches into the fire until Jerry told them to slow down.

"We've got plenty, guys. Take it easy."

Since Denisha had been the last one to add to the flames, Austin ran back for another load and returned holding a small piece of white plastic.

"What's this from?"

"Let me see that, Austin." He handed it to me. "Where did you find this?"

"In the driveway. Is it a clue?"

"Well, I don't know. It might be."

Immediately, Denisha ran around the house and down the driveway. Austin yelled, "Hey!" and followed.

Jerry took a closer look at the plastic. "Is it part of a bottle cap?"

"I think so." There was something along the rim of the piece that peeled off like webbing. I rolled this stuff in my fingers. "This looks like dried glue."

"Bottles aren't usually glued shut, are they?"

"They are if you want to put something inside."

"But wouldn't you be able to tell if the cap was glued on?"

"I just happen to have some glue in my studio. Let's experiment."

I went upstairs. As I hunted for the glue, the faces in the half-finished portrait caught my eye. Damn, they weren't bad. I stopped for a moment and examined the picture with a critical eye. Yes, it was just as good close up. I could do this. But not right now.

I found the glue I wanted, the white all-purpose kind, and brought it back to the campfire. Austin and Denisha had returned and were trying to see who could get the most marshmallows on a stick. I opened a bottle of Coke, took the cap off, and then put it back on, carefully sealing the edges of the cap with glue. I set the bottle aside to dry.

Austin's mouth was full of marshmallow. "Why'd you do that?"

"I want to see if it will stay fresh."

"It's easier just to put the cap back on real tight." His stick, overloaded with marshmallows, popped off into the fire. "Oh, man."

Denisha licked her sticky fingers. "Ha, ha."

I thought Austin might try to stab her with the remains of his stick, but he surprised me by laughing. "Look, Denisha. It looks like the Bubbling Blob from *Super Spies*."

The glob of marshmallow heaved and crackled in the fire. "It wants blood," Jerry said. "Give it some ketchup."

I checked my watch. "You'd better take care of the blob

and put out the fire. Jerry and I are due at the theater in about an hour."

After stuffing themselves with hot dogs and marshmallows, Austin and Denisha helped clean up. Austin used the garden hose to pour water on the fire and then he piled dirt on the wet ashes.

"To make sure the Blob doesn't rise again," he said.

The kids thanked Jerry for the hot dogs and rode off on their bikes. I put my glued bottle on the kitchen table. I wanted to leave it overnight. Now it was time to shower, change clothes and get in the pit with Jerry.

THE NOISE AND CONFUSION backstage at the theater gave me flashbacks to my pageant nights. The dressing rooms smelled of powder and hairspray; trays of deli meats and cheese lay on top of doughnut boxes and plates of cupcakes; people ran in frantic searches for safety pins and tape; microphones refused to work or exploded with sudden booms of sound.

Jerry led the way past all this, pulling back a section of the heavy gray curtains to reveal a small flight of steps down into the orchestra pit. Members of the orchestra included a flutist, a trumpet player, a drummer and two violinists. Jerry introduced me to everyone.

"Just pull up a chair, Mac. I don't need you to turn pages, thanks. You can watch the show."

"Not the best view in the world," the trumpet player said, "but an interesting angle, nonetheless."

"He likes to look up the girls' skirts," one of the violinists said.

"Jerry, don't forget Kenna made another cut in 'Wells Fargo,'" the other violinist said. "It's from eighty-six to one hundred thirty-two."

"She still wants a vamp at eighty-five, though."

"Yes, and everyone comes in at letter B."

"Is that cut time there?" the trumpet player asked.

"Just through the second repeat."

The orchestra members continued to speak their special language as I unfolded a metal chair and sat down near the piano. The curtains opened. The dancers stretched their legs, and the cast came to the edge of the pit for a vocal warmup. Donna Sanchez gave me a little wave.

As far as I could tell, the dress rehearsal went well. I spent most of my time watching Jerry play and wondering how I could channel his love of music into a paying job. At intermission, we climbed out of the pit to get some colas from the drink machine in the lobby. Flynn Davis was sitting in the auditorium.

"I didn't know you were in the orchestra," he said. "You guys sound pretty good."

I couldn't imagine what allure a community theater production of *Music Man* would have for Davis. "I'm just visiting. What are you doing here?"

"Gotta have some way to pass the time. Are you leaving?"

"I'm going to get a Coke."

"I'll come with you."

At the drink machine, Jerry put his money in and got his bottle. Kenna hurried up, clipboard in hand.

"Jerry, I need to go over a few cues with you."

"Okay," he said.

They went off together. I would've liked to have followed, but Davis's unexpected appearance made me curious. I put in my quarters and punched my choice of Coke. "Are you a fan of musical comedy?"

"I've done my share. Nothing like live theater."

My bottle rolled down with a clatter. I wedged it out. "This is probably too amateur for you."

"It's where all the good-looking gals hang out."

Now I remembered. Davis was interested in Donna Sanchez.

"And," he said, "I may be able to help you solve the crime."

I knew he wanted to pin Gaskins's murder on Henderson. "Not unless you can prove who did it."

"It's hard to choose between that goofy girlfriend of yours and Stephanie."

"Stephanie? Why Stephanie?"

"Oh, I know she gave this big sob story about being Josh's right hand girl and not caring about being in front of the camera, but that's a bunch of bull. He'd promised her a leading role in his next film. When she heard he'd contacted Vivian Montrose, she was furious. I heard her giving him hell."

"When was this?" I asked.

"Couple of days ago."

"Did you tell the police?"

"No." He leaned forward. "I'm telling you. We kinda got off to a rough start. I thought this might make things better between us."

I began to slowly shake my bottle of Coke. "You won't get anywhere by referring to Twenty as my goofy girlfriend."

He eyed the bottle. "Sorry."

"Or by lumping her in with your prime suspect."

He took a step back. "We can talk about this."

"Nope," I said, still shaking the Coke. "We're not going to talk about anything else. As far as I'm concerned, you had just as much cause to kill Gaskins. You were just as angry over Henderson's narration as Stephanie may have been over Vivian, and believe me, I'm going to ask her about that."

Davis backed further away. "You'll find out I'm telling the truth."

The lobby lights blinked to signal intermission was over. "Why are you really here, Davis?" I asked.

He smirked. "I've got a date with Marian the Librarian."

"Donna Sanchez?"

"She's a hell of a lot more agreeable than you are."

Boy, were those two well suited. "I'm so happy you've found each other."

I went back to the orchestra pit and carefully set the Coke bottle down beside my chair. It would be a while before the drink settled. I felt the same way.

"What's up?" Jerry asked.

I indicated Donna Sanchez. "Flynn Davis is seeing Miss Congeniality."

Jerry whistled. "Hope he's got insurance."

Interesting, yes, but it didn't get me any closer to solving the mystery. Davis was the kind of man who could work anything to his advantage, even being stuck in a small town. He didn't seem to be the kind of man who'd take unnecessary risks. True, he'd been with me when Gaskins drank his last soda, but the poison could've been put into the drink earlier in the day.

Act Two went smoothly, although Kenna had to stop the last scene to reblock where the band members would stand for the finale of "Seventy-Six Trombones." The cast rehearsed the curtain call, and everyone sat down in the auditorium for a few notes. Afterward, Jerry asked if we could stop by Georgia's.

"I promised Hayden I'd get in touch with his poltergeist."

"Okay."

Georgia's closed at ten, but most of the lights were still on. Hayden unlocked the front door. "Come on in. I'm straightening the kids' books."

"Have you had any problems today?" Jerry asked.

"No, it's been pretty quiet." He stooped to pick up one of the many magazine inserts that littered the floor. "Do you want to start in the same section? I'm going to turn out the lights in the back."

"Let me see what I can do."

Jerry sat down in the New Age aisle. Hayden went to the back. He was turning off the lights over the magazines when we heard him yell. An avalanche of books fell with a crash. Something long and white streaked past, making an angry "duke-duke" sound. Jerry ran after the something. I hurried to Hayden.

"Are you all right?"

He pointed a shaking finger toward the front of the store. "It's in here! It ran right by me."

Jerry disappeared out the front door. I snapped on the rest of the lights and looked up and down every aisle. When I came back to Hayden, he was sitting in one of the little chairs in the children's section. He leaned forward, his head in his hands as if he were going to faint.

I dug into my pocket for my cell phone. "What happened?"

"Something rushed past, screaming. It was horrible. Its eyes were glowing."

"Are you hurt? Do you want me to call nine-one-one?"

Before he could answer, Jerry returned. "You okay, pal? I've got your ghost."

Hayden raised his head. We stared at the scrawny white ferret trying to struggle free from under Jerry's arm.

"Is that what's been causing all the racket?" I asked.

"Footsteps, whispers, strange cries, missing food, shelves knocked over? Yep, I'd say Snowball here's your culprit."

"But how did it get in?" Hayden asked. "Georgia's very careful about the building."

"Didn't you have to repair the ceiling?" I said. He nodded. "I'll bet it got in that rainy night when the tiles were loose, and it's been hiding somewhere in the shop."

Now that the ferret had calmed down, it didn't seem to mind Jerry holding it. "It's pretty tame. Does somebody around here have a pet ferret?"

"I'll bet it got away from the pet shop that closed."

To my relief, Hayden began to laugh. "A ferret."

Jerry set the ferret down. "Let's see if it'll run to its hiding place."

The ferret took off, leaped over a shelf and disappeared behind one of the magazine racks. Jerry pulled the magazines aside. "There's a nice ferret-sized hole back here."

Hayden looked at the hole and straightened, shaking his head. "I feel like a complete idiot."

"Don't worry," I said. "If you're not expecting a ferret to come dashing past your legs in the dark, it can be unsettling."

There was a look of entreaty in his blue-green eyes. "I'll pay you any amount of money not to mention this to Shana."

"I won't say a word," Jerry said.

I agreed. "If you promise not to get so carried away with your ideas about ghosts."

Hayden sighed. "I know, I know."

"Are you all right? Do you want us to take you home?"

"I'm fine," he said. He put his hand on his chest. "Heart's still beating. I was sure it had stopped."

Just to make sure he was all right, Jerry and I waited until he'd closed the store and gotten into his car.

"Think we ought to follow him home?" I asked.

"Wouldn't hurt."

We followed at a discreet distance. When we saw the red taillights turn onto the road to Autumn Fields, we decided Hayden could make it the rest of the way.

"Now we can go Mantis hunting," Jerry said. "Where's Kirby's hideout supposed to be?"

"Half a mile beyond the covered bridge, we're looking for a sign that says Lucky Lakes. Past the sign and some big rocks, we start looking for Mantis activity."

Jerry rolled down his window. The night air smelled of clover and honeysuckle. "I'll be on the lookout for gleaming red eyes."

Poppy Farrington's directions were accurate—up to a point. Half a mile past the covered bridge, we saw a worn wooden sign propped on a tree stump declaring, "Coming Soon! Lucky Lakes, A Luxury Development!"

"Are there any lakes, and are they lucky?" Jerry wanted to know.

"Apparently not. Do you see any big rocks?"

"I don't see rocks of any size."

We drove on. The road narrowed until paving stopped and dirt took over. Shadowy woods lined both sides of the road. Abruptly, the road went over a slight rise, dipped down and stopped. Just beyond a dark field, we could see the gleam of water.

"A lucky lake," Jerry said.

"Looks more like a lucky pond."

He pointed. "Big rocks."

Sure enough, at one edge of the small lake was a clump of large boulders. "Guess we continue on foot," I said. I turned off the car. Jerry and I picked up our flashlights and got out.

"This is just like on *The X-Files,*" he said, making his light dance on the trees. "You know, where Mulder and Scully go into spooky basements with nothing but flashlights."

"Somehow I think Willet is long gone from this place, but we're here. We might as well check it out."

Grasshoppers and other insects whizzed and jumped as we walked through the field to the rocks, which loomed large and black against the night sky.

"It's certainly a good place to have a hideout," Jerry said. Then he stopped. "Mac, do you smell peanuts?"

I sniffed. "I think we're on the right track."

I heard a thud and a groan. At first I thought, in true Jerry fashion, he'd run into a tree. Then I saw him sprawled on the ground. An impossibly tall, thin figure stepped over him. The figure had bulbous eyes and a wicked triangular face. It swung its long arms like clubs. I ducked the first arm and grabbed the second as it whizzed over my head. The arm felt like a solid lead pipe. For a moment, my feet left the ground. Something ripped. I fell, my hands full of ragged strips. For a horrible moment, I thought it was diseased alien skin. Then a heavy clunk nearby made me realize I'd torn the creature's arm off.

I snatched up the limb, aware of the cold texture of metal. The rest of the mantis recoiled. A male and very human voice said, "Don't hit me!"

I raised the arm. "Who are you? What are you doing out here?"

"First you tell me who *you* are and what you're doing out here."

I kept a firm grip on my weapon. "I'm Madeline Maclin. I'm investigating the disappearance of Kirby Willet."

"What?"

"You heard me."

The mantis took off its head. The pale, thin man inside the elaborate costume gulped and said, "I'm Kirby Willet."

Good lord, I thought. I'd just been joking with Shana when I said the Mantis was Willet. We stared at each other until a groan from Jerry made Willet jump.

"Is he okay? I didn't mean to hit him. I just wanted to scare you away."

I helped Jerry sit up. "I'm all right," he said.

"Suppose you explain yourself," I said to Willet.

"I want people to stay away. I have work to do, important work. People don't understand. I need my privacy."

His eyes and his voice were jittery. I tried to stay calm. "Okay, we'll leave you alone. I just want to ask you a few questions."

"I didn't do it. I didn't kill Josh. I know that's what everyone is saying. They think I'm still angry about that scholarship, but I'm not! I have other ways of getting money. I have lots of money safely hidden away. I wouldn't kill anyone. Why have you been looking for me? Are you some sort of policeman?"

"You left some things at Frannie Thomas's house."

His voice rose in panic. "Those are my things! What's happened to them?"

"In storage. She needed the room for her mother."

"Everything's in storage?"

"Except for the money. The police have that."

"That's *my* money!"

"Look," I said. "Is there someplace we can go talk about this?"

Willet looked left and right as if expecting someone else to attack. "No. You should leave. Right now."

"I can explain about the money," I said.

I could tell he was torn between his need for privacy and his need to know about his cash. Jerry helped me out by groaning artistically, his hand on his forehead.

"Gosh, I'm really dizzy. You might have to call for an ambulance, Mac."

The thought of an ambulance and possibly the police screaming up Lucky Lakes road was enough to make Willet say, "No, no. No more people. Come with me. You can rest for a minute and then you have to leave."

He turned and lumbered up past the rocks. Jerry shone his flashlight in his own face so I could see him wink.

"Thank you," I said. "I promise we won't stay long."

I had several ideas about Willet's lair, but I certainly wasn't expecting a shiny blue-and-white RV parked in a grove of pine trees. Inside, every possible surface was covered with wires, bulbs, bits of machinery and jars of peanuts.

Willet cleaned off a white plastic chair. "Sit there. I'll get you some water. There isn't room for you to sit, Ms. Maclin, but you won't be staying long."

Jerry was fascinated by all the gadgets. He pointed to a piece of folded cloth. "What's this?"

Willet radiated pride. He pressed a lever on the cloth and a small umbrella shot up. He tapped the clothespinlike attachment. "This is a book umbrella for when you want to read in the shower."

"Neat! And this?"

The next invention looked like two sets of metal claws. "A shoelace tier. It's for people who don't have time to tie their shoes."

"These are great. Have you sold any?"

"I'm very, very close to a breakthrough."

Very, very close to a breakdown, I thought. As Jerry continued to admire Willet's weird devices, the inventor relaxed. He brought Jerry a glass of water with an odd-looking piece of plastic.

"Is this a two-hole straw?"

"Yes, so you can share a drink with a friend."

"And this gadget?"

"It's a toothpaste-tube cleaner. You know how that extra gunk around the opening gets all hard and crusty? This scrapes the gunk away."

I was amazed that Jerry could keep a straight face. "I can see why you'd want to keep this place a secret," he said.

Willet reached for the nearest jar of peanuts and shook some into his hand. Crunching his favorite snack seemed to calm him even more. "It's extremely important neither you nor Ms. Maclin tell anyone about this."

"No problem."

Kirby looked at me. "I won't tell a soul," I said, "but you have to explain something. Jerry and I found a package of poison hidden in room sixteen of the Wayfarer Motel."

He didn't seem surprised. "Isn't it obvious? Someone is trying to frame me."

"Why?"

His gesture sent peanuts flying. "Because I'm a loner! Don't you people watch TV? It's always the loner. Just because I'm eccentric, keep to myself, have no close friends and only come out at night. It's not fair. I just want to be left alone to work on my inventions."

"What about your film, the one that lost the scholarship contest?" I asked.

"What about it? It was just an experiment. I'd rather pour my creativity into my inventions."

"I thought your movie was brilliant."

"Me, too," Jerry said. "It could've used a car chase, though."

Willet shook out another handful of peanuts. "Thank you, but it's not my thing. I want to know about my money."

"The police are keeping it for you," I said.

"Why are they involved?"

"Ten thousand dollars is a lot of money to keep in a box. I thought I'd better take the money somewhere safe."

His thin brows drew together. "What were you doing looking in my boxes?"

"Frannie didn't know where you were or how to get in touch with you. We thought we might find an address in one of the boxes. If you don't mind me asking, where did you get that much cash? Did you sell one of your inventions?"

Again he puffed with pride. "I won a contest."

"An invention contest?"

"No, I wrote the winning jingle for Blue Ribbon peanuts. 'Superior in taste and size, Blue Ribbon peanuts take the prize.' Pretty good, huh?"

"Who knew you'd won this contest?"

"I can't think of anyone I'd tell."

"You don't have any friends in town? What about Bernice?"

"I don't know if I mentioned it to her or not."

"But she's the one who suggested you store your things at Frannie's. Did she know about the money?"

"I don't know. Now that you mention it, she's the one who thought I should enter the contest, seeing as how I'm a fan of Blue Ribbon peanuts." He poured another handful from the jar. "If you see her, tell her I won. I really don't want to go into town. I've got things to do."

"Were you planning to give Gaskins the money?" I asked.

He nodded. "I was willing to take a chance on his movie. We made movies back in school, and his were excellent. I always knew he'd become a famous film director."

Not only was Willet a bad inventor, he wasn't much of a critic, either. "When was the last time you spoke with Gaskins?"

"He called me a couple of weeks ago and said he was coming to Celosia to film a movie." He crunched on the peanuts and swallowed. "I knew my money was safe, so I told him he could get it whenever he needed it."

"But didn't he contact you when he got to town?"

Willet took a sudden interest in a box of test tubes. "Well, he might have. I don't know."

A bad inventor, a lousy critic and not much of a friend. I looked around the cluttered workplace for all-purpose glue. I didn't see any. "He couldn't find you, could he?"

He wouldn't look at me. "I may have gotten involved with a project and forgot."

I was trying to understand the relationships here. "So why would anyone want to frame you for Gaskins's murder?"

Willet lined up the test tubes on the counter. "I have no idea. Someone must have the mistaken idea that Josh and I are enemies or rivals, which is ridiculous. We were up for the same scholarship in high school, that's all. I wasn't upset when he won. I told you, I thought his movie was excellent. He deserved to win." He finally looked up. "Eventually, I would've remembered to give him the money. I'm not stupid, just absentminded. I'm supposed to be absentminded. I'm a genius, not a murderer."

I was beginning to believe him. Even if the real murderer didn't have a grudge against Willet, the inventor was a convenient suspect. Everyone in Celosia knew Willet was strange and unpredictable. People would have no trouble accepting him as the culprit.

Now he glared at Jerry. "I trust you're recovered?"

Jerry set the glass with its goofy two-hole straw on top of a pile of scrap metal. "Yes, thanks."

"Then if the two of you would please go."

"I need to ask you one more question," I said. "The night Gaskins was killed, where were you?"

"Here, of course, doing my work."

"Can you prove that?"

"Actually, I can," he said. "I videotaped myself."

In anticipation of needing an alibi? "Are you in the habit of taping yourself?"

"Yes, I am. I need a record of my attempts to perfect my inventions. Last night, I was here, fine-tuning my musical tweezers." He leaned over and snapped on a TV, pressed a few buttons, and there he was on screen, hunched over a tangle of metal and wires. I could hear the first few bars of "Hair" twanging faintly in the background. Willet let us watch a while and then smiled a tight, unfriendly smile. "So you see, Ms. Maclin, I haven't let my filmmaking skills go to waste. I believe you and your friend were leaving?"

JERRY AND I TREKKED back to the Mazda, batting away the mosquitoes that swarmed up from the lake.

"Okay," Jerry said, "he's a genuine nut, but he's got a great alibi."

"He's a genius, all right," I said. "A genius at filmmaking, wasting his time on dead-end inventions."

"Do you think he did it?"

"No, but I can't think of anyone who'd go to all the trouble to frame him, either."

"It would have to be someone who knew about Willet and Gaskins and has the wrong idea about the Baker Scholarship."

We stopped in the tall grass and looked at each other. "Twenty," we said.

"But she's not the only one, remember?" Jerry said. "County Maxwell said the whole senior class hated Gaskins."

I started walking. "It has to be someone else, someone with a motive other than a bad memory from high school."

Jerry almost tripped over a clump of weeds. "Don't forget the film crew."

"But how many of them know Willet?"

"Maybe somebody's mad because they didn't get the money."

I stopped again, and Jerry almost ran into me.

"What?" he said.

"What did you just say?"

"Maybe somebody's mad because they didn't get the money."

A face had appeared in my mind, a severe disapproving face topped with steel wool hair. "I need to talk to Bernice."

"You think she knew about the cash? Willet wasn't even sure she knew he'd won the contest."

"Everyone in town knows about the money."

"Yeah, but would Bernice think she's entitled to any of it?"

"That's a very good question."

When we got home, it was almost midnight. I'd have to wait and call the library tomorrow. Jerry and I were both too wired after our encounter with the Mantis to go to bed, so we got some cookies and cola and sat down in the living room. Jerry turned on the CD player. I passed him the bag of cookies. I pulled off my sneakers and sat back on the sofa, finally able to relax.

"Hey," Jerry said, "I just realized something. You found Kirby Willet. Another triumph for Madeline Maclin Investigations."

"Now I've got to find Gaskins's killer," I said, "and Willet has a great alibi."

He took another handful of cookies. I looked past the TV to the picture hanging over the mantel. The swirls of abstract flowers and crescent moon was titled *Blue Moon Garden*. I'd painted it in college. It was the most successful of my paintings. After my disastrous art exhibit, I'd thrown it away. Jerry had rescued it from the garbage.

He saw me looking at *Blue Moon Garden*. "How's your latest picture coming along?"

"It's not bad. How's your job search?"

"Well, I think from our experience tonight we can see that I have an excellent future as a Mantis magnet."

"Attracting eccentric inventors dressed as large insects doesn't count."

"I should've asked Willet if he knew my uncle. Maybe they belonged to the same eccentric club." He set the cookies aside. "I've been thinking about what you said. Why did Val leave the house to me? Why not Des? I mean, it's worked out great, because I like the house very much, but it's still a mystery."

"Let me solve it," I said.

"Okay, you're hired."

He smiled at me. The passionate music swelled. We were full of cookies and cola and safe after an adventure in the wilds of Celosia. Another perfect time had come.

Jerry covered a huge yawn with his hand. "All of a sudden, I'm beat. Guess the excitement of Mantis busting caught up with me."

"Me, too," I said.

He turned off the CD. "Good night, Mac."

"Good night."

And another perfect time had gone.

EIGHT

THE NEXT MORNING, I checked my glued soda bottle.

"I can't tell where I've glued it."

Jerry took the bottle and opened it. "It opens just as if it were new."

"Do you see any glue tracks?"

"Very little. If you were extremely careful, there would be none."

Extremely careful. Hadn't Bernice been extremely careful gluing the corners of a paperback book?

Before we went to the library, I helped Jerry pack the bat books into boxes.

"You're sure you want to give these away?"

"I know all I need to know about bats."

I held up a slim green volume. "What about this? It looks like a journal of some kind."

Jerry took the book and flipped through the pages. "It's probably about bats. Yep, right here on page thirty-five, 'September tenth. Found a large colony of myotis lucifugus roosting in the Fosters' barn.'" He turned another page. "And here we have a record of all bats sighted from 1975 through 1980. Useful stuff." He tossed the book into one of the boxes. "Maybe I don't want to know why he left the house to me."

"Have you called Harriet?"

"Not yet."

"Now would be a good time."

Jerry was actually reaching for the phone when Rick Rialto sauntered in. I'd been wondering where he was, but I didn't really want to see him, especially now.

"Hey, what's up, Hardy Boys?" He grinned. "Or should I say Nick and Nora? Anything new to report? You've found the real killer, right?"

"We found the real Mantis," Jerry said, "but we don't think he's the culprit."

Rick perched on the arm of the sofa. "Well, damn it, get cracking. I'm paying you good money to solve this crime."

"No, you aren't," I said. "I find the killer, you leave. That's our deal."

"Where have you been?" Jerry asked.

"Well, things are kind of slow down at the shop, so I've been pursuing other avenues. Tell me about the real Mantis. I'll bet his costume wasn't as good as mine."

"Kirby Willet. Eccentric inventor and all-around nut."

"You're sure he didn't kill Gaskins?"

"If anything, Gaskins would've killed him. Willet was supposed to back the movie, only he never showed with the money."

"Great. He welshed on Gaskins and then Gaskins couldn't pay me."

"So now we're tracking down other people who wanted that money."

"Which still doesn't look good for yours truly. I stopped by the other day, but you two were out."

"We went to Riverdale to try to find Willet's cousin. And Mac wanted to talk to Monroe McKittrick."

"McKittrick?"

"The fellow who painted that big picture of me, Des and Tucker."

"Why is he so important?"

"Seems he had an assistant named Jackson Frye who might know more about the fire."

"Jack Frye? I used to know a small-time hustler by that name."

"Do you know where he is?" I asked.

"No, but I could find out."

"What sort of hustling are we talking about here?"

"Oh, Jack loved the ladies. He'd flirt with them, promise them all kinds of stuff just to get into their bedrooms, only he didn't just want to sleep with them. He wanted to steal whatever he could find in the house, usually jewelry. He wasn't too particular."

"Let me get this straight, Rick. Frye would make women fall in love with him so he could rob their homes?"

"That was his m.o. Set up a midnight rendezvous. The gal lets him in. He takes what he wants, maybe gives her a kiss, and disappears into the night."

"Why didn't these women report him?"

"This is just my theory, you understand, but I think they were too embarrassed to admit they'd been taken in. I'll call around, see if I can locate him." He got up. "J, you want to scope something out with me?"

"Can't right now. I promised Mac I'd help cart these books to the library."

"The library? Sheesh. Catch you later."

As soon as Rick had gone, I said, "Midnight rendezvous? Sounds like our guy."

JERRY AND I CARRIED the boxes into the library. Bernice wasn't at the desk. Joan was in the back, still sorting through boxes of books. She held up a black-and-blue baseball cap.

"I know Bailey Seacomb's been looking for his Carolina Panthers hat, and here it is."

"Here are Val Eberlin's bat books," I said. "Do you still want them?"

"Oh, yes. Bring them in."

We set the boxes on the floor.

"Now, you've been through these, right?" Joan asked. "I don't need any of Val's old shoes."

"Just books. Jerry and I cleaned off a bookcase." I straightened and dusted my hands. "Is Bernice here today?"

"She'll be in later. She's finishing the cookies for the sale. We're closing early today to set up. She should be in around five." She took a few books from one box. *"Bats and Their Habits. Wild World of Bats.* You were right about this collection."

"All bats all the time."

She held up the green book. "Sure you don't want this journal?"

"It's a record of Val's bat activities. We don't need to keep it."

As she started to put it back, a small square of paper fell from the book and sailed to the floor. I picked up the paper. "To Jack with all my love" was written on one side. I turned the paper over. It was a photo of a dark-haired young girl with a severe expression.

Harriet Fairweather.

"Do you know her?" Joan asked.

Jerry nodded. "It's a picture of my sister."

Why would a picture of Harriet be in Val's journal? "Let me have another look at that journal, please," I said.

She handed me the green book. I looked through each page, finding nothing but bat facts and bat sightings.

"If I find any more pictures, I'll set them aside for you." Joan said.

"Thanks."

We sat in my car for a long while looking at Harriet's stern young face. I turned the photo over to look at "To Jack with all my love."

"I think we can figure out what happened, Jerry. She was too embarrassed to tell the truth. She must have let him in."

"So I get stuck with the guilt."

"We won't know for sure until we talk to her."

Jerry held out his hand for my cell phone. I gave it to him. He called his sister.

"Busy signal."

"We could stop by her place."

He handed me the phone. "I need some time to figure out what to say to her." Then he sighed. "What I really need is to go to the theater and just forget the whole thing."

"We're close to solving this, Jerry."

He looked at the picture of his sister's stern young face. "Maybe Harriet's right. Does it matter whose fault it was? It's not going to change what happened."

"It's time you moved out from under her influence. Once she admits what she did, you're going to feel a lot better about yourself."

He gave me his serious look. "If we do solve this and it turns out to be my fault, could you possibly consider living with someone like me?"

"I've been living with you."

"I mean in a more permanent arrangement." My heart gave a jump, but before I could say anything, he said, "You've been so faithful, no matter what, I just want us to start off without any baggage. I want everything to be perfect. You deserve that."

Was he talking about marriage? Was this what he'd been trying to tell me all these times we'd been interrupted? I was afraid to ask. "Jerry, I know I'm going to find the answer. Then you should feel free to say whatever you want to say." I reached over and gave his hand an encouraging squeeze. "All right?"

He nodded. "All right."

I started the car. "Where do you want to go?"

He put the picture in his pocket. "The theater."

Now I definitely wanted to prove Harriet was at fault. "Okay."

AT THE THEATER, we interrupted an argument between Kenna and Cathy Sloop. Cathy had a redecorated *Music Man* poster.

Marian the Librarian now wore a tiara, and Professor Harold Hill had sprouted antennae.

"But it would be so easy to change 'Music Man' to 'Mantis Man,'" she said. "We'd save so much in posters and other publicity."

Kenna gave me a look as if to say, "Can you believe this?" "Cathy," she said, "it still looks like a *Music Man* poster, a *Music Man* poster someone has obviously defaced."

"No, no, can't you see? It's Miss Mantis."

Kenna snatched the poster and tore it in half. "Make your own posters. Leave mine alone."

Cathy's lower lip went out. "It was just an idea."

"A screwy idea. Don't you have the Miss Celosia Summertime Pageant to get through first?"

"I thought you might be interested."

"No, thank you." Kenna motioned to Jerry. "I've got a few notes for you, Jerry. Let's use my office."

She and Jerry went up the aisle. Cathy turned her droopy face to me. "It was just a sample. She didn't have to tear it up."

I helped her pick up the pieces of poster. "Not everyone shares your vision, Cathy."

"I know." She sat down in the front row and heaved a sigh. Mitch wasn't with her today, so I couldn't tell if he had decided to wear aqua blue and peach. "There's not a lot in the budget for another pageant so close to Miss Celosia Summertime. I was looking for ways to save money."

"You might want to wait and hold Miss Mantis in the fall."

She sighed again. "It doesn't seem likely it'll happen now, not with the movie being cancelled." She crumpled the paper. "Why did that fellow have to go and get himself killed, just when things were going so well?"

Yes, Josh Gaskins should have planned his demise more carefully. "I guess he wasn't thinking."

Oblivious to sarcasm, Cathy nodded. "Are you any closer to solving the mystery?"

"I have a few more people to talk to."

"Well, I remembered something else."

"Okay." And how useful was this going to be?

"Mitch and I saw that assistant buying drinks in the Super Food the day Gaskins was murdered."

"I knew that already, Cathy. Stephanie always bought the drinks. I don't think she killed Gaskins."

"She didn't seem the type. Actually, she's quite attractive. Could be a good contestant. Her mother was really unpleasant, though."

"Her mother?"

"Some gray-haired lady was there with her. I assumed it was her mother. She said some very cutting things to Mitch and me about pageants, said they were a waste of time, and she didn't appreciate us being in town."

I sat down next to Cathy. "This is very important, Cathy. Can you remember anything else this woman said to you or to Stephanie?"

"I remember everything she said to me because she was so hateful. I don't think she spoke two words to Stephanie."

"But they were shopping together?"

"I thought they were. They were both in the drinks section. They each had about six of those big bottles in their carts."

Bernice must have been buying refreshments for the library used book sale. Could she have switched the doctored bottle with one of Stephanie's?

"Did they have the same kind of soda?" I asked.

"Whatever it was, it was dark with some red on the label. Mitch and I didn't stay to chat, not with that woman being so rude to us."

This was actually very useful information. "Thank you, Cathy." Now I needed to talk to Stephanie. With any luck, she'd remember a certain gray-haired woman buying the same brand of soda.

STEPHANIE WAS SITTING out by the pool at the Wayfarer Motel. Despite being in the shade of an umbrella, she drooped like a wilting flower. Several other crew members were reading or sunning themselves.

"How are you doing?" I asked.

"Not so good. I think it's finally hit me that Josh is gone."

"Do you feel like answering a few more questions?"

"I guess."

"When you were in the grocery store buying drinks, did a woman approach you, ask you anything?"

"A lot of people came up to me. I guess they thought I could get them into the movie." She shook her head. "This town's crazy."

"It can be at times. This woman would've been in her fifties, curly gray hair."

"That description fits nearly everybody. There were some kids, of course, and a few guys who mainly wanted to hit on me, but mostly it was older women. 'Is there a part for a mature woman? Someone who'd have a scene with Lance Henderson?' That's all they asked me. Lance must have been some kind of stud in his day." Her voice was scornful. "Look at him over there with those girls. It's revolting."

Henderson was stretched out on a lounge chair chatting with Sue Ann and another Wayfarer employee.

"There wasn't one who asked about something other than the movie? The woman I'm talking about would've spoken to you when you were getting Josh's drinks. She would've bought the same kind of soda."

She thought a moment. "I'm trying to remember."

While she thought, I watched the other members of the *Curse of the Mantis Man* crew. Gaskins's death didn't seem to have affected any of them. One of the cameramen cannon-balled off the diving board. Everyone laughed as the water sloshed over the sides of the pool. Two more crew members hopped into the water and began throwing a Frisbee back and forth.

I hadn't seen Flynn Davis. Now he strolled across the parking lot. Donna Sanchez was with him. They made a point of ignoring Stephanie and me as they passed. Donna looked perfect in her gold bikini. Davis was equally radiant in his red Speedo.

Stephanie made a disgusted sound. "Davis thinks he's God's gift."

"So does Donna."

"He does this everywhere. That girl's in for a rude awakening when he dumps her and leaves town."

"I don't think so."

Davis spread his towel on a chair for Donna. She sat down. They began to rub suntan lotion on each other. This was a production worthy of a porn film.

Stephanie looked away.

Something in her expression made me ask, "Were you ever involved with him?"

I didn't think she was going to answer me. Then she said, "For a while. Until I realized what a jerk he was. He used me, you know, to get on this project. His contract on *Days of Love* expired, and they killed off his character. He needed work. I thought he needed me, and he did, just not the way I imagined." She put her hand to her mouth and fought back a sob. "I wish he'd been the one to take that drink."

Before I could reply, she looked at me, her eyes wide. "Oh, my God. I didn't mean that. It just slipped out."

"It's okay," I said. "You're upset. Don't worry."

She covered her face with her hands. "That sounded awful. I'm sorry. I seem to be the only one who cares that Josh is dead."

Yes, you do, I thought. And is this a convincing performance? Was the poison meant for Davis? I could easily see several people wanting Davis out of the picture—permanently.

Stephanie lowered her hands. "Excuse me, Madeline. I can't sit here and watch those two." Her room key was on the table. She picked up the key and went back to the motel.

Davis and Donna had finished lathering each other. They lay back in their chairs, holding hands, their perfect bodies gleaming. I noticed Lance Henderson glaring at them from across the pool. Was Henderson just as annoyed that Davis was alive?

Stephanie hadn't answered my question about the woman in the store. With so many people pestering her about the movie, it seemed unlikely she'd remember another shopper in the drink section, but I would call her later and ask again.

I MET JERRY FOR LUNCH at Deely's. We ordered Mantis Burgers, and Jerry asked if I'd spoken to Bernice.

"Not yet," I said. "How was rehearsal?"

"Pretty good." He took Harriet's picture out of his pocket and put it face up on the table. "I kept looking at this. Why would Val have it?"

"I wondered about that, too."

"The house is a great place to hide things. Maybe she visited one time and stuck the picture in the bookcase."

"Why not tear the picture up? Why keep something to remind you of a tragedy?"

"That's what I'm going to ask her."

Alicia brought our order. Jerry was pleased by the size

of his cheeseburger. "How many mantises had to die for this, Alicia?"

"A quarter pound," she said. "Say, Madeline, that old man was in here for breakfast, the one you said used to be famous? He asked me out. Can you believe that?"

"You're the envy of every woman in town."

She made a face. "I told him no, thanks. It'd be like dating my grandpa. It sorta pissed him off. Now, if the other guy had asked me, I would've said yes."

"Do you mean Flynn Davis?" I asked. "He's hanging out with Donna Sanchez."

Alicia nodded. "I kinda figured that. They were in one of the booths the other day. They were both griping and fussing because she couldn't be in the movie."

"The Mantis Man movie?"

"Yeah, Mister Davis said he'd already asked you to take Vivian Montrose's place, and if he'd only known, he would've asked Donna. Then he said once Gaskins was out of the way, he could get her into a better movie."

"You're sure that's what he said? 'Once Gaskins was out of the way'?"

"Yeah, 'cause Donna said, 'When will that be?' and Davis said, 'I doubt he'll last much longer,' and then Donna said a lot of stuff about the pageant and how she was sure she was going to win because the other girls are all dogs. Davis said she shouldn't worry about pageants because being in the movies was way more glamorous."

Another customer signaled for Alicia. When she'd gone, Jerry said, "Well, that sounds suspicious."

I grimaced. "Guess this means I'm going to have to go back to the Wayfarer and talk to Davis. He and Donna are sunning themselves at the pool."

"You can wait till they're nice and crispy," Jerry said and crunched one of his fries.

"I don't want to talk to either of them." I took a bite of my cheeseburger. "Something else about Bernice. Cathy Sloop said she saw a gray-haired woman talking with Stephanie in the drinks section of the Super Food. I'm guessing this woman was Bernice. Cathy also noticed this woman and Stephanie had the same kind of sodas in their shopping carts."

"I don't believe it," Jerry said.

"That they had the same drinks?"

"That Cathy Sloop noticed anything not pageant related."

"What if Bernice poisoned a bottle of soda and switched it with one of Stephanie's?"

"When and how would she do this?"

"I haven't figured out that part yet. I do know it's possible to glue the cap back on, and Bernice is good at gluing."

"And why? What's Bernice got against Gaskins?"

"If she'd ever get back to the library, I'd ask her."

"Where does she live? Let's go by her house."

The next time Alicia passed our table, we asked her if she knew where Bernice Coleman lived. She didn't know. She brought us the phone book, and I looked through all the Colemans.

"There isn't a B. Coleman listed." I closed the phone book. "She'll be in the library later. Joan said they were setting up for the book sale." I sighed. "Guess I have to talk to Davis."

"You knew the job was dangerous when you took it."

BY THE TIME I GOT BACK to the Wayfarer Motel pool, Donna had gone. Davis gave me a self-satisfied smile as if he thought I just couldn't resist returning to him. Not many guys can wear a Speedo successfully. Lounging in the pool chair, Davis resembled a long stretch of road with a speed bump in the middle.

"Glad you came back, Madeline."

He patted the chair where Donna had been sunning herself, inviting me to take her place. I pulled up another chair.

"I need to ask you a few questions."

"Good lord, give it a rest," he said. "This inspector business doesn't suit you at all. You're much too beautiful."

"When you and Donna Sanchez were talking in Deely's, why did you say once Gaskins is out of the way, you could get her into a better movie?"

His reaction wasn't what I expected. He looked amused. "I might have known."

"Might have known?"

"That you'd be wondering why I offered her a better deal. Don't worry, Madeline. I'm just stringing her along. Stick with me, and I can open all kinds of doors for you."

Davis's parents must have made a deal with the Ego Fairy. "This isn't about the movies," I said. "This is about you wanting Gaskins out of the way, as in dead."

He pulled himself up and jerked off his sunglasses to stare at me. "For the last time, I did not kill Gaskins. If I said something about getting him out of the way, I meant when the distributors see the incredible mess he made of this movie, they'd yank him from Voltage Films and put him on some nature documentary." His eyes narrowed. "Were you spying on me in that diner? That's a pretty amateur trick."

"The waitress overheard you talking to Donna."

Davis was annoyed, but he tried one last play. "Yeah, well, why don't you leave the detective work to the police and go where you can be appreciated? You're wasting your talent and your looks in this stupid little town where you can't fart without making the front page of the paper."

"The only thing I'm wasting right now is my time."

Davis lay back and put on his sunglasses. "Fine. Stay here and rot. The sooner I can leave Palookaville, the better."

Amen to that.

As I went back to my car, I checked my watch. It was

almost two. I thought about finding Donna and telling her she was on the endangered species list. Then I remembered I needed to finish my conversation with Stephanie. I also remembered her room number from seeing the key on the table, so I went to room twenty-three and knocked.

"Stephanie? It's Madeline."

Muffled voices and thumps sounded from inside. Thanks to the Wayfarer's thin walls, I heard Stephanie say, "Oh, no!" and a man's voice cursing.

"Stephanie, are you okay?" I called. I banged on the door. "Do you need help?" More thumps and a crash. I started to run for assistance when I heard her say, "Wait a minute. I'm coming."

She opened the door a little way and made an attempt to straighten her hair. Her clothes were askew and her face was flushed.

"Are you all right?" I asked.

"Yes, fine. What do you want?"

Behind her, I caught a glimpse of a man struggling to his feet, his lower half tangled in a sheet. "Oh, sorry," I said. "I didn't mean to interrupt—" As the man turned to pick up the phone from the floor, I blinked to clear my vision. It was Lance Henderson.

I knew my amazement was obvious, for Stephanie blushed even darker. In the long silence that followed, Henderson looked up, saw me in the doorway and, as usual, made a production out of the situation.

"Two friends comforting each other in their hour of sadness, my dear Madeline. Two souls longing to purge the memory of another friend's passing."

Two souls longing for something, all right. "I apologize for interrupting."

He waved my apology away. "Not a problem, my dear."

Stephanie said, "Lance, make some coffee, will you? Madeline and I are going to talk out here for a minute." She came out and pulled the door shut. "I know I made some mean comments about Lance, but he saw how upset I was about Flynn, and—"

"Hold on," I said. "You don't owe me an explanation. I'm sorry I reacted like that, but hearing all the noises, it sounded like you might be in trouble."

"No, I'm all right." She sat down in one of the white plastic chairs the Wayfarer provided in front of each room. "Lance and I had a long talk. I feel a lot better. You wanted to know about the people in the grocery store."

"Did a woman approach you in the drink section?"

"Like I said, there were a lot of women, all wanting to know about Lance."

And you can give them the inside story now, I thought, but this was way too rude to say out loud.

"I told them if they came out to where we were filming, he'd be glad to sign autographs and take pictures and whatever. It was quite a crowd of them."

"Around your grocery cart?"

"Mainly around me. After I answered their questions, they went away. Oh, no, wait." She frowned as if trying to remember.

I didn't expect Stephanie to recall anything I could use, so her next words gave me a chill.

"There was a woman by my cart. I'd forgotten. In all the confusion, her cart had bumped into mine. She apologized for knocking over my bottles of soda. She straightened them all back up. I told her not to worry about it."

"Do you remember what she looked like?"

"Sure. She looked like all the other gray-haired ladies. I wouldn't be able to pick her out in a crowd."

But I would.

WHEN I ARRIVED AT THE library, Joan was locking the front door. "Sorry, Madeline. We closed early today, remember?"

"Did Bernice ever come in?" I asked.

"Yes, she's in there now, setting up the refreshments table."

"I really need to speak with her."

Joan unlocked the door. "Okay. Just pull the door shut when you leave."

The door closed behind me with a soft hiss.

I made my way to the back, stepping around the boxes of used books.

"Bernice? It's Madeline Maclin. I have a message for you from Kirby Willet."

The used books had been arranged on the tables. Bernice placed signs on each table with category and price information. She gave me a suspicious glance. "What sort of message?"

"He wanted you to know he'd won the Blue Ribbon peanut contest."

She paused for a moment. "Oh, I know all about that."

"So you knew he'd won ten thousand dollars?"

"Oh, yes."

Since Bernice's natural expression was one of bitterness, it was hard for me to tell what she was feeling, but she seemed more bitter than usual.

"Did you know the money was in one of the boxes he stored at Frannie's?"

"No." The signs in her hand trembled. "If I'd known, I would've taken my rightful share. Half of that money was to come to me."

Jerry was right. Someone was angry about the money. "Half?"

"I told him about the contest. I urged him to enter. He said if he won, he'd give me half."

Didn't she know how absentminded Willet was? "Did you remind him of this?"

She slapped the signs down. "Remind him! I can't find

him. I thought he'd run off with the money, and now I find out it was at Frannie's where I could've gotten it myself."

"I know where he is," I said. "You can go talk to him and get this straightened out."

"He has no intention of giving me my share."

"Are you sure? You need to talk to him—"

Her voice shook. "He was going to give it to Gaskins for that idiotic film! After all I did for him! We had a deal! We had a bargain!"

"After all you did for him?"

She started toward me. Something in her manner made me keep a table between us. "I took care of him. I found him jobs. I covered for him when he was off somewhere making some sort of machine. I washed his clothes, cooked his meals."

As she came around the corner of the table, I went the other way. "You were living together?"

"Don't you dare judge me! You have no cause to talk."

"I'm just trying to understand your relationship with Willet. You said you had a deal with him."

Light glinted off her glasses as she shook her head. "Oh, you wouldn't understand. You don't know what it's like. You've never had to work to get a man to notice you. All you have to do is smile that pearly pageant smile, and here they come like pigs to a trough."

"Hold on a minute."

She sneered. "You think I don't know what goes on up at that house? Strange men coming and going at all hours. You and that rich Fairweather fellow lording over the rest of us."

"Bernice, you've got it all wrong."

"Oh, no. I'm the only one in this town who sees things very clearly."

You could've bottled Bernice's look and sold it to exterminate rats. If she was this delusional, then maybe she was also desperate enough to kill.

"Did you put something in Gaskins's drink?"

For the first time, she smiled, and I wished she hadn't. "Me? Oh, my, no. It was that crazy inventor, the one who decided to finance a stupid monster movie. Everyone knows Willet is still angry about losing the scholarship to Gaskins. Everyone knows he's insane."

"Willet has an alibi. He videotaped himself inventing that night."

This stopped her for only a few moments. "That doesn't matter. When the police search his hotel room, they'll find proof."

"I'm afraid not," I said. "That little packet of poison won't be there."

"What?"

"Jerry and I already found it."

She lunged over the table for me. I tumbled backward, tripped and fell over a box. Books scattered. Before I could get up, Bernice was on top of me, pounding with her fists, her face distorted with rage. I tried to push her off. She was too heavy. I tried to dislodge her by rocking from side to side, but boxes of books limited my actions. As her hands closed around my neck, my flailing hand searched for a weapon and closed on something that felt like a stick. I brought it around and down on Bernice's wooly head and heard a satisfying whack. Bernice fell back. I gave her a couple more whacks and staggered to my feet. Bernice lay crumpled next to a pile of old encyclopedias. What had saved the day? An umbrella with a sturdy duck's head.

Oh, good, I thought as I rubbed my sore neck. Mystery solved.

I sagged back and steadied myself on a table, umbrella ready, but Bernice didn't move. During the struggle, my cell phone had fallen out of my pocket. Using the tables as support, I leaned down, picked up my phone and called the police. By the time Chief Brenner arrived, Bernice was conscious and curled in a corner, sobbing. Between sobs, she told him Willet had promised her half the prize money, and when she realized he planned to give it to Gaskins, she felt so betrayed she put the digitalis in Gaskins's drink and then switched bottles with Stephanie in the grocery store.

"But I didn't mean to kill him! I just wanted him to get sick and go away. He'd have to return the money and then I'd get what was rightfully mine."

"Willet never gave Gaskins any money," Brenner said. "We still have it at the station."

"It's mine! I insist on having it."

Brenner took her by the arm and pulled her up. "We'll talk about this."

As he took her out, she was still sobbing, "But I loved him. I did everything for him."

I stayed for a few minutes to pick up the spilled books. Then I sat down and took a few more deep breaths. Bernice's rage had been terrifying, but her sorrow choked me even worse. Bernice had been brokenhearted, but how could anyone have known? If only she'd been able to talk to someone, she would've realized that practically everyone experiences some heartbreak in life. But Bernice kept her emotions inside until they exploded, taking Josh Gaskins with her. Kirby Willet remained free and oblivious.

Do I sense a lesson here? I asked myself.

I did as Joan had instructed, and when I left, I pulled the library door shut. I arrived at the theater before the box office opened. I went down the aisle and leaned over the edge of the orchestra pit.

"How'd it go?" Jerry asked.

"Bernice did it to get Willet in trouble. She thought they had an understanding."

"Didn't she know all Willet loves is peanuts?"

"I think she knows that now."

Jerry gave me a closer look. "My God, Mac, what happened to your throat?"

"She tried to strangle me."

"Are you okay?"

"I'm fine. I'm more than fine." I held up my weapon. "I found Patricia's umbrella."

NINE

"I CAN'T IMAGINE WHERE you found it," Patricia said. She turned the umbrella over and over. "Dear me, the paint's a bit chipped."

"Yes, sorry about that," I said.

She opened the umbrella, dislodging several items off her desk. "Oh, that doesn't matter. It still works. Where did you find it?"

"Did you donate some books to the library used book sale?"

"Don't tell me it was in that box!"

"Joan said she found lots of things."

Patricia closed the umbrella and reached for her pocketbook. "I'm so glad to have it back. I really wish you'd let me pay you something."

"No, thanks," I said. "That umbrella saved my life. I'll tell you the whole story sometime."

I'd stopped by the Chamber of Commerce first thing the next morning. When I got to my office, Twenty was waiting at the door.

"Madeline, I need to apologize to you for anything I might have said. I know I was overbearing and crazy and just not right."

I unlocked my door. "You don't need to apologize. You felt strongly about the movie, and you were entitled to express your opinion."

"But if you hadn't solved this mystery, I could've been charged with murder. I'm your friend for life."

"Thanks. Come on in."

"I can't stay. I need to disband S.T.O.M.P. and apologize to everybody there, too."

As she hurried down the hallway, Stephanie and Lance came up.

"Madeline, I'm glad we caught you," Stephanie said. "We're all leaving today, and I wanted to thank you for catching Josh's killer."

"You're welcome."

"I wish I'd paid more attention in the store. Maybe I would've seen her switch bottles."

"I don't know if this will make you feel any better, but she just wanted him to get sick and stop filming," I said. "It was her way of crying out for attention. Unfortunately, the person she was trying to attract hadn't a clue."

"I'm just happy to be getting out of this town," Stephanie said. "No offense. Lance and I are going to continue with Voltage Films. Our next project is to go ahead with *Pastel Memoirs*."

"Yes, now I can return to the quality projects my fans expect of me," Lance said.

"I hope so, Lance. I wish you the best of luck."

He looked pleased. "You suspected me for a while, didn't you, my dear?"

"I suspected everyone."

He took my hand and kissed it. "The role of murderer is one I never played, not on television, not in real life."

"I'm glad to hear that."

"Good day."

As soon as Lance and Stephanie left, Ted walked in. "Was that Lance Henderson?"

"He stopped in to say good-by."

"Too bad the movie didn't work out for him."

"I don't think he's too torn up about it. Have a seat, Ted."

"Just for a moment." He sat down in the armchair, and I

took my place behind my desk. "Congratulations on solving the murder, Madeline. I can't believe Bernice capable of such a thing."

"Unfortunately, she did it for love."

"Love or money. Those are usually the reasons, aren't they?"

"Actually, this was for love and money, although I think she would've been happy with love."

Ted shifted in his seat and straightened his tie. Plain blue, I noticed. "Um, Madeline, while we're on the subject."

Uh-oh.

"We haven't known each other very long, and I hope I'm not misreading the signals, but is there a chance for us? Can we take our friendship to the next step?"

Is there a chance for us? The very words I wanted to ask Jerry. "Ted, I really don't know."

He held up his hand. "Now, I understand. I don't want to rush things. We've both been through rough relationships, and the last thing I want to do is pressure you."

"It isn't that." Ted had been so patient and kind. I needed to be honest with him. "It's Jerry."

"Oh," he said. "I didn't realize."

"It's a little complicated."

"Oh," he said again, and this time the "oh" was a long, sympathetic "oh." "But aren't he and Olivia—?"

"That's over."

"I'm sorry, Madeline. I had no idea."

"Please don't apologize." I couldn't help but smile. All the women I know had immediately seen my predicament. Ted, bless his heart, was in his own way as clueless as Jerry. "Ted, you're one of the kindest men I've ever met. I'd hate to lose your friendship, but that's all I can offer you."

He smiled back. "You're not going to lose anything. If Jerry's crazy enough to let you go, I'll be first in line."

"Thanks, Ted."

THE MISS CELOSIA SUMMERTIME Pageant was at three, so I met Jerry at Deely's for lunch. Mantis Man Burgers were still on the menu. We ordered two.

"I've had a busy morning," I said. "Everyone came to say good-by."

"Even Davis?"

"I didn't expect him."

I'd taken a big bite of my Mantis Burger when Denisha ran in, spotted us and bounced up to our table. "Guess what, Madeline? We're going to be rich!"

"You are?"

"And all we have to do is have a party!"

"What kind of party?"

"Pocketbooks! Isn't that neat?"

Jerry coughed as if he'd choked on his lunch. His eyes widened, and he seemed a few shades paler. I knew he'd done something more than swallow wrong.

"Would this have anything to do with that conversation you had with Rick the other day?" I asked him.

"It's the brand name scam, one of Rick's favorites."

Along with his Mantis Man merchandise, Rick must have gotten his hands on some famous brand knock offs he intended to sell at Tupperware-like parties around town. "It's one of your favorites, too, isn't it?"

Denisha frowned. "What's a scam?"

"A trick."

"Is it a trick? My auntie says it sounds like a good way to make some money. She doesn't usually trust people when they talk about things like this, but she likes you, Jerry, and Mister Rialto said you think it's a good idea, so she's gonna do it."

I'd never seen Jerry look so disconcerted. "Did your aunt give Mister Rialto any money?"

"She's going to the bank first thing tomorrow."

"Is your aunt home now?"

"Yes, she'll be fixing lunch. But I'd rather have a Mantis Burger. Madeline, call her and see if I can."

Jerry got up. "Come on. I'll take you home."

"Jerry!"

"I'll buy you a Mantis Burger later, okay?"

He left, tugging a reluctant Denisha, and came back alone about a half hour later.

"Did you explain things?" I asked as he slid into his seat across from me.

He nodded. "I told her I'd made a mistake and she shouldn't invest in anything Mister Rialto suggested. She was very nice about it. Denisha kept looking at me funny, though."

"What changed your mind?"

"The other times, it wasn't people I knew."

I decided not to say anything else. Had he finally learned this valuable—and to me, always obvious—lesson?

He inspected his now soggy french fries. "Rick's going to be pissed."

"He can find another village to plunder."

Jerry looked at me. "You know, you're right. I don't want him pulling that scheme here. I got all caught up in the excitement, just like old times, but it's different now. I know these people."

"Does this mean no more séances?"

He grinned. "Well, let's not go overboard. I may cut back gradually."

"You won't have time for séances once you find a job."

"I hear there's an opening at the library."

Jerry in the library. I suppose it could work. "I'm afraid your ties are too loud."

"I've got other plans," he said.

Oh, dear. "Are you going to tell me what they are?"

"No. I want it to be a surprise."

"I think I want to know now."

He checked his watch. "Isn't it about time for the pageant?"

"Jerry."

"Come on," he said.

THE *MUSIC MAN* SET HAD been taken down and replaced with a backdrop of silvery sparkles and giant flowers. The auditorium was full, but Jerry and I found seats at the back. As the contestants paraded through the opening number, singing about confidence and pride and hooray for womanhood and America, I felt my stomach roll with the memory of pageants past. I gripped the arm of my seat, wondering if I was going to heave Mantis Burger and fries.

In one of his rare moments of intuition, Jerry patted my hand and said, "That's not you anymore."

No. No, it wasn't. I took a deep steadying breath and managed to watch the rest of the pageant objectively. Most of the contestants followed my advice, stood up straight, wore their best colors and smiled their best smiles. Donna's smile was tight and forced. She looked worried. But the real surprise was Rose Farrington. Somewhere between my talk and this evening, Rose had transformed into a real beauty queen, so no one except Donna was shocked when Rose won and another girl took first runner-up. Donna was a furious second, barely containing her anger on stage, her smile now as rigid as a doll's.

"I think there may be another murder in your future," Jerry said as we stood to applaud the winners.

BACKSTAGE, THE GIRLS hugged me and thanked me for my help. Donna had already flounced out without a word to anyone. I found out later she left with Flynn Davis.

I congratulated Cathy, Mitch and Evan on a successful pageant. I noticed with amusement that for the evening, Mitch had adopted Evan's lavender suit and signature yellow handkerchief in the jacket pocket, and Cathy's evening gown was purple and yellow.

"We have big exciting plans for the fall," Cathy said. "We're thinking Miss Celosia Autumn, then Miss Celosia Wintertime and Miss Celosia Springtime. An entire season of pageants!"

Whether I liked it or not, the Pageantoids were going to be in town. "No Miss Mantis?"

"I really couldn't get my head around the concept."

Evan shook my hand. "Thanks again, Madeline. I really appreciated all your support. What did you think of the results? I was pleased and surprised. Rose will be a wonderful queen. I couldn't be happier. She has a bright future ahead of her."

"Yes, she does," I said.

Out in the parking lot, I saw Poppy Farrington dressed in a tight pink dress that made her look like a tattooed sausage. She was standing by a large, black motorcycle with Benjy Goins, one of the judges, and he had his arm around her shoulders. She gave me a wink.

I laughed.

"What's so funny?" Jerry asked.

"This town," I said. "I love it."

"Me, too."

"Really?" I said. "Is that your surprise?"

"My surprise is at Georgia's," he said.

At Georgia's Books, the white ferret was sitting by the cash register, no longer scrawny and dirty, but fat and fluffy.

"This is Poltergeist," Hayden said. The ferret slid under his hand. As he rubbed its head, it made a soft clucking sound. "Poltey for short. Now any time I hear a strange noise, I just say, 'Oh, must be the ferret,' and you know what? It usually is."

Shana was helping Georgia fix the cardboard display

holding Shana's latest historical romance. "If I'd known that, I would've bought a ferret a long time ago."

Hayden scratched the ferret behind its ears. "I've gotten really fond of it. I never had a pet because of my mother's allergies. Poltey sits right up here with me most of the day."

"A very calming influence for a ghost," Shana said.

"This is a very nice surprise," I told Jerry.

"Oh, Poltey's not the surprise," he said. "Starting tomorrow, I'm gainfully employed at Georgia's Books. Hayden wants some time off to write."

I stared at him and then stared at Hayden. "Is this true?"

"Jerry and I have been talking about it, and I think it's going to work out for both of us."

I don't know why I hadn't thought of this before. The bookstore was a perfect place for Jerry. It was always busy, he could interact with people all day, and he loved to read. "That's great."

"You need to sign a few papers for tax purposes, Jerry," Georgia said. "Come to the back, and we'll get that taken care of."

I was going to congratulate Hayden on his decision to spend more time writing when I saw Rick Rialto walk past the store.

"I'll be right back," I said.

I caught up with Rick at his Mantis Man shop. To my relief, he was packing the tee shirts and key rings.

"I hear J's going legit," he said.

"He's got a job at the bookstore."

"Good luck to him, I say." He closed one box and started filling another with caps and coffee mugs. "This town's too small for the really big schemes, anyway."

"Your shop wasn't doing too well, was it?"

"The murder kinda put a damper on things. It's funny, 'cause usually something like that makes people want to buy stuff." He shrugged. "Oh, well."

"You're taking all the fake handbags, too, I hope."

"Yep." He reached for the Mantis Man salt and pepper shakers. "So the old broad at the library did it, huh? She wasn't even there that night."

"She only meant for Gaskins to get sick."

Rick didn't seem concerned that Gaskins was dead. "Too bad. Thanks for solving the mystery, though. Got me off the hook."

"You're welcome."

I had turned to go when he said, "Oh, I found out what happened to Jackson Frye, if you're still interested."

"Yes, I'd like to know."

He paused in his packing. "Don't know how you feel about irony."

"It has its place in my life."

"Then you'll appreciate this. Seems Frye pulled one too many schemes and was finally caught and sent to jail. You remember that prison that caught fire about ten years ago? Killed about fifty inmates? Frye was one of them."

"Doesn't that make you want to rethink your life, Rick?"

He laughed. "Nah. I'm not going to get caught."

"Well, thanks for the information."

"I thought I'd do you another favor and tell J how you feel."

What the hell? "How I feel?"

"Yeah, you know, about him getting a job and everything. He's cool with that."

"Oh, the job."

"What'd you think I meant?" Rick gave me a look that was surprisingly serious. "When are you going to tell him?"

"Tell him what?"

"That you love him. You always have."

I was suddenly interested in the stack of Mantis Man dishcloths. "We're at an odd place right now."

"You think he'll turn you down?"

"I don't know what he'll do."

"So you're just going to go along the same old way until what? You're roommates at the nursing home?"

The dishcloths were too soft; otherwise, I would've thrown the whole pile at his head. "Get lost, Rick."

He grinned. "Or you find something better? I'm available."

"No," I said. "You're leaving. We had a deal."

He gave me a salute. "Unlike our friend Kirby the Mantis, I keep my end of all bargains. See you later, Mac."

I was so glad he was leaving town, I didn't correct him.

AND I WAS SO PLEASED about Jerry's job, I thought I'd press my luck. When I came back to the bookstore, I asked him, "Now what about Tucker's wedding?"

"I think I'll go."

I took in some air. "I don't think I can take any more surprises today."

"Harriet will be there. You hold her down, and I'll ask the tough questions."

JERRY STILL DIDN'T WANT to go inside the Fairweather home, so it was fortunate that Tucker's wedding was held in the garden. Delighted, Tucker asked Jerry to stand with him. Des played the piano. Harriet, dressed in her usual dark clothes, sat by herself on the front row. I watched her face as Tucker's gorgeous bride, Selene, floated down the aisle in a shimmery gown, accompanied by her equally attractive father. All through the brief ceremony, Harriet's expression remained fixed. Afterward, as Tucker and Selene cut their wedding cake, she stood off to one side as if poised for flight. Jerry brought her a piece of cake.

"Harriet, I need to talk to you."

"I'm very glad you decided to come," she said. "Let's not spoil things."

He took the picture out of his pocket and turned it over so she could see the words "To Jack with all my love." "I just want to know about Jackson Frye."

She paled. She would've left if I hadn't been there to block her way. "Harriet, we know about the robbery. We know Frye came to the house that night to steal some things. He caused the fire, didn't he?"

Her mouth trembled. She put her hand over her eyes for a moment, and when she looked at us, her eyes were shiny with tears. "I let him in. May God forgive me, but I let him in."

Jerry took her arm and led her to a chair. "We just want to know what happened."

She kept her head down. "I was so mortified. The first boy I ever cared about, and he didn't care about me. He only wanted inside the house. He ran, the candles fell over. It happened before I could think. I couldn't bear the thought of being blamed. I'm a Fairweather! These things don't happen to people like us." She gave Jerry a glance and then avoided his eyes. "You were always playing with matches. It was easy to make people believe you had done it. You were so little, I didn't think it would matter."

"Good God, it did matter, Harriet. I've spent my whole life thinking I killed our parents."

"I'm sorry, I'm sorry. Didn't you believe me when I told you it was an accident?"

"Yes, but what kind of an idiot causes huge flaming accidents? No wonder I never thought I could do anything right."

She was crying now. Jerry handed her his handkerchief. She wiped her eyes. "I tried to make it up to you. When Uncle Val was making out his will, he asked me if I wanted his house, and I told him to leave it to you. I knew you wouldn't come back here, and I thought you might like his place."

"Harriet." He stopped and took a deep breath. "I can't decide if I'm angry or relieved."

She grasped his hand. "Please don't be angry."

The photographer came up. "Excuse me, folks. I'd like to get a shot of the family."

Des, Tucker, Selene and her father stood waiting at an archway covered in roses. Jerry hesitated and then pulled Harriet to her feet.

"Come on," he said. "You need to be in the picture."

She wiped her eyes and even managed a smile for the camera. Then she kissed her brothers one by one and left.

"That was nice," I told Jerry.

"I can't hate her," he said. "She's all alone. At least I got a house out of the deal."

"Now we know why Val left the house to you."

"And I have you."

Tucker strolled up in time to hear this. "Is there a possibility there might be another wedding soon?"

To my surprise, Jerry caught my hand and held it tight. "Yes," he said. "If Mac will have me."

I didn't know what to say. My heart started beating so fast, I'm sure the front of my dress was flapping.

"I've been trying to tell you for days, and somehow the time never was right," he said. "You're my best friend. You've always been here with me, and now that I know I'm not a complete idiot, I can't let you get away. You found the answer, so now I'm going to say what I've been wanting to say. Will you marry me?"

I could hardly speak for laughing. "Yes!"

"Deal." He put his arms around my waist and pulled me to him. "But we're not going to shake on it. I have something better in mind."

* * * * *

REQUEST YOUR FREE BOOKS!

2 FREE NOVELS
PLUS 2 FREE GIFTS!

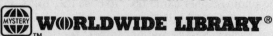

WORLDWIDE LIBRARY®
Your Partner in Crime